DANRITE WILLOCKY

HALF GIANT – HALF DWARF

ALL HERO!

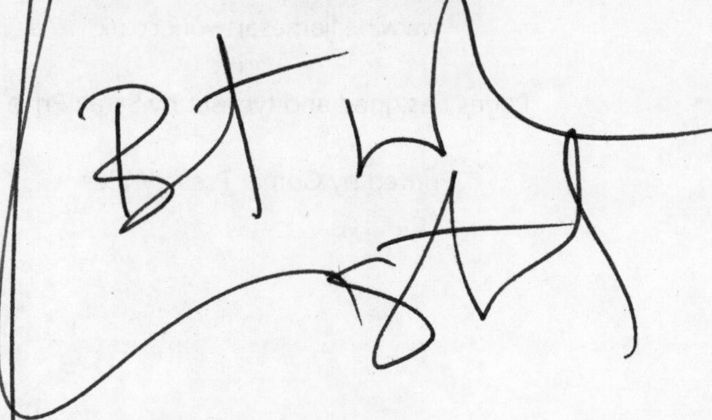

Published in 2016 by Zygmunt Stanley

ISBN 978-0-9574625-1-9

In this work of fiction the characters, places and events are either the product of the author's imagination or they are used entirely fictitiously.

Cover illustration by Neil James
www.neiljamesartwork.co.uk

Pages designed and typeset by Sarah Price

Printed by Gomer Press, Wales

Other Titles

By

Stefan Jakubowski

*

Supernatural comedy starring Richard Ross

STRANGE RELATIONS

DEAD PECULIAR

*

Fantasy comedy nonsense

MISCREATION

*

Time travel comedy starring Tom Tyme

ONCE UPON A TYME

TYME AND TIME AGAIN

*

Comedy tales of the short kind

NOT JUST FOR CHRISTMAS

Three Christmassy short stories to be enjoyed at any time including Tom Tyme in

"The Missing Christmas Sock"

THE AUTHOR

Originally from Reading, Stefan moved to Wales in the latter part of the last century. (He wishes to point out that he is not as old as that makes him sound.) (Nia, his wife, wishes to point out: ‘Oh yes he is!’) He lives with Nia somewhere in Carmarthenshire.

For

Friends

Large

*

For

Friends

Small

*

For

Friends

Furry

*

For

Friends

All

*

Special thanks to
Sarah Price
and
Neil James

It is written that if myth, fantasy, and make-believe should ever threaten to fade from the earth, to become but shadowy memories on its surface, a champion will arise; a hero who will face the dark and lead the creatures of the fantastic from its depths, and back into the world of the light.

Sadly, the time of shadows is nearly upon us. With books, the small and silver screen, devoid of new ideas, and machines that think for their owners, imagination is on the ropes. Dirge is the name of the game, and sadly that game will sell in its millions. Myth, fantasy and make-believe are skulking deeper and deeper into those shadows. The time is nigh. A champion is needed, now, before myth, fantasy and make-believe become just words in a dictionary no one will bother to look at.

But who is this champion, this hero who will heed the call to arms? It is said he will be mythical; the hero of legends. A superhero, who will rise and storm forth across the face of the earth, spreading imagination before him, putting light into the darkest of corners. He will be fearless. He will be a creature of myth; half giant - half dwarf. He will be …

Hang about. Half giant – half dwarf? Oh dearie me, I have a bad feeling about this. I fear imagination may be in a worse state than first thought.

CHAPTER 1

'When will he come?' asked a small chap, who stood covered head to foot in a hooded robe. It was a question he had asked many a time in recent days. So much so, it was fast becoming the new, "Are we there yet?"

'Soon, Vlad, soon,' replied a voice, steeped in exasperation.

'And how will we know him?' said Vlad, the question, as always, following hot on the heels of his other question.

A deep sigh accompanied the answer. 'As I have said on numerous occasions, Vlad, it will be as the prophecy foretells.'

'Why does it have to be a he?' enquired a female voice.

'It?' questioned the exasperated voice, missing the point being made.

'Our hero,' said the female voice, patiently. 'Why does our prophesised, all-conquering hero, have to be a he?'

The owner of the exasperated voice looked at her as if she were mad. 'Because it is written,' he said.

'By a man, no doubt,' said the female, sitting back in her chair, her massive bulk in danger of overflowing as she squirmed to get comfortable. 'And isn't it time we invested in some decent seating?'

'There's a two-seater sofa in the lounge Twinkle; we could bring that up for you,' suggested Vlad, innocently. Twinkle glared at him, as she demolished half her lunch in one go; a large pork pie. 'I was only saying,' said Vlad, backing away.

'If you're both quite finished?' said the exasperated voice.

'Only half to go,' said Twinkle, holding her decimated pork pie out for examination.

'I meant the bickering,' said the exasperated voice, on the verge of terminal exasperation.

The small fellow in the robe shifted uncomfortably, but it was nothing to do with his chair. 'Sorry, Salor, I didn't mean…'

'No, you never do, do you, Vlad,' said Salor, keeping the exasperated tone.

Vlad pulled his hood a little lower.

'Now,' said Salor, all businesslike, 'if there are no further questions, I suggest we go about our business. We all have jobs to do.' And before anyone had a chance to think of another one, he briskly set about leaving the room. The door swung shut behind him.

Twinkle and Vlad exchanged glances then followed suit. The table they had been sat around duly did the same. A horse followed the table. The chairs stayed where they were.

CHAPTER 2

'It's a girl!'

'Oh no it's not!'

'It's a boy!'

'Oh no… oh, it is. Anyone can make a mistake you know!'

Enough said.

CHAPTER 3

Time passed.

As it does.

CHAPTER 4

The table was feeling a tad anxious as Salor, Vlad, and a glitter-sprinkled Twinkle, took their places around it. Behind them an equally anxious whinny announced the presence of the horse.

'Well Vlad?' said Salor testily, as the three sat. He was a busy man. He was head of all things mythical, magical, and make-believical. A lot rested on his shoulders, and he could do without another of Vlad's almost weekly panics. Vlad's "When will he come?" mantra had, over time, changed to "The time is upon us." It appeared it was upon them again. 'Please pray tell, why you have felt the need to call an emergency meeting?'

Vlad stood up and cleared his throat. 'I believe the time is upon us,' he said, 'ready or not.' Behind him the horse whinnied in support.

Eyeballs that had started rolling, stopped mid-roll; something was different. Vlad hadn't delivered his speech in his usual dramatic way, he appeared almost panicked and he had support this time. The hairs on Salor's neck rose.

'What do you mean, "ready or not"?' said Salor. The table shifted nervously, it knew what Vlad was about to say.

'I'm sad to say, Percy's brown bread,' said Vlad, solemnly.

Salor stared at him with a bemused, yet stern look on his face. 'You called a meeting to tell me you're sad about saying something?' Or was he trying to say that Percy had taken up baking?

The table did another quick shift.

'When?' said Twinkle.

Salor looked at her.

'Less than an hour ago.'

Salor looked at Vlad.

'Good grief,' said Twinkle, ashen-faced.

He now looked at Twinkle again the bemused look deepening. 'Good grief?' said Salor. 'What *are* you talking about?'

Twinkle told him.

'What?' said Salor, jumping to his feet. 'What do you mean dead? Why didn't you say? When? Why wasn't I informed?' His face had turned white, then red, then a sort of pinkish colour; quite pretty really, then white again.

Vlad's hood lowered a little, the shadows within darkening. 'I only just found out myself,' he said. 'It happened less than half an hour ago. That's why I called the meeting.'

A silence fell upon the room as the sad news sunk in. And as with all silences it was then broken, by Salor. Fate had dealt a hand and it was now time for action. 'The boy is open to attack,' he said.

'I've taken steps,' said Vlad.

'Who?' said Salor.

'Jose.'

'Good grief!'

'No one else really,' said Vlad, shrugging.

'Then we had better move quickly.'

Twinkle, who had been quiet up until now, suddenly leaned forward, glitter falling onto the table top. She raised an eyebrow. 'But are we *sure* he's the real deal?' she whispered.

It was an old road much travelled and Salor was loathe to travel down it again, especially with the news of Percy's recent demise. Salor sighed. 'I thought we had sorted that out,' he said.

'Yes,' said Vlad, valiantly sucking-up. 'It's as the prophecy foretold.'

'Oh yeah,' said Twinkle, sitting back, 'I forgot, a champion will blah-blah. *He* will come and blah-blah-blah.'

'This isn't the time,' snapped Salor.

'Then make time,' Twinkle snapped back. 'Who really knows what a half giant, half dwarf looks like? And before you say anything, I know, it's written, but really?'

Salor angrily slapped his fist into his palm. 'Enough!' he demanded. 'He was born in the right place, the right century, down to the right second. What more proof do you need?'

'Yeah,' said Vlad, 'what more?'

'Shut up, Vlad!' said Salor and Twinkle in unison.

'I was only saying.' Vlad slumped in his chair feeling sorry for himself; no one ever listened to him.

‘But a baby, think about it Salor, it doesn’t make sense,’ said Twinkle. ‘Having to wait eighteen years; to wait for the champion to grow out of nappies, I had expected someone a little more hands on; bigger. Someone with attitude, dressed in shining armour, and with a whacking great sword.’

‘And who is to say he won’t be like that, one day,’ said Salor, slightly calmer. ‘But until that day, we have what we have, and we make the best of it. It is written, so be it.’

Twinkle tutted and crossed her arms. ‘I am only saying.’

‘And such is noted,’ said Salor. He took a breath. ‘Now, it would appear that fate has dealt from the pack and we each have a hand to play. So I say, we shovel those cards and play the game out.’

‘Shovel?’ said Vlad, not sure he understood what Salor had just said.

‘Whatever,’ said Salor, not sure he did either.

‘He means we should get on with things,’ Twinkle explained.

‘Oh,’ said Vlad, realising the old duffer had meant shuffle.

‘Exactly, Twinkle,’ said Salor. ‘I believe it’s time for us to claim back our place in the world.’

‘Yes,’ said Vlad, nodding, his thoughts turning to mirrors.

‘Then onwards we must go.’ Salor stood and dramatically waved a hand towards the door.

The horse, whose name was Sid, whinnied.

‘What’s that?’ said Salor.

‘Haven’t you forgotten something?’ said Twinkle.

Salor looked confused. ‘Forgotten something?’

‘Percy.’

‘Good grief. Yes, poor Percy.’ Salor looked suitably embarrassed, but pulled himself together. ‘Let us bow our heads in reflection and draw good thoughts and energy from the memory of our good friend, wherever he may be.’

‘Be,’ said Vlad, bowing his head.

‘Be,’ said Twinkle, doing likewise.

Sid whinnied, and bent a knee.

The table, named Rosie, tipped its top slightly sending a small shower of glitter cascading to the floor.

Salor raised his head. 'And now,' he said solemnly, 'it is our turn to look after the boy. But we will not let ourselves be known to him until Percy has been laid to rest. Until then it is business as usual.'

Moves were now made to vacate the room, but Salor had one more thing on his mind.

'Vlad,' said Salor, as Vlad made to leave.

'Yes?'

'Make sure Jose doesn't do anything stupid.'

'I will,' said Vlad, fingers as crossed as he could get them.

CHAPTER 5

Danrite Willocky, Dan to his friends, not that he had any, so mostly known as Willocky, was a strange boy. This though wasn't entirely his fault. But we will come to that.

'Oi! Willocky! 'eard any voices lately?' was bellowed after Danrite as he trudged home. This was a not an uncommon question as it was well-known in the confines of the world that Danrite existed in, that Danrite heard and saw things. Or so he had said; which hadn't been an entirely wise move on his part. The question was then followed by a not uncommon round of cruel laughter. Danrite trudged on, head down, eager to ignore the jibes, but the deriding continued.

'Ha-ha, next he'll be seeing….' There was a brief silence as the derider wrinkled his brow.

This silence brought about a question from his companion; also a derider, but more a follower than an instigator. 'Seeing what?' he asked.

The brow wrinkled further. 'Thingy things.'

'Thingy things?' repeated his fellow derider, not being very helpful.

'You know,' said the instigator.

It appeared neither did. So while foreheads wrinkled and brows beetled, Danrite took the chance to make with rapid leg movements. It was an often necessary course of action that had on repeated occasions stopped him from being pulled this way and that, and generally pummelled.

Danrite made for open ground, and was on it and putting good distance between him and his would-be assailants before they had any inkling their quarry was making good his escape. By then it was too late. One thing Danrite could do right was run. To be fair he had had a fair amount of practise. He had never been caught when given a head start. A head start that was sometimes provided by forces he knew nothing about.

Danrite didn't stop running until he was home. But this wasn't the usual. Usually he would appraise the situation, and when sure the danger was past would slow back to a walk. But today was different. Chest heaving, temple pulsing, Danrite steadied his hand and put key to lock. He opened his front door and stumbled inside.

Inside, he leant against the hall wall, his back to it, and waited for his heart to return to normal. It didn't take long. It never did when he was home. He was safe when he was home. The familiar pictures on the walls. The fading carpet. The paint-chipped doors. The stairs at the end of the hall, always welcoming; especially after a particularly stressful day. All, always welcoming. All helping to calm him. All was part of his home. And this day, this moment in time, he needed to feel his home around him, more than ever.

CHAPTER 6

Danrite was sat on his bed, his knees tucked under his chin, his arms embracing them, staring at the small alarm clock he kept on the bedside table. It was about to display two o'clock on its digital face. The solicitor had said he would call on him at three. Danrite sighed. It had been a long day so far; a long week; a long life. The numbers on the clock changed; an hour to go. Danrite let his mind wander.

Everything had been going along great until he was eight years old. Then his world had come crashing down around him. No one knows to this day what happened to his parents, only that they had disappeared without trace one day. Off they had gone one morning, after dropping him off at school, to never return. His mother had kissed his cheek, his father had waved. It was his last memory of them.

Danrite shifted a buttock and reached beneath it. He had sat on something. To his surprise it was an old fob watch. It was Uncle Percy's. Funny, thought Danrite, how did that get there? He was certain it hadn't been there when he had sat down. He stared at it for a long moment and his mind turned to the day the strange man had suddenly appeared from nowhere, barging his way into Danrite's life.

Percy Willocky had arrived, not known, unannounced and not long after the powers that be had decided that the young Danrite should be placed into care.

He had breezed in, flashing to all and sundry his credentials, to wit, proof that he was the long lost brother of the poor child's missing father and therefore the legal guardian of the said poor boy. Danrite had never heard of him. Couldn't remember any mention of him. Yet all appeared to be in order, so it was job done, and Percy became Danrite's legal guardian. The weirdest chapter of Danrite's short life thus far, had started.

Percy took enthusiastic charge of his young charge as soon as, and immediately moved into Danrite's home. But any fears Danrite may have harboured about the strange man that had suddenly entered his life were soon dispelled as Percy proved himself to be as likable as a sugar mouse wearing a silly hat. Eccentric, like a sugar mouse wearing a silly hat, but likable.

The first year with Percy was a bit of a blur, but Danrite could remember looking up "eccentric" in his father's dictionary and feeling disappointed when there was no mention of Percy.

The next year was a little less chaotic though. Danrite put it down to becoming used to Percy's eccentric ways.

There was the case of the hammock. Strung across the landing at the top of the stairs because Percy said it reminded him of his days at sea. 'Couldn't be doing sleeping in a bed that didn't move' he would say. Not that Percy ever slept in it of course. No, that would be too "normal". At first Danrite had thought it odd. All things Percy did were odd. But gradually Percy's oddness became the norm in Danrite's house; the accepted thing where Percy was concerned. And sometimes things he did seemed to have a degree of sense to them. Unless, that is, Danrite was becoming odd. Danrite had decided, when thinking this, that perhaps he shouldn't think too hard about it.

Some things though didn't change; the everyday, ordinary, mundane things. The house. The furniture. The curtains. Going to school. Which, in a world full of Percy was comforting in a way. But that wasn't to say there wasn't some oddness among the mundane. Danrite had never seen Percy dust or clean, or do the washing up. Nor had he seen Percy doing the weekly shop; but the larder and fridge were always full, the house neat, tidy, and dust free. Oddly, just as the day his parents had disappeared.

Now Danrite wasn't at home twenty-four seven. No he wasn't. Percy could have done it all while he was at school, or out playing. But Danrite had this feeling. A feeling that had him hiding away one Saturday in a kitchen cupboard, to watch for Percy to do the washing up. He stayed all day. He had sandwiches, a bottle of orange squash and a pile of comics. Oh, and he also had a bucket for emergencies; the orange squash. Danrite was on a serious stakeout. But wait as he did for all that day, he never saw Percy do the washing up. Yet it was done. Had he inadvertently fallen asleep? He didn't think so. So things continued as they did, and Danrite kept his feeling.

And another thing, as mentioned before, the house appeared to remain in the same state as when his parents had disappeared. You hear of people keeping a loved-one's room just the way it was before they were lost, but a whole house? Nothing changed. Nothing appeared to wear out. Even the hall carpet never got any tattier. It was as if an invisible covering constantly protected everything, protecting it from the wear and tear of time. But again, in its way, it was somehow comforting; odd, but comforting. So Danrite never felt the need to mention it, and Percy, in turn, never said anything either.

By the next year, Danrite was generally taking things in his stride. Until, that is, he started hearing things. Nothing solid; nothing he could quite catch. This was closely followed by the seeing things, just on the peripherals; always a breath away, but something, now and again.

At first Danrite thought he might be going mad; something to do with being an orphan. Then he wondered perhaps if it might be something to do with Percy; his oddness rubbing off on him. But every time he began to doubt his sanity, contact with Percy somehow made him feel alright again; his fears fleeing like a butterfly from a net; all okay with the world again. After a while Danrite decided he was worrying about nothing. It wasn't as if he was talking to himself or anything like that. He didn't have hair growing on the palms of his hands (a well-known sign of madness), nor did he look to see if he had hair on his palms (another sure sign so he had been told). So all was still well with the world, until that is, he told someone.

It was understandable. He wanted to talk about what he thought he heard and saw. But Percy would not do. No adult would. So he told, as all children do, his best friend. Children can be so cruel. One minute you are besties, the next you are worsties. It can happen in a blink of an eye. Overnight, Danrite Willocky had become Danrite weird. And so the teasing and running began.

As Danrite sat on his bed staring at, but not seeing the digital clock, his memories playing through his mind like some tragi-doc, he began to gently rock back and forth. The movement began to build momentum. A second or two later Danrite returned to the here and now as he fell off the bed and landed on the floor. He picked himself up, dusted himself down, and wondered if perhaps rocking was perhaps the first sign of his going bonkers.

Deciding not to dwell on his impending madness, Danrite went to the window and peered outside to the street below. All appeared as it usually did, another normal day, but he knew it wasn't. Today was a sad day. He was alone again. Percy Willocky, eccentric uncle, loveable loony, had been laid to rest that morning; a week to the day of his accident. What Percy had been doing on the roof before he fell off was as much a mystery as the man himself. Fitting then, felt Danrite, in a way. He turned from the window.

Percy's fob watch was on the floor. Danrite picked it up and squeezed it, gaining something from doing so; reassurance maybe. Danrite wondered what would become of him now. What changes lay ahead? He couldn't think of anything good. Danrite gave the fob watch another squeeze. He doubted the teasing or chasing would change. He had already had to run that day, and on his way back from the chapel of rest. Is nothing sacred anymore?

But it wasn't the time for feeling sorry for himself, he had the rest of his life for that. Danrite placed the fob watch on the bedside table and left the bedroom to head downstairs. The solicitor would be here soon and he had to practice keeping a straight face. He could do it; he knew he could do it. But every time Danrite imagined Percy's solicitor getting to the part about Percy being of sound mind, he couldn't help but smile. He doubted he could do it.

CHAPTER 7

'You know, thingy things.'

'Still don't know what yer going on abo- 'ere, he's legged it!'

'After him.'

The two would-be pummelers chased after Danrite. Together they ran. Together they suddenly fell forward and landed on their faces.

'Nice one, Twinkle,' said Vlad, admiring her handiwork.

'Ditto, Vlad my man,' said Twinkle, holding up a hand. They high-fived and looked to where Danrite had skedaddled.

'Jose still with him?' said Vlad, peering.

'Must be,' said Twinkle, also peering, 'unless he's fallen down a hole again.'

Vlad surveyed the area between themselves and where Danrite had fled. 'Can't see any holes,' he said.

'That's the trouble,' said Twinkle, 'neither does he.' Twinkle guffawed at her witticism, causing a shower of glitter that landed at her feet.

Vlad tittered and offered his hand high again. They high-fived and headed in the direction Danrite had taken.

Behind them, floundering in the dirt, the two bullies peered about them trying desperately to see who it was that had tripped them up. There was no one to be seen. They got to their feet. They dusted themselves down. They exchanged worried looks. They made sudden and quick tracks to anywhere far from where they were. On the way, as they made those quick tracks, they wondered if they should mention the voices they thought they had heard.

This scenario, as may well be obvious, occurred but a short while ago as Danrite travelled home from the chapel of rest. What isn't so obvious is that this small episode in the life of Danrite Willocky was just a small taste of the strange occurrences and odd happenings, he had been experiencing the last nine years; ten if you counted the arrival of Percy.

You see, Percy and the hearing things, glimpsing things was only the shallow end of the pool. The deep end was far weirder, and thankfully Danrite never mentioned anything that happened in the deep end, otherwise who knows where he would have ended up.

There was the time he had forgotten his gym shorts. A nightmare for any eleven year old boy when you were privy to the school rule: no shorts, no excuse. You would have to do gym in your underpants. But as luck had had it, just as the stricken Danrite had been thinking of hiding in a cupboard for the duration of the lesson, a pair of shorts, and just the right size, had blown in through an open window and onto his shivering lap. Lucky boy. Not a totally impossible thing to happen, granted, but these just so happened to have Danrite's name written on the inside in Percy's handwriting. Very lucky boy.

Another example of the strange was when Danrite had sneaked from the house one evening to go fishing. Percy had shown no interest in the sport, so Danrite had gone out behind Percy's back. Percy didn't like Danrite going out on his own. Danrite had put it down to Percy being overprotective. So Danrite, his father's rod in hand, had wandered down to the river, baited his hook, cast his line, and next moment found he was back in bed, staring up at a fish mobile he had, until then, never possessed. To further compound the mystery, he was now in his pyjamas. Had his fishing trip been nothing but a dream? A very realistic dream? For sanity's sake he had decided it must have been. But that of course didn't explain the fish mobile, or that when he got out of bed he found he was wearing wellingtons with his pyjamas tucked into them.

But the strange had gradually become the norm and that was then and this is now, and Danrite is no longer a child but a young man of eighteen years of age, waiting for his uncle's solicitor to arrive.

'What time is the solicitor supposed to arrive?' asked Twinkle, applying fresh glitter to her face.

'Three,' said Vlad, pulling his hood tighter around his face.

'I don't know why you do that,' said Twinkle, frowning at Vlad, 'it's not as if anyone on this side can see you.'

'You can,' said Vlad.

'Only your cape. If you took it off even I wouldn't be able to see you.'

'It's not my fault,' said Vlad.

'I didn't say it was,' said Twinkle, putting her pouch of glitter away.

'We've got time,' said Vlad, getting back on topic.

'You suppose Jose is there already?'

'He had better be,' said Vlad, 'there's no one else.'

'Bit lax I say,' said Twinkle, 'if he's all they say he is.'

'Jose?'

'Danrite.'

'Oh, what's that supposed to mean?'

'What do you think I mean?'

'It's because you've never seen a being half giant, half dwarf before. He's a first.'

'He's that all right,' said Twinkle.

Vlad decided to ignore her. Just because she didn't believe Danrite was the one, didn't mean he wasn't. His thoughts instead turned to Jose. 'Perhaps we should get a move on,' he said, picking up his pace, 'just in case Jose's been sidetracked or something.'

'He'll be fine,' said Twinkle, gathering her tutu to her. 'Jose won't let us down.' But just to be on the safe side; you never knew, a hole here a tree there. 'Here give me your hand.' She held out her left hand.

'You sure?'

'Wouldn't ask if I wasn't.'

Vlad took hold of Twinkle's outstretched hand and closed his eyes. When he opened them again they were outside Danrite's house. 'Still got some of the old magic then,' he said.

'A little,' said Twinkle, smiling sadly, 'but not as much as yesterday and less again as the day before.'

Vlad, who was still holding Twinkle's hand, gave it a reassuring squeeze. 'Everything will be okay, you'll see.'

'I hope so,' said Twinkle, letting go of Vlad's hand. 'I sincerely hope so.'

CHAPTER 8

'Do we have him Mister Fix?' said a sharp-suited dude, sitting behind an expanse of desk that used to be a large oak tree.

'Yes, sir,' said Mister Fix. He wore a not so sharp suit that screamed minion.

The sharp-suited dude appeared to muse for a moment on this piece of information before asking another question. 'Anything interesting I should know about?'

'No, sir, nothing out of the ordinary to report.'

'Who's taken his place?'

'Mister Project, sir.'

The sharp-suited dude sat back and steepled his fingers. 'Who has he got with him?'

'Rogi and Ergo, sir.'

A look of concern passed across the sharp-suited dude's face, but it was fleeting. 'Are they stable?' he asked.

'No deterioration noted, sir.'

The sharp-suited dude smiled grimly as he got to his feet. 'Let's get it done then,' he said, 'but keep those two monitored.'

'Yes, sir, Mister Power, sir,' said the minion, suddenly displaying a modicum of nervousness as Mister Power moved in his direction.

'Leave me.' Mister Power waved a hand towards the door.

'Yes, sir,' said the minion, eager to do as he was told.

Mister Power, he chose the name himself, turned to face the massive wall to wall, floor to ceiling window, that he usually had his back to. He stared at the vista beyond the glass without looking at it. 'Just one more thing Mister Fix before you go.'

Mister Fix stopped, rooted to the spot. 'Yes, sir?' he managed to say without too much quiver to his voice.

'Send Miss Manager in. I wish to know how it goes with the new line of autobiographies.'

'Right away, sir,' said Mister Fix, mustering an enthusiasm he didn't realise he possessed.

CHAPTER 9

Danrite was in the kitchen when the front doorbell rang at three o'clock on the dot. The dishes had needed cleaning and he had doubted they would do themselves, even if he was to hide in the cupboard all day. He dried his hands and went to the door.

'Mister Willocky?' the suited gentleman standing on the doorstep enquired.

'Yes,' said Danrite, thinking that the man looked more like a teacher than a solicitor. A science teacher; all eagerness and a top pocket brimming with pens and pencils. Danrite had expected a silk handkerchief at least, but then Danrite had never met a solicitor before. And, as he hadn't met Percy's solicitor before, could be jumping to conclusions. Who was to say the man standing on the doorstop was the solicitor he had been waiting for; he could be anyone. At least the man was wearing a suit; dishevelled as it was.

The solicitor held out a hand. 'My name is Mister Law,' he said brightly. 'I am… sorry was… sorry is, your late uncle's solicitor.'

He was the solicitor, and as first impressions went, Danrite wasn't; impressed that is. And what sort of name was Law? Apt, Danrite supposed, but really? Danrite stepped aside and ushered the man inside.

'Where is he?' whispered Vlad, as he and Twinkle watched the solicitor enter Danrite's home.

'How should I know,' said Twinkle.

'Do you think he's already in the house?'

'I don't see why he should be. We told him to wait in the garden until we arrived, unless there was an emergency and I don't see any emergency, do you?'

Vlad didn't, so where was Jose? Then a thought struck him. 'How many gardens does the house have?' he said.

'How do I know?' said Twinkle, who obviously didn't know a lot about anything. To be fair though, she had only ever seen the front of the house. 'Two maybe, back and front, who knows?' A second later the penny dropped. 'Ah.'

'Now, Danrite, I can call you Danrite?' asked Mister Law as he and Danrite sat at the kitchen table.

Danrite didn't really care what the dishevelled man called him because he wanted this meeting over as soon as possible, so he nodded.

'Good,' said Mister Law, looking in his briefcase. 'Now, where did I put it?' He rummaged further. 'Ah, here it is.' Mister Law looked up at Danrite and smiled. It wasn't an overly friendly sort of smile, and quickly disappeared as he pulled something from his case, something that most certainly had no resemblance in the least to a last will and testament. 'I want you to have this.'

But before Mister Law had a chance to give to Danrite, whatever it was he wanted to give him, the kitchen window imploded, spraying the room with glass. With the glass was something else; something that landed on the top of the table.

Danrite stared, open-mouthed, as he tried to disentangle his legs from the chair he had just been sitting on, but which was now somehow wrapped around his ankles.

Mister Law meanwhile, was backing away from the thing on the table. The object he, just a moment ago, was so keen to give to Danrite still in his hand. He pointed it at the something on the table. The something on the table growled and showed rows of sharp tiny teeth.

Danrite's eyes had widened; he had never before seen such an angry chihuahua.

Twinkle and Vlad's arrival at the back garden was instantly greeted with the sound of breaking glass.

'Oh grief,' exclaimed Twinkle, who had seen what had caused it. 'Quick, give me your hand.'

'But the…'

'Hand!'

He did what he was told and the next second he was robeless and knocking a gun out of the hand of someone that looked suspiciously like a teacher.

'Wah!' wailed Mister Law, as the gun he had been going to threaten Danrite with, and had then been trained on the chihuahua, suddenly flew from his hand.

'Wah!' yelled Danrite, as a sudden cloud of shimmering glitter arrived between him and the kitchen table.

'Wah!' shouted Twinkle, as the door to the kitchen suddenly burst open, revealing two humongous suited creatures.

'Wah!' repeated Mister Law, as those two humongous creatures in suits, each grabbing an arm, carried him, sharpish-like, from the kitchen, stepping on Vlad as they did.

Vlad, who had had his back to the kitchen door when it had flown open and had been knocked to the floor, sadly hadn't had time for a "WAH!" but did manage something somewhat similar when a humongous size twenty boot inadvertently stepped on him. 'Waaa!' howled Vlad.

Another voice now entered the fray, a comical Mexican voice that would have been at home in any cartoon where a comical Mexican voice was needed. 'I chase them, sí?' snarled the chihuahua.

'Wah!' said Danrite, continuing the theme; and why shouldn't he, when faced with a talking dog?

'Naw, better not,' said Twinkle, who was on hands and knees looking for the invisible Vlad, 'could be more of them.'

'Wha-what's that?' stammered Danrite, recovering the ability to speak, but to no one in particular, while pointing at the chihuahua. He had gone as white as one of those sheets you see in a washing powder advert.

'A chihuahua,' said somebody with a boot imprint on his invisible body.

Danrite spun round to see who had spoken, but there was no one there. He spun back, eyes large as saucers. He had just noticed the huge woman on the floor. A huge woman, who was covered in glitter, wearing a tutu and a tiara, and was staring straight at him. Where had she come from? He had never known the hearing, seeing things to be this bad before. Everything seemed so *solid*. Perhaps this was it, the tipping point. Any moment now, people wearing white coats would pour through the gap left by the stricken kitchen door and cart him away. His knees, obviously not liking the idea of being carted away, decided to have nothing more to do with the situation. As they buckled and Danrite found he was no longer as tall as he was a moment ago, his mind and the rest of his body decided, unanimously, to join his knees in their decision; so one out, all out. Danrite collapsed in a heap.

'He all right, you think?' said Vlad, as he picked up his robe which, for some unknown reason, had arrived a little later than he had.

'I think he's fainted,' said Twinkle, getting to her feet. 'You okay?'

'A bit bruised,' said Vlad.

'I didn't think you could,' said Twinkle.

'I was speaking metaphorically.'

'Ah,' said Twinkle, as she headed to where Danrite lay. She reached down and felt for a pulse. 'Yep, our hero is still with us.'

'Not that confident he'd fainted then?' said Vlad.

Twinkle ignored Vlad and stared hard at the chihuahua. 'This is your fault,' she said, sternly.

The chihuahua shrugged. 'Why, I am only doing my job?'

'You spoke, you shouldn't have,' said Twinkle. 'He wasn't ready.'

'She's right you know,' said Vlad.

Jose the chihuahua glared at Vlad. He couldn't actually see him, but his doggy senses and the hovering robe, helped to point him in the right direction. 'And you have no blame, Mister voice from the thin air?'

'He's right,' said Twinkle. 'You're both to blame. And for goodness' sake Vlad, put your clothes on.'

'No one can see me.'

'Not the point,' said Twinkle, tut-tutting.

Vlad donned his robe and made a face at Jose.

Twinkle righted the chair Danrite had been sitting on and then heaved his limp body back on to it, sitting him upright. 'This could be serious,' she said, lifting one of Danrite's eyelids to show the white of his eye. 'It was way too soon.'

'What is serious?' said Jose, jumping from the table.

'It wasn't time.'

'Time for what?' said Jose, sniffing at Danrite's right leg.

'For him to see us,' said Twinkle, checking under Danrite's other eyelid.

'Well that lets me off the hook,' Vlad joked.

Twinkle reached across to where the robe was hovering and slapped the side of the hood; just where Vlad's ear should be.

'Ow!' said Vlad.

'Now's not the time,' Twinkle scolded.

On the floor Jose took a precautionary step backwards, he knew the dangers of getting too close to an angry Twinkle.

'So what do we do now?' asked a rueful Vlad.

'Perhaps we should be telling Salor,' said Jose.

'Good idea,' said Twinkle. 'Off you go then.' Twinkle expected Salor would be none too pleased with developments. Better someone else told him.

'Me?' said Jose, suddenly smelling a rat.

'I don't see any other talking chihuahuas, do you?' said Twinkle.

'But…'

'No buts, Jose, off you go.'

Jose's tail dropped between his back legs. If Twinkle thinks things are bad, it is bad. Salor would not be happy then. When would he ever learn to keep his mouth shut? 'Very well, I will be going.' Jose dragged his feet as he headed towards the broken window. There he stopped and looked round, his big round eyes watery under their lids. 'I will then wish you both a fond farewell, adiós amigos.' And then he was through the window and away.

'Talk about dramatic,' said Vlad.

'Tell me about it,' said Twinkle.

CHAPTER 10

'Come,' said Mister Power, as the door to his office quivered under the knocking of a humongous fist. It was one of the reasons the office door was made of steel.

The door opened and a huge figure in a suit squeezed through the gap. Mister Project, aka Law followed, his feet some two feet from the floor. Dangling Mister Project from a huge fist was another huge figure in a suit. He too squeezed into the office. Mister Project, limp as a newborn kitten, was duly dumped in a heap in front of the oak desk.

Mister Power toyed idly with a Newton's Cradle; the clacking helped him think. But this wasn't the time for thinking; it was the time for doing. He grabbed the steel balls mid clack and cast a steely eye over the prostrate Mister Project. Mister Project had assumed a rather professional grovelling position. Rather impressive, thought Mister Power, but futile. He hated failure, and no amount of grovelling, however impressive, was going to sway his decision. Mister Project was to be disposed of. But first, out of professional courtesy, he would hear him out. Besides, who knew what bit of useful information might be gleaned.

'Well?' said Mister Power.

'It wasn't my fault,' whined Mister Project, nose to the carpet, eyes firmly averted.

'It never is,' said Mister Power, inspecting a manicured fingernail.

'He was guarded.'

Mister Power glanced at Rogi, who he felt was the more intelligent of the two humongous suits; but only if you were comparing the intelligence of a slug to that of a peanut.

'He was, sir,' said Rogi, sounding remarkably posh.

'Ah,' said Mister Power, rounding his desk.

On the floor, Mister Project, foolishly so, took his bosses comment as a positive. He took a chance to back up his excuse. 'Heavily so, sir,' he said, his lips touching carpet.

'By what pray tell?' asked Mister Power, stepping to within a couple of feet of his prostrate underling.

And here the delusion Mister Project had been clinging so dearly to, evaporated. His mind suddenly darted here and there, trying desperately to think of a way of escape he knew didn't exist.

'Well?' said Mister Power.

Mister Project's Adam's apple bobbed frantically as he mumbled something into the carpet.

'What was that? I didn't quite catch what you said.' said Mister Power. 'Has the cat got your tongue?' He paused a second, 'Or should that be the chihuahua?'

Mister Project wailed.

'Take him away,' ordered Mister Power, waving a dismissive hand in Mister Project's direction. He turned his back on the terrified man.

'And where would that be to, sir?' said Rogi, grabbing an arm.

Mister Power half turned, as if listening for something. 'Recycling I think,' he said, 'seems to be the thing these days.'

'No!' screamed Mister Project, 'Anything but that.'

Mister Power was back facing him in a flash. 'Anything?' he asked, sinisterly.

The remaining colour in Mister Project's face immediately drained. Was there something worse than being recycled? His mind decided it didn't want to know. Mister Project slumped in a faint.

'Recycling it is then,' said Mister Power. 'Take him away.'

Rogi and Ergo, the other suited humongous, each grabbed an arm and picked the limp Mister Project from off the floor before sidling sideways through the doorway.

'Oh and,' said Mister Power, as an idea struck, 'take him via the stairs.' The stairway was the most visible exit, and there was nothing like a bit of visible recycling to keep everyone on their toes. He was then struck by another thought. 'And don't…' But Mister Power was a second too late. The huge steel door slammed shut, shaking the walls and everything in the room. The Newton Cradle clacked like a thing demented.

As Mister Power picked himself up from the floor, there was another knock at the door; a gentle knock this time; a more delicate hand. It was a knock he knew and, although loath to admit, looked forward to. 'Wait a moment,' he said, quickly putting a comb through his hair and generally titivating. 'Okay, come in.'

The door opened and Miss Manager entered the room. A tall vision of loveliness with playfully swaying tousled auburn hair and the bluest of eyes. She also wore spectacles of the horned-rim variety. She was also far from stupid, as she knew what Mister Power's idea of loveliness was, right down to the horn-rimmed glasses; she had done her homework. She also knew that what Mister Power didn't like, didn't usually last very long.

'Ah, Miss Manager, is that the information on the new line of autobiographies I asked for?' asked Mister Power, straightening his tie.

'It is,' purred Miss Manager. 'Shall I place them on your desk?'

Mister Power was staring.

'Mister Power?'

'Yes?' He gathered himself. 'Oh. Yes, that will be fine.'

Miss Manager did as she was told. 'Will that be all, sir?'

Another Adam's apple now bobbed. 'For now, thank you,' said Mister Power. He watched her leave the room and sighed as she closed the door behind her. He wondered how she had ever come to be working for him. She was unique you see. She was the only human he had ever employed.

CHAPTER 11

In his unconscious state, Danrite was riding a rollercoaster ride; a rollercoaster ride that was travelling way too fast; a rollercoaster ride on the verge of becoming a runaway.

Danrite was sitting alone in the first car, holding on to the front bar for all he was worth; safety restraints that may have existed in the real world were sadly lacking in this, his unconscious one. Behind him, sat in the second and only other car, was his Uncle Percy. Percy was standing up and frantically trying to tell Danrite something important. But as loud as he might shout, his voice was being drowned out by the noise of the wind rushing by and the rattle of the rollercoaster.

The cars suddenly shook. Danrite's knuckles grew whiter. There was a bump, followed by a jolt. The cars bucked violently, the wheels lifting from the track. Danrite gasped. Somewhere behind him Percy screamed. Somehow, the cars stayed on the track.

Gripping tightly, a petrified Danrite started to turn in his seat. Slowly, agonisingly, inch by inch, he eventually managed it. And what he saw when he had, filled him with horror. A screaming Percy was no longer in his car. A screaming Percy was now hanging from the back of it; holding on for dear life; flapping about like washing in a force nine gale.

A choice had to be made. Did Danrite sit tight or go to Percy's aid? Danrite wasn't a brave lad by any stretch of the imagination, but he gritted his teeth and decided on the latter. Trouble was, that was easier said than done. Danrite found his hands were locked tight around the bar. As much as he wanted to help Percy, his hands just wouldn't let go. Percy had stopped screaming now, but was still making a noise. He was shouting something; something Danrite couldn't quite make out.

'I can't hear what you're saying!' yelled Danrite, still trying to coax his hands into letting go of the bar. Then suddenly there was a lull. The noise the wind and the rollercoaster were making had eased. They had slowed slightly. They were going uphill. And with the lull Percy's voice at last was able to reach Danrite's ears.

'They're coming!' yelled Percy. 'They're coming for you Danny boy!'

'Who is?' yelled Danrite, the hairs on the back of his neck rising, reacting to the look of terror on Percy's face.

'They are!' shouted Percy. 'They are!' He took a hand from the bar and managed to point towards Danrite; past Danrite. It was dramatic. It was a mistake. As soon as he had, his other hand started to lose its grip on the bar. Percy tried to grab hold again with the hand he had pointed with, but to no avail. He lost hold. He screamed. He was gone.

'No!' wailed Danrite, but it was too late.

With tears in his eyes he faced forward again. The summit of the upward slope he was travelling along was fast approaching. What had Percy meant? The car reached the summit. Tears now started to flow; tears that disappeared as quickly as they appeared, the wind tearing them away as the car hurtled down. What was it Percy had been pointing at? Danrite wiped away a tear that had managed to creep into his left nostril. He had seen nothing when he had turned away, and all he saw now was a huge tunnel, looming dark; so dark.

And then there was light; or lighter as it happened, which gradually started to grow even lighter. Danrite was suddenly aware of the lack of movement; a lack of rollercoaster. All was now bright light. Now, amongst the light, shapes were appearing. Vague shapes. Blurry shapes, but gradually becoming clearer. Oval shapes, round ones, with features of growing definition, becoming faces. Faces were all around him. Some of which he recognised; his parents', Percy's. Some he didn't recognise. He didn't know the large one, looming as the tunnel had. Looming and covered in what looked like glitter. Now the faces started to fade; all but one, the large one. It loomed larger. LARGER. Danrite screamed like he had never screamed before.

'Yaaaaa!!' screamed Danrite, screaming like he had never screamed before.

Twinkle, face glitter blown to the four corners of the room by the force of Danrite's outburst, blinked and then grabbed Danrite by the shoulders. 'Whoa there big boy,' she commanded, 'you'll do your tonsils a mischief. Everything's fine now.'

But everything didn't look fine, not to Danrite. Not when a woman he didn't know was holding him down with the strength of ten men. A woman who was the size of a sumo wrestler, a large sumo wrestler, wearing heavy red lipstick that was only inches from his face, a tiara set at a jaunty angle on her head and a tutu that looked on the verge of turning into an experience no amount of couch counselling would be able to put right. No, things did not appear fine to Danrite. And what was with all the glitter? He instinctively tried to struggle which, under the circumstances, got him nowhere, but did manage to dislodge some glitter from the tip of his nose. Danrite then proceeded to breathe said glitter into his left nostril. The resulting sneeze did not help matters.

'Why you little…'

'Twinkle!' snapped Salor, as Twinkle clenched and raised a huge fist. He had just arrived and was stood in the kitchen doorway, a picture of shock on his face, Jose between his feet.

Twinkle was aghast. What had she been thinking? Yeah her face was covered in spittle. Yeah she was angry. Yeah she didn't believe for a minute that the gangly youth she had been about to whack was their saviour. But man alive, that was no reason to raise her fist. Head hanging, eyes averted, shocked by what she might have done, Twinkle put down her fist, got to her feet and waited for the rightful ear hammering she expected to receive.

But Salor, as horrified as he was at what he had just seen, controlled his anger. Everyone was on edge. No point in making a bad situation worse. He softened his voice. 'What happened here?'

Twinkle sagged as the tension in the room took a deep breath and relaxed a little. 'Didn't Jose tell you?' she said. She looked at the chihuahua.

'Not fully,' said Salor, looking down between his feet. 'You know how he gets when he's excited.' Jose whined, his tail dropping between his back legs. Salor looked up again. 'Rosie was cleaning it up when I left.' There followed another pathetic whine from below. 'But I'm here now, so fill me in.'

Whilst the telling of the tale took place, Danrite started to regain what senses he had been given at birth. He stirred slowly. He felt a little dizzy. What had happened? He gingerly opened an eye. He could hear people talking; in his kitchen. What were people doing in his kitchen? He then remembered the solicitor that looked like a teacher. This led to other recollections. He shut his eye again. He needed a moment. There had been… the window had broken… then there had been… the talking… Danrite's mind suddenly wanted to shut down again. No, he wouldn't let it, there had to be a reasonable explanation. Danrite cogitated, and analysed. And then he had it; a conclusion. He knew what had happened, and was currently happening to him. It was the only thing it could be; so obvious. He opened one eye again and had a quick shufti around the room. He had been, and was still, hallucinating. It was truly the only explanation for what had, and was, happening.

It had been a hard day after all, a rough day on the senses; a stressful one. It was little wonder then he was displaying doolallyness. Who wouldn't? He was tired, mix that with the stress and it isn't too much of a leap to conclude a more than possible amplification of his usual seeing and hearing episodes; something way beyond the norm; if you could call such episodes the norm?

Happy with his self-diagnosis Danrite, ignoring all that was going on around him, got up to make a nice cup of hot sweet tea. Just what the doctor might well have ordered, if apt to the occasional misdiagnosis. Not that he needed a doctor. No, a cuppa would suffice.

Dodging his hallucinations - they weren't there, but Danrite felt it rude to just walk straight through them – Danrite went to prepare that cuppa. He filled the kettle, switched it on, took a mug from the mug tree, shoved two spoons of sugar and a teabag into it, and waited; tapping his foot and whistling under his breath as he did so.

Danrite was still waiting for the kettle to do its stuff when a worried Jose jumped up onto the draining board Danrite was leaning against and stared up at him. Danrite didn't bat an eyelid. Why should he? Something that wasn't there couldn't startle. Jose had been watching Danrite. Had noted him leave his chair. Noted the way he dodged everyone as he went about whatever it was he was about to do. Noted Danrite appeared to be looking straight through him as he sat there. 'Is he okay?' said Jose, cocking his head to one side. He also noted, as he aired his worries, that Danrite didn't appear to hear him.

The tale tellers, who had been at it for about ten minutes now; nine minutes bickering, one to tell it, had just finished. They and Salor, all of whom had failed to notice Danrite was up and about, looked across at Jose.

'Come away,' said Salor, frowning at the little dog.

Jose jumped down from the sink unit. 'I think he sleeps on his feet,' he said, shrugging bony shoulders. He went over to the broken door, sat on it and decided the back of one of his ears needed a good scratch.

Salor decided it might be time to make introductions, along with the odd explanation. He ambled over to where Danrite was standing and stood beside him.

'Who's asleep?' asked a puzzled Twinkle.

'I think introductions are in order,' said Salor, offering his hand. 'My name is Salor.' But the offer was ignored; as was the introduction. Salor did some more frowning and coughed. Again he was ignored. Salor's frown deepened. He decided to try something. He slowly raised a hand which he then carefully placed in front of Danrite's face.

Danrite had heard the voice, seen the hand, but hadn't, because they didn't exist. Come on kettle, he thought, the sooner I get some tea inside me the better.

Nothing; it was if his hand was invisible. Salor tried it a little closer, waving it, almost touching Danrite's nose; again nothing.

Danrite steeled himself as the hand that didn't exist started to get closer. He mustn't blink. Because if he did that would mean… mean what? Danrite didn't rightly know what it might mean, but he doubted it would be good.

Salor took his hand away and looked at the others, his face showing slight concern. 'I'm not totally sure, but I believe Danrite here might be experiencing something along the lines of shock.'

Ha! thought Danrite. Knew it would go away if I ignored it. What did he just say? But thankfully, before the illusion that surrounded him could suck him in, he was saved by the timely ringing of a bell; or whistle as it happened. The kettle had gone above and beyond. It had boiled Danrite's water and stepped in when he was on the brink of all out total doolallyness. Saved by Percy, thought Danrite, as he recalled what Percy had said when he appeared with the kettle one day. "A kettle isn't a kettle, my boy unless it can whistle while it works." And how glad was he now that Percy had insisted on its use. The noise from the kettle was real; a beacon amongst the shadows of the unreal. He smiled to himself as he picked the kettle up and started pouring its contents into his cup.

'He's gone ga-ga,' said Vlad, noticing the smile.

'Sí,' Jose seconded. 'Ga-ga.'

Ignoring the sounds that bounced against his eardrums, because they weren't really there, Danrite squeezed the teabag against the side of the cup. Then, teabag squeezed to within an inch of its tealeaves, he deposited it in the little plastic box the council had supplied for just such eventualities. He then, as he poured the milk, had a sudden and worrying thought that sent a shiver running down his spine. How could you ignore what wasn't there? You couldn't ignore what wasn't there, could you? He stirred the contents of his cup and then took a sip. The thoughts drifted away. Just what the doctor ordered, but not the couch variety of course.

Danrite turned; he had decided he needed a sit down to fully appreciate his cuppa, but not here; too many things to ignore that weren't really there; the lounge then. He started across the kitchen, weaving when needed because it was only polite, and headed out the door.

Salor and the others watched him go. 'Definitely in shock,' said Salor, stroking his beard thoughtfully.

'Then he's doing the right thing, drinking sweet tea,' said Vlad.

'Poppycock,' said Twinkle, 'just an old wives' tale.'

'Is not.'

'Is.'

'And you'd know?'

'Why you…'

'Enough,' said Salor, stepping between Twinkle and Vlad.

'Ga-ga,' said Jose, not to be left out.

'I think not,' said Salor. 'Follow me.' He headed after Danrite.

They found him sat in the lounge, sat on a sofa, sipping his tea and staring straight ahead. Salor pulled up a chair and sat directly in front of Danrite.

'I have the feeling Jose might be right on this one,' said Twinkle, after a couple of minutes of Danrite staring right though Salor. 'He's lost it.'

Jose wagged his tail.

'No,' said Salor, steepling his fingers under his chin, 'something else. Something has disturbed him greatly.'

'I knew it,' said Twinkle. 'I told Jose it was too soon. Didn't I tell him, Vlad?'

'She did,' said Vlad, climbing back aboard the merry-go-round that was their relationship. 'It's Jose's fault.'

Jose said nothing. Just gave his accusers the evil eye and thought unhappy thoughts.

'It's no one's fault,' said Salor, coming to the chihuahua's defence. 'Jose was just doing his job. If he hadn't acted, who knows what might have happened. I doubt young Danrite here would be about to enjoy that cuppa.'

'Sí, he is right,' said Jose, quick to big himself up in front of Twinkle and Vlad. He grinned, a huge doggy grin.

'I was the one that knocked the gun from the baddie's hand,' said Vlad, quick to latch on to the acclaim bandwagon.

'I used some of my magic,' said Twinkle, not to be left out. 'And that's not something to be sniffed at.'

'Yes-yes,' said Salor, smiling at them, 'you all did very well and I'm sure the world is truly grateful, but I feel we must turn our minds to Danrite and what it is that might be afflicting him.'

'What is this *afflicting*?' said Jose.

'What's wrong with him,' said Twinkle, explaining.

'I do not know,' said Jose.

'Don't know what?' said Twinkle.

'What it is that is wrong with him,' said Jose.

'What?' said Twinkle.

As Twinkle and Jose were happily crossing their lines, Salor was studying Danrite's face. He didn't think he liked what he saw. Perhaps it would help if they took him somewhere else. Remove him from the scene of his trauma. At least for safety's sake, another attempt on his life could be just around the corner. 'I think we should take him home,' said Salor.

Home? thought Danrite who, although he was doing his best to ignore what wasn't going on around him, wondered at this. He took another sip of his tea; a long thoughtful sip.

'How are we going to do that?' said Vlad.

'Sí,' said Jose, who had wandered over and was now sat at Danrite's feet, 'how?'

Danrite's eyes had a quick look south. It was that talking dog again. But dogs don't talk. It had earlier. Grief, thought Danrite, his eyes quickly resuming their earlier position, I don't see any dog. Sugar needed. He quickly sipped his tea.

'His eyes moved,' said Twinkle, catching Danrite's quick glance. 'When Jose spoke. He looked at him. I'm sure he did.'

Salor had also noticed Danrite's eye movement. He stroked his beard and wondered. A wondering that brought a sudden realisation. He wasn't was he? He is you know. He was bally well ignoring them. But why? Unless… Salor suddenly clapped his hands together, causing Jose to jump and Danrite to sip his tea with a new vigour. The boy thinks he's seeing things; the only explanation for it; that and maybe shock. But why? Salor took to more wondering and even a little deep thinking. Unless… unless he's seen things before, or thinks he has, but really has. Was that possible? Of course it was possible. Vlad and Twinkle have been shadowing him for years. He's caught something in the corner of the eye. Not quite there but… not quite sure what but… the episode with the shorts! He had torn them off a strip for doing that. But it all adds up. He thought he saw something here. He thought he heard something there. And then… blammo! He slammed fist into palm making Jose jump again. He had it. All Danrite's here and there's had suddenly come home to roost, all at once, every single weird one of them; all solid, no longer peripheral. No wonder he couldn't take it.

Salor did a sort of little jig. Now he understood. And why not? One minute Danrite thinks he is seeing and hearing strange things, and the next he is. Only he can't take it. Salor stopped his jig, a frown formed. "*But why is he ignoring **me**?*" Salor pondered. "*I'm not weird or strange.*" It had to be something else then? "*Surely it's not my attire? My wonderful hat festooned with stars and crescent* *moons. Or cloak adorned with the same, with its gold and silver flecks set to catch the light and match my eyes, surely not?*" He pondered more and then looked perplexed. "*Not the lipstick and eye shadow? Surely not, blue is my colour.*" He pulled a small mirror from one of his sleeves and peered into it, just in case it was smudged, but no. "*Then why does he ignore me?*" He looked at the others. And then he had it. "*Of course, it had to be; association. I arrived with Jose; spoke to the others, so naturally I'm tarred with the same brush.*" He shook his head. What was poor Danrite to think? He glanced at the others. "*You only have to look at them.*"

Danrite's eyes were far from moving now, fixed as they were on Salor as he went about having his eureka moment. He had also adopted a rather gormless, mouth open look. His cup dangling from a finger, set to drop at any moment.

Salor, finished looking at *them*, was now looking at Danrite, who was looking a bit odd and staring straight at him as if he was mad or something. What now? he thought. He looked at the others again. 'Why is he staring at me like that?' he said.

But the other two faces and hood in the room were also staring at him, though in quite a different way, something on the lines of reproachful with a touch of anger would best describe.

'What?' said Salor, puzzled by the looks. 'What's going on?'

'"*But why is he ignoring **me**?*"' said Twinkle sarcastically, resting the back of a hand against her forehead.

'"*Association,*"' said Vlad, equally sarcastically.

'"*You only have to look at them,*"' growled Jose.

Salor was aghast as a horrible realisation suddenly hit home; everyone had suddenly developed telepathy. That or he had been saying things out loud.

The cup now fell from Danrite's finger, bounced on his knee, spilling what contents were left and landed on the floor where it broke into two. Oblivious to the tea soaking into his trousers he stood up and mouthed something no one in the room could quite catch.

'What did he say?' said Vlad.

'You're real,' said Danrite, answering Vlad's question. He looked from one to the other, stopping at Jose. 'You're all real.'

Heads and hood nodded.

Danrite staggered as this sunk in. He then joined his cup on the floor.

CHAPTER 12

Mister Fix fiddled nervously with his tie as he waited for Mister Power to look up. Mister Power wasn't a happy bunny.

Finally, Mister Power did look up. 'You're here then?' he said.

'I came as quickly as I could,' said Mister Fix.

'Of course you did,' said Mister Power, the hint of a smile on his lips. He stood up and walked to the front of his desk. There he rested a bottom cheek and perched on the desk's edge. He smiled again. 'So what are you going to do about the little problem you've landed us with?'

Mister Fix gripped the knot of his tie. 'I've… um, sent two of our best to watch the house,' he said.

'Not…'

'Oh no, sir,' said Mister Fix, anticipating. It was a dangerous thing to do where Mister Power was concerned. 'I mean… sir. Sorry, sir.' He was now gripping the knot of his tie so tightly he was going red in the face.

'Go on,' said Mister Power, an amused twinkle in his eye.

'Yes, sir. Sorry again, sir. 'I've sent Nomed and El Yograg.'

Just for a moment Mister Power looked startled, his usually steely composure dented. 'El Yograg? Is that wise?'

'Nomed knows how to handle him sir, and he is the best tracker we have, should Salor try to hide the boy.'

Mister Power's composure was back. 'On the Otherside you mean?' he said.

'Yes, sir.'

Mister Power lifted his buttock from the desk and casually strolled over to Mister Fix. 'But we wouldn't want that to happen though, would we?'

'No, sir,' said Mister Fix, now almost purple from his tie fiddling. 'What I meant…'

Mister Power reached up and loosened a flinching Mister Fix's tie before he could do himself a permanent mischief. 'But if it did come to that, something I may add I would not be very happy about because I would expect the boy to be in our hands before that is allowed to happen, I would expect you to follow and get him back before things, shall we say, got out of hand.' He patted his handiwork. 'There.'

His face returning to a colour more normal to what it should be, Mister Fix gave Mister Power a look of awe bordering on terror. 'Me, sir? Going over to the Otherside, sir?'

'If that is what it takes.'

'With Nomed and El Yograg?'

'With Uncle Tom and all if needs be,' said Mister Power, smiling. 'But don't let me down Mister Fix.'

'No, sir. I won't, sir.'

'No you won't, because Mister Fix,' said Mister Power returning to his chair, 'because I can just as easily tighten ties as loosen them.' One of Mister Fix's hands went instinctively to his throat. 'So, what are you waiting for? Off you go then.'

Mister Fix went to go.

'And don't slam the door after you.'

Mister Fix didn't; he didn't dare.

Alone, a thoughtful Mister Power pondered the situation; the boy. Was he really the hero those idiots of myth and magic thought he was? Who knew, but whatever, he couldn't risk ignoring the problem, just in case. His empire, which grew larger day by day, had been built over the years on ignorance and laziness. The last thing he wanted was every man, woman and child suddenly rediscovering their imagination. He had worked so hard at relieving them of it. His head now hurt. He sighed, reached forward and touched the ornate beading decorating the edge of the desk.

A small section of the desk, between the top drawer and the beading, flipped open revealing a shallow drawer of the secret persuasion. Mister Power pulled it open and removed the contents; something wrapped in the finest red silk. Carefully placing it on his desk he pressed a button on the office intercom.

'Yes, sir?' said Miss Manager.

‘I’m not to be disturbed until I say so,’ said Mister Power, eyeing the silk-covered object. ‘Whatever the reason. Is that understood?’

‘Yes, sir,’ said Miss Manager, seemingly not in the least bit curious or interested as to why, as she eyed the magazine she had bought to read in her tea break. The intercom connection went dead.

Mister Power picked up the object. Full of loathing for it, but loath to put it back in the drawer, he eagerly removed the red silk. He shouldn’t really, but he was stressed and really didn’t need an excuse; he wanted to.

Silk removed, he smiled at the object it had covered and instantly hated himself for doing so. The smile dropped. He should really destroy it. Wanted to destroy it, but it wasn’t that easy. He needed it. But it was a need he didn’t fully understand. He had always had it, or so he had been told; the only thing that was with him when he was found as a baby. A foundling with a secret. A weak helpless being. Mister Power hated weakness. The object a sore reminder perhaps?

He fingered the object. Held it. Then decided he had seen enough, so as quickly as he had removed the object, he now replaced it back in its wrap of red silk. He put it back in the secret drawer and closed it; hid it away. He realised he was breathing heavily. He should destroy it, but he had the nagging feeling, a feeling that gnawed at his very being, that if he did, or it was discovered, it would be the end of him. Something deep inside of him whimpered and hid. Mister Power shuddered.

But the object now safely hidden away, Mister Power was able to regain composure and he sneered at his stupidity; his weakness. He stood up, but his eyes were drawn back to the place where the secret drawer lay hidden. What if someone knew it was there? What if Salor knew it was there? And in that moment the two banes of his life came together for an instant. But he was being paranoid. Who could know? He was a fool. Salor was a fool. Everyone was a fool.

Mister Power sat down again. Everyone was a fool. The thought stayed with him. A doubt formed. Fools could not be trusted. Mister Fix was a fool. He suddenly doubted Mister Fix would deliver on his promise; him and his two buffoons. So why send them? Who else was there? They were all fools. So who could he trust to see out his orders? He realised there was only one answer to that. He reached for the intercom.

'Yes, sir?' said Miss Manager, unable to hide the surprise in her voice at being summoned so soon. She put her magazine down.

'I've decided to take a holiday,' said Mister Power, on the other end of the intercom.

'A holiday, sir?' said a now astonished Miss Manager. Such a thing had never been heard of.

'Yes, I'll be going today,' said Mister Power. 'And while I'm away you're in charge.' In his office Mister Power stared at the intercom; he hadn't the foggiest why he had just said that. Perhaps it was those darned horn-rimmed glasses? But she would be as good as anyone, so he stuck with the notion. Besides, he didn't really trust androids or monsters.

As for Miss Manager in her office, the surprises just kept on coming. 'Today?' she mouthed, quietly. 'Me, sir?' she said, as what Mister Power said sank in. 'But…'

'No buts, Miss Manager,' said Mister Power, putting his hand up at the intercom. He looked at it then frowned. 'But…' he cringed as he said it, 'before I go, fetch me a list of the shortlisted autobiographies and the like, and those we discarded earlier.'

'But…'

'I said no buts, Miss Manager. I don't care what I decided earlier. I don't care how young the subject, or how many times they've been done before, or how boring. As long as they have some modicum of fame attached, I want them.'

'Yes, sir,' said Miss Manager, more than a little taken aback by it all.

The connection clicked closed.

Mister Power sat back in his chair. While he was away, he was going to flood the market; flood the bookshops; flood the internet. The world of imagination was on the edge of extinction. It just needed a little push. He stood up. And it should be he that did it.

CHAPTER 13

There had been no rollercoaster this time, just a gentle, peaceful, whiteness. Danrite, in his unconsciousness, felt he might like to stay in this white for evermore; succumb to its serenity; forget the real world and its woes.

But this couldn't happen, and as Danrite lay in his whiteness he noticed what appeared to be a dark speck on the horizon. Danrite watched it; watched as it started to grow; appeared to be heading straight at him. Suddenly this world of white wasn't so comfortable. Danrite shifted his weight, trying to get away from the steadily growing speck. But try as he might it got closer, and bigger, until it looked to engulf him, until it…

'Ow!' said Danrite, as something poked him in the eye, rousing him from his stupor.

'Told you, your finger was too close,' said a voice Danrite thought he recognised.

'Hello, Danrite,' said another voice. 'Sorry about that.'

Danrite, not sure what was going on, warily opened the eye that hadn't been poked. He stared for a moment, getting his bearings; he appeared to be on his back, staring at the ceiling. Now something, someone, was moving into his eyeline.

'How are you feeling?' said Salor, that someone, peering down at him. And then Danrite remembered. Grief and little kittens, he thought. What now? How did he play this? Danrite continued in the position he had found himself in, but knew he couldn't stay there forever.

'Perhaps he would like another cuppa,' said Twinkle.

'Would you?' said Salor.

Cautiously, that is how he would play it, Danrite decided. It wasn't often that one found out his imaginary friends might in fact be real; not that they were his friends. He raised his head and gave a tentative nod.

‘Cuppa for Danrite,’ bellowed Salor, to somewhere over his shoulder.

‘Coming up,’ shouted Vlad, who was in the kitchen, having been given the job of clearing up the mess in there.

Danrite struggled to his feet, declining the offer of a helping hand from the bloke in the wizard get-up, and sat on the sofa. He now noticed he had a damp patch in an embarrassing place.

‘Tea,’ said Salor, noticing the look of horror on Danrite’s face.

‘Oh,’ said Danrite, mightily relieved. He now recalled the incident.

‘Now,’ said Salor, ‘how do you want to play this?’

Danrite started at the question, but not enough to be noticed by anyone. Hadn’t he just been thinking that? Nothing but coincidence. Let it lay. He had enough on his plate. He suspected his mind was jumping at shadows. He settled. Okay, he thought, let’s get this over with. ‘How about from the beginning?’ he said, hardly able to believe he was speaking to someone he was hardly able to believe existed.

‘Good idea,’ said Salor, beaming at Danrite, ‘no better place to start.’

It had been foretold that a hero, half giant - half dwarf, would save myth, magic, and make-believe in its direst of moments. That moment arrived.

The foretelling told of when the hero would appear. Told of the place the hero would make an entrance. That moment also arrived. *But it never foretold it would all take place in a maternity ward. But so what, did it matter? Yeah, the hero’s arrival had been announced by wailing and not the expected fanfare of trumpets. Again, did it matter? No, not really, unless you really thought about it, but who was? A hero had arrived to save them! Hurrah!*

Time passed, the baby grew into the fine young hero they had expected. *Okay, that’s not strictly true, but hey-ho.* But then something unexpected happened. A circumstance of tragic consequence occurred. It saw Percy step into the breach. He would be the hero’s guardian until such time as it was written.

Sadly, Percy was now no more; a victim of the onslaught of progress. *He had fallen from the roof; it was a mystery.* This meant that the hero was once more alone; easier prey to the danger that sought to destroy the saviour of myth, magic, and make-believe.

This danger, festering in the world of man, was a power that hated and sought to destroy all things fantastical. A power that would do all it could to bring about the demise of imagination, to destroy the world of the Otherside where the characters of Myth, Magic and Make-believe lived. This danger, this power, had a name. Mister Power. *Thus proving the destruction of imagination had already begun!*

Head of the most powerful publishing-entertainment house in the world, Mister Power sought to flood the world with mediocrity. Batter it into submission with the mundane. Into it he would bring brain-achingly boring autobiographies, biographies of nonentities and then serialise them. He would take reality television to new depths of drivel. Produce mind-numbing gaming for the youth of the world. He wanted to rid the world of imagination and bring it under his heel.

And it was working. Hardly anything fresh or new was wending its way into the world of entertainment. Old films were being re-written. Old television programmes re-hashed. Kids no longer knew the meaning of playing outside when the sun was shining. Imagination was waning. He was winning. But to be able to claim total victory there was a little something he would have to do first. Put an end this hero he had heard about. Put an end to Danrite Willocky!

And no better way to finish a story was at the end, which Salor had just done. It had taken awhile; three cuppas and a round of cheese and pickle sandwiches to be precise. The room was now filled with an expectant hush. Apprehensive faces looked on; Vlad with the help of a mirror. Would their hero stand up and be counted, or would he do a runner for the nearest exit?

Danrite, for his part, was feeling remarkably calm considering; especially as someone wanted to put an end to him. He casually took another sip from his cup and placed it on the coffee table. He looked from face to face to mirror to face. He spoke. 'Half giant, half dwarf?' he said, which surprised everyone. They had been expecting something along the lines of "Me?!!!" or "Why me?!!!".

'In the mythical sense,' said Salor.

'In the mythical sense?' Danrite repeated. What did that mean? he thought. 'What does that mean?' he asked.

'It means… eh…' Salor began to falter in his explanation and looked for help amongst his peers. He got a couple of shrugs for his trouble; one draped in a robe, the other cascaded glitter. He was on his own.

Oh no he wasn't. 'He means like the books and films,' said Jose, coming to the rescue. 'Not everyday big persons and small persons,' he further explained.

'Yes,' said Salor, eagerly agreeing. 'Like what Jose just said.'

Scenarios played through Danrite's mind of giants throwing huge tree trunks, and dwarfs in armour who were fond of the underground; in the mythical sense. 'Really?' he said, as the last tree trunk flew overhead.

'Sí,' said Jose.

'Yes,' said Salor.

'Oh,' he said, cocking his head to one side and appearing to stare into space. Another tree was thrown in Danrite's mind's eye. 'Tree throwing and hole digging types,' he said, returning his thoughts to the here and now.

'Er… yes,' said Salor, looking to the others again. This time he got three shrugs for his effort.

Again Danrite took on a faraway look. He had a problem with this whole giant dwarf thing. 'I don't remember my parents moving trees about, or being big in excavation?' he said.

'Er…,' said Salor, which was fast becoming his word of the day. He furrowed his brow and crinkled his eyelids, causing creases in his eye shadow.

'Ah,' said Twinkle, who was standing in the doorway between the lounge and the hallway. 'I think I know what Danrite is trying to say.'

'You do?' said Salor.

'He's talking about not being able to recall his mother or father being of the giant or dwarf persuasion,' she said. 'Which means, I think, he has some doubts about being the hero we have been waiting for. I think he has a point.' Which meant *she* had a point; Twinkle having not so secretly harboured doubts about Danrite being the hero from the start. An opinion she frequently aired.

'Well I…' said Salor, eyelids crisscrossed with lines of congealed eye shadow caused by his earlier crinkling; it wasn't the most expensive. He glanced at Twinkle, who was giving him a *told you so* look. 'But…' Suddenly Salor was having doubts. Surely he hadn't been wrong about the boy, had he? But it had been written. Salor was confused.

'Perhaps it's metaphorical,' said Vlad, drawing a scowl from Twinkle. He turned his mirror so Danrite could see his face.

'Metaphorical?' said Salor, looking puzzled.

'About him being half and half,' said Vlad.

'He's not a curry side,' said Twinkle.

Jose sniggered.

'No, I'm not,' said Danrite. 'Nor half giant and half dwarf, I'm just an ordinary boy - I mean man.'

Salor stroked his beard thoughtfully. Vlad could have a point. A hero didn't have to wear armour to be a hero. And it had been written, and Danrite had been there at the right place and at the right time.

'No!' said Salor suddenly, causing Jose to do a little mischief on the carpet. Jose could always be trusted to do some sort of mischief in times of stress and duress and… well, any time really. 'You are the one! It is written, so it is. It is you that will save us in our darkest hour!' Salor had become quite animated. Hands swishing, robe billowing. He had gone quite Shakespearian.

'Ooo!' said Twinkle, as she turned to get something from the kitchen to clear up Jose's little mischief, 'listen to him.' She of course wholly doubted it, but what did she know? And if she was honest, she had about given up on the real hero turning up; therefore the boy would have to do. She just wanted things back to how they were. She wanted her magic back; all of it. And if that meant travelling to wherever if need be with a deranged old man who couldn't put his make-up on properly and a, what had Vlad said, oh yeah, metaphorical side dish, then so be it. She then suddenly stopped in her tracks and looked back into the lounge, at Danrite; a little lost boy. A lost boy she had spent most of his life looking out for. And whatever the danger they faced, she was going to darn well make sure he was safe. She sniffed. Her little lost boy was all grown up. Twinkle quickly scurried to the kitchen before anyone noticed how wet her eyes were. Flipping canine ammonia!

In the lounge, as Salor stared expectantly at Danrite, Danrite was staring at the little puddle that Jose had deposited on the carpet. A carpet that was so threadbare it was unable to soak it up. He wanted to laugh. Amazingly, after all that had happened to him recently, he found he didn't want to cry. Others might have crumbled. But then, others hadn't lived with Percy and all his weirdness. He now suspected his time with Percy may have been some type of grounding, to ready him for what was to come. So, even though he didn't feel much like a cross between two persons of the mythical persuasion, or a hero of any description, he suspected that somehow it was his fate to be whatever it was that had been written.

'Okay,' said Danrite, looking up at Salor, 'I'll buy it.'

'Buy it?' said Salor.

'The hero thing,' said Danrite. 'I believe you.'

'You do?' said Salor.

'He means welcome aboard,' said Vlad, holding out an invisible hand. 'I'm Vlad.' He had never had a doubt where Danrite was concerned.

Danrite gripped the proffered sleeve and shook it. Jose, who had been a little downcast since his accident, now brightened up and bounded over to Danrite, tail wagging.

But Salor, eyes filling up, but only because of the cheap mascara, nothing else you understand, now become all serious and leader like. 'Time enough for all that,' he said, stepping forward and pulling Danrite from his seat. 'I believe circumstances dictate the need for a safer environment. Let's head home people.'

And although Danrite thought he already was, he fell in step and let the others lead on.

CHAPTER 14

Home, it transpired, was a way station, a stepping stone, a portal from one realm to another; a gateway to the Otherside, where the creatures and peoples of Myth, Magic, and Make-believe lived. It was also different things to different people. To the general world at large, those that did not know what it was they were looking at, home was something of inconsequence; something to be ignored; glanced at, but never really seen. But to others, who could see it, really see it…

For Salor as he followed a path towards it, it appeared as a single white tower, one that's top disappeared amongst the clouds that gathered high around it. Twinkle saw it as a golden castle; silver pennants flying in the wind upon its turrets. To Vlad it also appeared as a castle, but this one of grey stone; brooding, set against a stormy background of thunder and lightning. Alas to Jose no such romanticism attached itself to what he saw, as lights flashed bright across the fascia of a huge kennel, announcing it as the world's best cantina, and boasting the best tequila-flavoured dog biscuits this side of Mexico. His little tail wagged so hard it was in danger of coming loose. Danrite, who had been, shall we say, a little surprised when he stepped from his front door to find he wasn't stepping out onto his garden path - he would enquire later as to the circumstances of his sudden change of scenery, but for the moment he was going with the flow - saw a small white cottage with climbing roses, red and rambling about its front door.

Each stepped across the threshold into something totally different. There was no great hall, or sawdust-covered wooden floor to greet them, instead they each stepped into a world of warmth, a homely welcome, a home from home. There was the smell of freshly baked bread straight from the oven, coffee brewing, a grandfather clock chiming. No, nothing like one would expect, unless you were Danrite that is who, as it worked out, *had* been expecting the scene that awaited him as it matched the cottage completely; but perhaps though, not the drabness and aging worn-out décor.

'Wow!' said Danrite, sniffing the air as he entered. 'Something smells good.'

'Ah,' said Twinkle, pointing to a wall socket, 'sorry to disappoint, but it's one of those plug in and smell thingies.'

Danrite looked puzzled, then disappointment. 'I didn't know they made ones that smelled of baking and coffee?'

'We've also got "Sunday Roast" and "Marrowbone Jelly". Jose chose that one.' Twinkle lowered her voice, 'But we try not to use it if possible; gets him over excited.'

'Oh,' said Danrite, not quite knowing what Twinkle meant, and happy to leave it that way.

'Now,' said Twinkle, 'what did you see?'

'See? said Danrite.

'When we led you up the garden path, so to speak,' said Twinkle, smiling.

Danrite frowned at her. 'I don't understand,' he said, suspecting that it might be some sort of test.

'What was the image presented to you?' said Salor, muddying the waters further as far as Danrite was concerned.

'What sort of building was it?' said Vlad, chipping in.

'Building?' said Danrite, a tiny tad confused.

'Yes,' said Twinkle. 'What did the building look like before you came through the door?' She turned to Salor and whispered, 'Not too bright this hero is he?'

'Sí,' said Jose. 'What is it you see before you come in? I see best cantina this side of Mexico.'

'You did?' said Danrite.

'I saw a castle,' said Vlad.

And then it dawned on Danrite what they were going on about. 'It was a cottage,' he said, 'with roses around the door.'

'A cottage, eh?' said Vlad, sounding a little disappointed.

'Not much in the way of aspiration then?' said Twinkle.

'What do you mean?' said Danrite, lost again.

'The image projected is supposed to reflect your heart's desire,' said Salor.

Danrite couldn't remember ever wanting a cottage. He told them so.

'You do,' said Twinkle, 'in here.' She put a hand to her chest. 'You just don't know it yet.'

'Precisely,' said Salor, who had picked up a stool from somewhere. 'Now, if you would be so kind as to follow me please.' He turned and headed for a staircase.

As Danrite and the others followed, he whispered a worry to Twinkle. 'Is inside here my heart's desire as well?' he asked, worryingly eyeing the tatty wallpaper.

Twinkle laughed. 'No, and thank goodness I say,' she said. She explained. 'We all see the same on the inside. It is what it is. It's only outside that reflects our inner desire.' Her smile faded a little. It's supposed to give all that enter hope.'

Phew, thought Danrite, who for a moment had been worried his taste in décor would become seriously flawed somewhere along the line. 'Thank goodness for that,' he said, missing the tinge of sadness in Twinkle's voice. He picked at a piece of peeling wallpaper then, suddenly realising what he was doing, apologised. 'Sorry, I didn't mean to…'

'Forget about it,' said Twinkle, her smile back to full strength, 'it's just a sign of the times.'

Danrite wondered at her comment, but said nothing. Then he had a thought. 'Can anyone see their heart's desire?' He now visualised all the people in the world queuing up outside, all patiently, or not so patiently, waiting to make a claim to their dreams.

'Heaven no,' said Twinkle. 'The gateway's shielded. Only those that need to see it, see it; safer that way.'

Danrite imagined it would.

They reached the top of the stairs where Twinkle gestured towards a doorway. She ushered him in.

'Sit here,' said Salor, as Danrite entered. He pointed to the stool he had been carrying. 'Now,' he said when he felt all were giving him their full attention, 'time for those introductions I think.' He nodded towards Vlad. 'Vlad you have already been acquainted with.' Vlad shook the sleeve of his robe and turned his hand mirror just so, so Danrite got a glimpse of a pale smiling face. 'He's a vampire.' Danrite instinctively moved his stool an inch or two away, causing Salor to smile. 'But a friendly one, and before you ask, yes, ordinarily you can't see vampires in mirrors, but times have changed and some things aren't what they used to be. Well, not entirely.'

Not overly convinced he *was* going to ask that particular question, Danrite sat tight and smiled a forced smile.

Salor now started to go walkabout around the room. 'Myth and magic, you see,' he continued, elaborating on the story told earlier to Danrite in his house, 'are fading; losing cohesion. Poor Vlad here can only be seen in mirrors, where once he couldn't.' Salor stopped, stroked his beard and looked to the ceiling. 'It's a curse, truth be told. The world of fantasy is being turned on its head; in danger of becoming extinct.' A pained expression settled on Salor's face as he continued to stare upwards. 'So, so, sad.' He put a hand to his brow.

'A bit of a pain really,' said Vlad, ignoring Salor's ham acting, his reflection frowning. 'Can't get the girls you see, if they can see right through you.' He laughed at his little joke revealing, to Danrite's dismay, a lovely set of fangs.

'I'm Twinkle,' said Twinkle, holding out a hand. As she did she bent forward and whispered in Danrite's ear. 'Don't worry about Vlad; his looks are worse than his bite.'

Danrite doubted it, but smiled again and shook Twinkle's hand. 'Pleased to meet you,' he said.

'She's a fairy,' said Vlad, glaring, via the mirror at Twinkle. Her whisper had hardly been that. 'Not quite what you'd expect, eh?' he sneered.

'Oh,' said Danrite, trying not to stare too hard at Twinkle.

'And what is that supposed to mean?' Twinkle demanded, hands on hips, chin thrust forward.

'Now, now Vlad,' said Salor, the sudden heat in the room crumbling his moment with the ceiling, 'we've all got our little problems.'

'And what is *that* supposed to mean?' snapped Twinkle, angrily turning on Salor with the speed of a cobra.

Salor shrivelled at the sight. 'I just meant…' he managed to stammer.

'And I am Jose,' said Jose brightly, jumping between the warring factions and on to the table they were sitting around. The table gave an indignant shake as he landed. 'I am a chihuahua; a werechihuahua. I used to be a werewolf, but that is life.' He sat and offered his paw.

'No way, Jose,' said Danrite, stuck for anything else to say.

'Sí way,' said Jose, cocking his head to one side. 'It is all true. It is the myth and magic being played with. I am a man again in the full moon.' He suddenly looked very sad and downcast. 'I am then naked.'

'Ah,' said Danrite, disengaging his hand from the chihuahua's paw as politely as he could.

'So you see,' said Salor, Jose's interruption giving him the chance to wriggle away from Twinkle's ire, 'not all is rosy in our little garden.' He cast a wary eye towards Twinkle who thankfully appeared to be calming down a little. 'Vlad used to be a vampire, Twinkle a fairy and Jose a werewolf. And that only leaves me to introduce my…' The table they were sitting around had suddenly taken to shaking, stopping Salor's flow.

'Oops, forgotten someone,' said Twinkle, back to her old self again.

Danrite watched wide-eyed, as Salor now conversed with the table. It was a short and sharp conversation that ended with the table stamping on Salor's foot with one of its legs.

'Ow!' yelled Salor, hopping on one foot.

'This is Rosie,' said Twinkle, enjoying Salor's comeuppance. She lightly patted the table.

'Rosie?' said Danrite.

'She's a wood nymph.'

The table lifted a flap.

'That means hello,' said Twinkle, looking sad. 'Poor girl's had a rough time of it since… well, since.'

'Hello, Rosie,' said Danrite, reaching forward with a tentative hand.

'Go on,' said Twinkle, 'she won't bite.'

Danrite patted the table, which shook slightly.

'She likes you,' said Twinkle, approvingly.

There now came a whinnying from the doorway and a horse popped its head into the room. It showed its teeth in a horsey grin.

'And this is Sid,' said Vlad.

‘Don’t tell me,’ said Danrite, entering the spirit of the introductions, but sadly jumping in with two feet, ‘he used to be a rocking horse.’ The room went quiet.

‘A unicorn,’ said Twinkle, grimacing.

‘Oh,’ said Danrite, cringing.

But Sid neighed the equivalent of a laugh and the tension instantly dropped from the room. Sid, it appeared, had thought the idea of him being a rocking horse hilarious. He ambled into the room and nuzzled Danrite’s shoulder.

‘Looks like you’ve made a friend,’ said Twinkle, laughing. Sid whinnied in agreement, nodding and shaking his head from side to side.

‘Sí,’ said Jose, doggy laughing.

The shoulders of Vlad’s robe heaved up and down.

Danrite smiled the smile of someone not sure why everyone was laughing so much.

Salor, who had been nursing a badly bruised big toe, and waiting for an opportunity to finish what he had been trying to say before his “accident”, took his chance as the laughter in the room started to subside. ‘And I am Salor.’ He thrust a hand towards Danrite. ‘I am a Grand Wizard, and the leader of our little band.’

The room once more filled with laughter, but of the more stifled, behind the hand, persuasion. Salor seemed to ignore it, but Danrite, as he shook Salor’s hand, couldn’t help but notice and wonder which of the two statements it was aimed at; he decided perhaps both. Shaking over, Danrite took his hand back and discreetly wiped it on his trousers. Salor’s hand was a tad sweaty.

‘But not so grand now,’ said Vlad, not meaning it quite the way it sounded.

Salor tutted. ‘What he means is, I’m not as powerful as I was.’

‘That’s what I said,’ said Vlad.

‘But still powerful enough to magic us home,’ Salor pointed out, puffing out his chest.

Ah magic, thought Danrite, that explains that; which it didn’t really, but after all that had gone on so far that day Danrite decided to let the matter drop. Weird was as weird is; or something like that.

‘Lost his ability to choose decent makeup though,’ Twinkle whispered in Danrite’s ear.

Danrite smiled, but wasn't sure if she was being serious or not.

'But I have been luckier than most,' said Salor, frowning at Twinkle, 'I may have lost some of my magic but I am still as I was.'

'Yeah, he's the "normal" one, 'said Twinkle, making quotation marks with her fingers.

The room once again filled with titters, but these were scarcely guarded this time.

'Yes, very funny,' said Salor, sounding downright sniffy. 'But now, if you've all quite finished, and as the introductions are over, I suggest we get down to the serious business at hand.' He looked at Danrite. 'Now Danrite my boy, how do you plan to save us?'

CHAPTER 15

Mister Fix waited outside Danrite's house. He knew the boy was in there, he had seen him through the window with Salor and his little gang. All he had to do now was wait for them to emerge, grab the boy, and get back to Mister Power as soon as. It was the option he preferred, he didn't want to travel to the Otherside; he had heard stories. Mister Fix fiddled with his tie, loosened it a tad, and then glanced at the roof of the house. He was nervous and El Yograg sitting atop the chimney like he was, wasn't helping.

'Does he have to sit up there like that?' said Mister Fix.

'It is what he does best,' said Nomed, resting on his haunches beside Mister Fix. His voice was deep and unnerving; something else that didn't help Mister Fix's current disposition.

Mister Fix threw a quick glance sideways; he had always made sure he kept his distance from Mister Power's pets as he liked to think of them. They looked dangerous. Close up they looked much, much worse. He couldn't wait for this to be over; for the boy to be safely in the clutches of Mister Power.

'He is moving,' said Nomed, suddenly.

'He is?' said Mister Fix, his attention snapping back to his surroundings. 'Who is?' He peered through the hedge he was hiding behind, a hedge owned by Mister Power. A hedge bordering the garden of the house that Mister Power owned, that just happened to be next door to where the boy lived. He could have waited inside, watched from a window, but Nomed wasn't someone you wanted to share an enclosed space with.

'El is,' said Nomed.

'Why?' said Mister Fix, his mind filling with sudden forebodings as he watched El Yograg clamber down the side of the boy's house.

'We shall soon find out,' said Nomed, as El scampered towards them.

El sidled up beside Nomed and started to grunt and snort at him. Mister Fix looked on as Nomed listened intently to the noises El was making. When El stopped his grunting Nomed nodded at him and then looked at Mister Fix.

Mister Fix, who suspected some sort of communication had taken place, but had no idea what had been said, spoke. 'Well?' he said. 'Did you make any sense of that?'

'Yes,' said Nomed.

There followed a stretch of silence that was in danger of extending beyond belief.

'And?' said Mister Fix, his nerves at breaking point.

'He said the boy and his companions have gone.'

Mister Fix looked from Nomed to El and back again. 'What?'

'Everyone has gone,' said Nomed, showing no sign of concern at the news.

Mister Fix's hand went to the knot in his tie. 'But how?' He stood up and stared at the house next door. 'We were watching. He was watching.' Mister Fix pointed at El who growled. Mister Fix quickly withdrew his hand.

'Yes,' said Nomed, in his unnerving voice. 'El watched them go.'

'But… but!' Mister Fix looked as if he was going to have some sort of fit, the way he was gripping the knot in his tie not helping. 'Why didn't he tell us?'

'He just did,' said Nomed.

This wasn't good, thought Mister Fix, who was beginning to think his surname was starting to reflect the predicament he was in. But perhaps El was wrong. 'I didn't see anyone leave,' he said, straw-clutching.

'No,' said Nomed.

'Then how?'

'Magic.'

'Magic?'

'Yes.'

'They've still got some?'

'So it would appear.' Nomed turned to El and attached a leash to his collar. 'Seek,' he said.

El immediately attempted to pull Nomed's arm from its socket. But Nomed was as strong as he looked. 'We go now,' he said.

‘The office?’ said Mister Fix, gulping. He had been wondering what he would say to Mister Power when he got back. Not much he suspected; he doubted he would be given the time. His hand went to the knot in his tie again.

‘The portal.’

‘Portal?’ said Mister Fix, who had been distracted by thoughts of his imminent demise. ‘Did you say portal?’

Nomed reached out a large scaly hand and placed it on Mister Fix’s shoulder. ‘We go now.’

And they did. Instantly.

And as they arrived at their destination Mister Fix threw up the entire contents of his stomach, together with a few shiny bits and pieces that perhaps shouldn’t have seen the light of day.

‘What the-’ Mister Fix started to say, as he rocked unsteadily on his feet.

‘The portal,’ Nomed announced, pointing.

Mister Fix, eyes watering, squinted at something in the not so distant distance.

‘The portal,’ Nomed repeated.

‘Yes, yes,’ said Mister Fix, head spinning. ‘I heard you, but what the heck just happened? How did we get here?’

Nomed stared at Mister Fix with his big red eyes. ‘El seeked the boy.’

Mister Fix stared back through watery ones. He had the feeling that that was about all he was going to get on the subject in question so, as he wasn’t feeling entirely one hundred percent at the moment, he decided to forget that line of enquiry and instead embark on another. ‘What is it?’ he asked.

‘El?’ said Nomed, patting El on its head.

‘No,’ said Mister Fix, rolling his eyes and instantly wishing he hadn’t as pain flashed across his temple, ‘not El, that there. The portal thing.’ He managed to point without falling over.

Nomed looked at the portal and then looked at Mister Fix, fixing him once more with those big red eyes of his. What he was thinking was anyone’s guess, but from his body language it appeared he felt he was working with an idiot. ‘What does it look like?’ he said.

Not the answer Mister Fix was expecting. What did it look like? Surely he knew what it looked like. They were both looking at the same thing weren't they? And what did it matter what it looked like anyway? He wanted to know what its purpose was. Still, feeling as he did, he decided to play along.

'Well?' said Nomed.

Grief, thought Mister Fix. 'Okay, hold your horses, I'm getting there.' He looked at the portal. 'It looks like a huge advertising hoarding, with a door in it.'

'Is that all?' said Nomed, who obviously had been expecting more than a hoarding with a door in it. He raised an eyebrow the size of a large mouse.

'Yes.' What did he expect him to say?

The mouse-sized eyebrow lowered. 'It is the doorway to the Otherside.'

Mister Fix's eyes grew wide. A question was forming on his lips. A question he didn't particularly want to ask. But he did anyway. 'Is that where the boy went?'

'Yes.'

'To the Otherside?

'Yes.'

'Bother.' It was the best he could muster.

'We have to follow and get him back for Mister Power.'

Mister Fix swallowed hard at the idea. At least he would have Nomed and El with him, but the thought wasn't entirely comforting. If he did make it back, and in one piece, he would still have to face Mister Power. His hand went once more to the knot in his tie. It was lose, lose all the way. He took a faltering step forward.

After another step, he stopped. Something was bugging him. He had to know. 'What did you mean when you said is that all?' said Mister Fix.

Nomed looked down at the pathetic being beside him. 'It is said a portal has the power to show your inner-most desire.' He looked back at the portal. 'But I don't think it worked for you. Perhaps you have to be magical.'

'Oh,' said Mister Fix. He wasn't.

Mister Fix looked at the hoarding. He hadn't strictly told the whole truth of what he could see. Maybe he wasn't magical, but he had seen his inner-most desire. He started to walk towards the hoarding with a little more purpose in his step.

Nomed fell in beside him. 'I saw home,' he said.

Mister Fix stopped again. He thought he'd caught a tinge of sadness in Nomed's voice. 'Home?'

'Maybe.'

'Maybe?'

'Perhaps.'

Mister Fix shrugged and continued on until he was standing before the door. But instead of reaching for the door handle he stepped back a pace to read again what was written on the hoarding, what he hadn't told Nomed. A large painted arrow shape was pointing down towards the door, above it, written in large black letters was: THE WAY OUT. Perhaps he wasn't magical, but he had seen his greatest desire. He wanted out; this could be the way. He smiled and removed his tie, stuffing it in his jacket pocket. That felt better. He reached for the handle.

'There are other portals,' said Nomed.

Mister Fix's hand hovered above the handle. Why was Nomed telling him this now? 'And?'

'There might be traps.'

Mister Fix thought on this for a second. 'But the boy went through this one?'

'Yes.'

He couldn't win; whatever the outcome. Mister Fix knew this. No choice really. Besides, it had shown him his heart's desire. In for a penny he thought, almost smiling. His mind was made up. He reached for the handle again.

'Wait!' said Nomed, 'You must say the words as you open it.'

'Words? What words?'

'Say what I say.'

Not sure why, but saying what he had been told to say, Mister Fix slowly turned the handle. He wanted a way out. He was going to get it.

CHAPTER 16

Danrite sat there, waiting for the punchline; because surely there had to be one. Surely Salor was jesting with him. But when the waiting continued, without a punchline making an appearance, and with the silence in the room starting to border on the embarrassing, Danrite started to think that perhaps he had misheard. 'Sorry?' he said, knitting his eyebrows.

The expectant faces that surrounded Danrite clouded slightly, their eyes, some mirrored, bright a moment ago, now started to shine less brightly. Those eyes now shifted, nervously, to look at Salor's face. Salor's eyes remained fixed on Danrite - because to do otherwise would have meant a visit to an optician - one must be careful when trying to look at one's own face without the aid of a mirror. 'Sorry?' said Salor, having trouble comprehending Danrite's reply.

'I don't understand,' said Danrite, eyebrows still taut.

'How are you going to save the world of Myth, Magic, and Make-believe?'

'Danrite?' said Twinkle, whose eyes had wandered back to Danrite, sensed a problem. She had noted his knitted eyebrows. 'Is there a problem?'

'What he just said,' said Danrite.

'Me?' said Salor.

'About saving you.'

'Me?' said Salor.

'And everyone else,' said Danrite.

'Yes?' said Salor.

Twinkle, seeing that they were going to get nowhere fast with Salor at the helm, intervened. 'What about it, Danrite?' she asked. She had suddenly acquired a horrible sinking feeling.

Danrite looked at Twinkle as if he had never seen her before. 'Der!' he said, '*Everything.*'

Danrite's words caused murmured stirrings, a puzzled whinny and a worried four-legged shuffling of the wooden variety, in the room.

'What does he mean?' said Vlad.

'I have a feeling he means what I think he means,' said Twinkle, her sinking feeling at her knees.

'He does?' said Salor, not quite following.

'Ay caramba,' Jose suddenly exclaimed. 'I am suddenly thinking that he means what Twinkle thinks he means which means I think I know what he means also.' His little ears flopped down beside his head; his tail flopped between his back legs. 'I go lay down.'

'He means, she means, what means?' said Salor, trying to get to the bottom of what was going on around him, by any means possible.

'I think what Danrite is trying to tell us, is that he doesn't know,' said Twinkle, airing her and Jose's fears.

'He doesn't know?'

'No,' said Danrite.

There followed more murmured stirrings, or rather a murmured stirring as Vlad was murmuring by himself, another whinny, this one expressing surprise – a whinny "what!" if you like – and more four-legged of the wooden variety shuffling; this time with added nervousness. There was also mixed, within the various expressions being expressed, a pitiful whining, emanating from the corner of the room Jose had chosen to lie down in.

Slowly it sank in. Salor looked from one to another. It can't be. 'You don't know?' said Salor, looking aghast at Danrite.

Now, thought Danrite, how do I answer? What more could he say? How did he put it? He plumped for the short sharp quick plaster removing technique. 'No,' he said; again.

'No!' said an ashen Salor.

Danrite shifted nervously on his seat.

'I told you,' said Twinkle, her jaw set. 'Didn't I say?' She turned to Vlad. 'Didn't I say he wasn't the one?'

Vlad said nothing. As did Salor, but for him it wasn't for the want of trying. He sat there, his mouth opening and shutting; nothing coming out.

'So you know nothing?' said Twinkle, about to climb on her high horse. Sid, noticing this, stepped hastily to one side just in case; there was only so much a horse's or unicorn's back could take: it had needed but a single straw where the camel was concerned.

'I wouldn't say that,' said Danrite, bringing a wince to Vlad's face; he knew what Twinkle was like if you rubbed her up the wrong way. 'But it's true what I said concerning the saving of the world of Myth and Magic.'

'What about Make-believe?' said Vlad hopefully. Twinkle gave Vlad a backhander across his hood. 'Ow!'

At last Salor found his voice. 'But I thought…' He lost it again. He looked up at Twinkle; at the others, he was floundering. He looked at Danrite and found his voice again. 'But it is written,' he managed.

'It is,' said Vlad.

'Sí,' agreed Jose.

He didn't want to say; he really didn't, but… 'But surely if it's written it must say something about how I save you?' said Danrite, reluctantly.

The eyes in the room settled back on Salor. The owner of one particular pair, with deeply furrowing brow above them, who had now forgotten about her mounting a high horse – much to Sid's relief – had suddenly realised something. Twinkle had heard it time and time again, "It is written", but she had never been told exactly what it was that *was* written. How could she make a judgement if she didn't know all the facts? Perhaps it was time to find out. 'Yes,' said Twinkle. 'What is written?' Her stare hardened. 'And I mean exactly, word for word; verbatim.'

'Isn't that some sort of paper?' queried Vlad. He was quietened by a glare.

Salor suddenly looked older; if that was possible; which it was, because he did, and started to stutter. 'I… er…' He was desperately looking for the right words. 'I must confess… I…' Oh-oh thought Twinkle as Salor struggled to find the best way to describe exactly what he didn't know. He eventually found the words he was searching for; nobody was going to like them. 'Truth be…' he said, then looked down at his hands and gulped. 'The truth is….' He looked back at a room full of worried faces; one reflected in a mirror. He twiddled his fingers. There really was no way out. 'The truth is I don't know,' he finally conceded. He felt as deflated as a balloon that had been discovered weeks after the festivities had finished.

'What?' spluttered Vlad.

'Oh, don't start all that again,' snapped Twinkle, who this time was far too angry with someone else to bother clumping him. She turned to Salor. 'You don't *know!*' She was shaking. 'Then what do you know?'

'I just know what I have been told. That it is written, that a hero would come to save us. I've never actually seen anything.'

It was written. It had been written. It had been passed down from generation to generation that it had been written. And that was the problem, all Salor had was the knowledge that something had been written. No one had thought to pass down exactly what was written. How the hero was going to save the world of Myth, Magic, and Make-believe? And the further it passed down, the more the next recipient of what was written thought the hero would know; until now that is. The buck stopped here. Someone had asked the question no one had thought would be asked. Which begged the question: just *how* was the hero going to save them?

Then the ground suddenly shook beneath everyone's feet.

'Ay caramba!' said Jose, swiftly getting to his feet.

'What was that?' said Danrite, looking worried.

Salor and Twinkle exchanged hurried looks. Salor then spoke with some urgency. 'It would appear we had an uninvited guest.' He went to the door. 'Time to move I think. To the Otherside people!' he said, and then strode quickly towards the stairs.

'"Had?"' said Danrite, not entirely happy with the sound of that.

'Come on,' said Twinkle, grabbing hold of Danrite's hand, 'we have to go.' She pulled him to his feet.

But Danrite dug his heels in; he wanted to know what was going on; why the sudden panic?

But all Twinkle would say was, 'Safety first Danrite, safety first.' And then he was lifted over her shoulder. Danrite was going whether he wanted to or not.

CHAPTER 17

Mister Power grumbled to himself as he watched Mister Fix remove his tie. He would be having words with him the next time he saw him. Which would be never as it happened, as the very next second Mister Fix was no more, disappearing suddenly in a sheet of bluish flame. El Yograg and Nomed, who had been standing just behind Mister Fix, suffered similar fates an instant later. There followed a noise like a sonic boom.

Ears ringing, Mister Power cautiously made his way over to where his minions had been standing. There he ran the toe of his shoe through a pile of ashes and the odd titanium screw that was once Mister Fix. Messy, he thought, but impressive. Although it did throw up a small problem or two; had his minions' demise been caused by a powerful spell guarding the portal, or had Mister Fix simply said the incantation of safe passage wrong?

Erring on the side of self-preservation, Mister Power decided on two things as he stood there staring down at the three piles of ashes. He would find another portal; with magic failing surely not all would be as protected as this one was, if that had been the reason behind the flames. He had also decided he needed cannon fodder; if anyone was going up in smoke again, it wasn't going to be him.

Mister Power removed the handkerchief from his breast pocket and wiped the dust from his shoe with it. He then shook it and returned it to his pocket.

CHAPTER 18

The Otherside, which Twinkle had explained to Danrite albeit briefly as she carried him, was where Myth, Magic and Make-believe lived. His mind had then gone into overdrive as he wondered what fantastic things he would see there. But when he arrived, with a bump as Twinkle deposited him on the ground, he found it was nothing like he had been expecting it to be; no mists, no forbidding darkened forests, no daunting castles, no strange creatures – present company excepted. Instead he found himself standing in a daisy-strewn grassy meadow that stretched away as far as the eye could see. The sky above was blue, the sun that shone down a warm yellow. It was all rather nice. But as nice as everything was, Danrite was determined to get answers, and so it seemed did the others. Twinkle's voice was the loudest.

'But it is as I said, it is written,' said Salor, cowed by Twinkle's pressing.

'We know that,' said an exasperated Twinkle, clenching her teeth, 'but it's not helping, is it? If our so-called saviour doesn't know what he's got to do to save us.'

'I thought he would know,' said Salor, as if repeating the words over and over again would help.

'Perhaps we should look at the book,' said Vlad.

Twinkle and Salor stopped their bickering and starred at Vlad as if he had suddenly grown another hood.

'I mean,' said Vlad, 'it has to be written somewhere; I heard it was in a book.'

'That's just a myth,' said Salor.

'What is?' said Twinkle.

'That there's a book that all is written in,' said Salor.

'I didn't know there was a book,' said Twinkle. Though now she thought about it, as it was written, it therefore had to be written somewhere, or else it wouldn't be written, would it?

'Sí,' said Jose, 'I too did not know this.'

Sid whinnied an acknowledgement of his lack of knowledge of a book.

The table did a little dance. It appeared Rosie was also ignorant of the fact.

'So where do you think the book is?' said Vlad.

'But it's a myth,' said Salor.

'What is?' said Twinkle.

'The existence of the bo- oh good grief,' said Salor.

It was at this juncture that Danrite decided to join the others and climb aboard the merry-go-round of debate, taking the opportunity of asking a question, or two, or three, of his own. 'If I may,' said Danrite, pushing between Vlad and Twinkle. 'I've got a question or two I want to ask.' Salor suddenly looked as if was going to burst into tears. 'Why did you bring me to the Otherside? What did you mean when you said we *had* uninvited guests? And what are we going to do now?'

A look of relief appeared on Salor's face as a chance to escape the book questions presented itself in the guise of questions he thought he could answer. Because of this he decided to ignore Danrite's mathematical failings. 'Ah, now,' said Salor, wringing his hands, 'good questions Danrite.' He positioned himself so he had his back to Twinkle. 'Safety my boy is the answer to your first question. We can't have our hero falling into the wrong hands now, can we?'

Danrite gave thought to the solicitor and his gun. He decided it made kind of sense. 'Fair enough,' he said.

Happy to help, Salor continued. 'As for the uninvited guests we had, well, shall we say they were shown the door and then disposed of.'

'Disposed of?' said Danrite.

'Poof! No more,' says Twinkle, making a face; her tongue poking out of the side of her mouth.

'No!' said Danrite, clearly aghast. Both at the thought of someone going "poof!" and the sight of Twinkle's tongue lolling onto her cheek.

'It was painless,' said Salor.

'A painless poof,' said Vlad.

'Sí,' said Jose, 'it was a quick poof!'

Nevertheless, however quick and painless the poof was, Danrite felt a shiver travel down his spine. 'But who were they?'

'Some of Power's lackeys no doubt,' said Salor. 'Looking for you, I shouldn't wonder.'

Danrite had found something else he didn't like the sound of.

'And the answer to his third question?' asked Twinkle, not at all liking the sickly colour Danrite's face had turned. 'What are we going to do now?'

Salor did more wringing of the hands and then spoke with all the crypticism of an idiot. 'I know a man!' he said.

No, no one was any the wiser.

What Salor had meant was, was that he knew a man that might be able to help them answer Danrite's third question. So Salor's answer wasn't the correct answer, because, the real answer to Danrite's question was in fact, that they were going on a journey to find a man that might be able to help them answer the question they all wanted to know; how was Danrite going to save the world of Myth, Magic, and Make-believe?

The man, as it happened, wasn't a man at all, or at least not in the sense of an ordinary man that is. This man was extraordinary. This man was a magus. A seer. A soothsayer. A woman.

'So he's not a he, he's a she?' said Danrite, giving Salor a funny look.

'Sort of,' said Salor.

They were sat on the grass. Sid was nibbling at it. Rosie had lowered her flaps.

'She is or she isn't,' said Twinkle.

'It's a man's job you see,' said Salor, making his point clear, to no one but himself.

Danrite, who had managed to make a daisy chain as they talked, which interested Jose no end, endeavoured to look even more puzzled than at any time since the episode in the kitchen. He succeeded. He put the daisy chain around Jose's neck. Jose immediately waltzed off to show Sid, who took an instant liking to it and ate it. Jose howled the howl of the disconsolate. Danrite frowned at the chihuahua and then looked back at Salor. 'And she'll be able to help us?'

'If anyone can, *he* can,' said Salor.

'*She'll* know where it is written?' said Twinkle.

'He is called the Font, a famous magus of considerable knowledge.'

'So she's a font of all knowledge,' said Twinkle, winking at Danrite.

'Like the ones they have in a church?' said Vlad.

'No,' said Salor. He had wanted to say stupid boy, something he had heard it said somewhere, but as he didn't actually know how old Vlad was, he refrained from the comment.

'If she's so famous, why haven't I heard of her then?' said Twinkle.

'His existence is on a need to know basis,' said Salor, tapping the side of his nose.

'Whatever,' said Twinkle, with a dismissive wave of her hand. She wondered whether the old fool believed half of what he said himself.

'Then all we've got to do is find her, this magus, and she'll show us what's written so I can save everyone?' said Danrite, doubtful it wasn't going to be as easy as he made it sound.

'Just so,' said Salor, looking his happiest since leaving the portal.

Danrite discovered he had yet another question, a nagging one. 'But what about this Power bloke, won't he try to stop us?' said Danrite, managing to put the smile on Salor's face into reverse.

'Least said about him the better,' said Salor, doggedly trying to cling to his happy thoughts.

'That won't help,' said Twinkle, 'the boy's got a point. All head in the sand, you are Salor. Stick it in and all will be all right in the morning. But what if it isn't?'

Salor crossed his arms, mumbled a reply that no one caught, and then sat brooding.

Ignoring the sand-dweller everyone concentrated on Twinkle and Danrite; the boy did have a point. Mister Power had to know about the Otherside, and that that is where they would go with Danrite. He had surely sent someone after them already; the poofs were proof of that. He would send more no doubt.

'So what do we do now?' said Danrite.

'We wait,' said Twinkle.

'For what?'

'That,' said Twinkle, pointing behind Danrite.

Danrite turned, and noticed for the first time a door shape thing in the distance, hovering and quivering a couple of feet off the ground like a summer heat haze.

'What is it?' said Danrite, squinting to get a better look.

'The door to the Otherside.'

'But I thought…'

'Everyone does, the first time they arrive,' said Twinkle, giving Danrite a knowing smile. 'Technically, I suppose, we are on the other side, but we are not yet in the Otherside. The cottage was the portal, this…' she waved her hands at their surroundings, 'is the staging area. We have to wait here until the Otherside is ready for us. It has to align you see.'

Danrite didn't see, but decided he didn't need to. He got to his feet. 'Shall we go then?'

'I don't see why not,' said Twinkle, joining Danrite. She then looked at Salor. 'So,' she said, 'where do we find this Font?'

Salor was struggling to his feet, his knees making weird popping and cracking noises as he did. 'Well,' he puffed, once up. He arched his back; more popping and cracking.

'Well?' said a frowning Twinkle.

'At the centre,' said Salor, stretching. Pop. Crack.

'At the centre!' said Twinkle. She cast a nervous look towards Danrite. Thankfully he was way too interested in the quivering doorway to notice. She repeated what she had just said, but this time in a hushed voice. Jose's ears had pricked up.

'Yes,' said Salor.

'But we'll never make it. It's way too dangerous.'

'Never said it would be easy,' said Salor, now shaking his arms.

'We'll have to go through all the lands?' Twinkle whispered. She looked worried.

Finishing his warm down with finger wiggling, pop, pop, crack, Salor nodded. 'Afraid so.'

This wasn't good. Twinkle gave Danrite another nervous glance. They were taking him out of the frying pan into the fire.

CHAPTER 19

The secret entrance was only known to Mister Power. It was rarely used; for emergencies really, should he need to make a hasty exit for example. In this instance he needed it to get back into the office without being seen.

Carefully closing the secret hatch to the secret entrance behind him, Mister Power made his way to the secret staircase. This would lead to a secret chamber that was secreted directly below his office. Mister Power liked secrets, but only the ones he kept, except that is the one in the secret drawer in his desk, which was now secreted on his person in a secret pocket. He wasn't so keen on that secret; it was one secret he could well do without. Mister Power started to climb the stairs.

At the top, Mister Power carefully opened the door to the secret chamber. It was doubtful anyone would hear the door open, but Mister Power was ever the careful. He slipped into the chamber and closed the door behind him; carefully.

Apart from several switches and monitor screens dotted here and there on the walls, and a pole in the centre of the room that reached from floor to ceiling, the room was empty. Mister Power went to one of the walls and flicked a switch, a monitor sprang to life. At the same time, hidden surveillance cameras in his office did their job, leaving no nook or cranny unobserved. Mister Power studied the screen; the room was empty, as he had expected it to be; one could not be too careful. Plus, he had told Miss Manager to manage the place while he was away, and as much as he liked her, not trusted mind, he trusted no one, she might take the opportunity of his absence to have a snoop around for the sake of it; he knew he would. Besides, he had told her he was going on holiday and had waved her a cheery ta-ta not so long ago; it would look pretty odd if he suddenly appeared in his room again as she was there. Goodbye secret entrance. Sadly it would also be goodbye Miss Manager; however much he liked her. He did like her though so he hoped that would not be the case. Perhaps that was why he was checking the screen again. Happily the room was still empty.

Mister Power now reached for a switch that would scramble the lock on the door to his office so he would not be disturbed, and then another that opened hatches in the ceiling, one either side of the pole. He stepped back and watched as his office chair lowered into the room on the end of the pole. Once the chair was resting on the floor of the secret chamber, Mister Power climbed aboard. He pressed a secret button under one of the chair's arms and held tight as the chair headed back up to the office.

Chair back where it should be, Mister Power wasted no time in getting what he had come for; a staff list. It contained names addresses – email and snail – and telephone numbers. More importantly it also contained the serial numbers of the micro-chips he had had planted in each of them; staff, whoever they were, sometimes tended to tell porkies as to their whereabouts now and again. This of course he could understand from the flesh and blood minions, but the androids? Perhaps he had made them too human? Never mind, more important than the micro-chips was the asset evaluation sheet; it was hardly good business getting rid of useful staff. He put the list into his pocket, sat back in his chair, pressed the secret button under the arm, and disappeared into the chamber below.

CHAPTER 20

Miss Manager, the tall, horn-rimmed bespectacled, blue-eyed, tousled auburn-haired, everything Mister Power likes, but she isn't, secretary but now in charge, was leaning on the door to his office, trying to still her pounding heart. She didn't know why she had left Power's office when she did, sixth sense perhaps, but she was glad she had.

She listened, but the reinforced door was hindering her. Someone was in the office, she was sure of it, but where had they come from, and more importantly, who was it? Did she call security? No. Because deep down she knew who was in there; Mister Power; sixth sense again? Now what did she do? It was late; way past her finishing time. If he came out there would surely be questions as to why she was still there. Should she leave? No. Miss Manager decided to go back to her desk and sat at it looking busy. If he came out, she was sure she could come up with any amount of viable excuses why she was still there.

After a while, Miss Manager ran out of things to shuffle on her desk. She looked at the door, almost mesmerised by it. She had been expecting it to open. Miss Manager looked at her wristwatch; she had been shuffling paperwork aimlessly for over five minutes. What now? Perhaps she should leave? No, curiosity was getting the better of her. She should knock. She would knock. Miss Manager got to her feet and went over to the door, giving it a couple of raps. Nothing. She knocked again, and then pressed her ear to the door. Nothing. Heart rate rising, she decided to try the door handle. It was locked. That was strange, the door was never locked. She then heard a faint click. Wondering at the sound, she tried the handle again. This time it turned, allowing her in.

To Miss Manager's surprise, the room was empty. Did she imagine someone inside? She sniffed the air. No she hadn't. Mister Power had been here, in the room, moments ago, and she didn't need sixth sense to know that; she could smell his cologne; eau de *slick and slimy*. Cologne so cheap its scent was barely able to cling to him, let alone linger. He would have had to have been in the room in the last half-hour for it to still be polluting the air like it was and he had left on his holiday ages ago.

Her thoughts turned to how he could have got in without passing her. A secret entrance no doubt. But she wouldn't be wasting her time looking for it, if Mister Power had a secret entrance then a secret it would stay; he was too much of a professional to make it easy to find, and besides she didn't have the time to look. She had things to do. Instead, she shrugged her shoulders and left. She left the room. She left the building. And would soon be leaving the world.

CHAPTER 21

'So,' said Danrite, speaking over his shoulder, as he stood a few feet before the shimmering doorway, studying it, 'how dangerous is this going to be?' One thing Danrite wasn't was stupid. He also had rather good hearing. They were going to the centre, he presumed, of the Otherside.

'Dangerous?' said Twinkle, nay batting an eyelash.

'I heard you and Salor talking.'

This time eyelashes were batted. 'Ah,' said Twinkle. She was now standing beside Danrite. She gripped his arm and looked into his eyes. 'Very, I'm afraid.'

'Ah,' said Danrite. The thought of stepping through to the Otherside had suddenly lost its lustre.

'Look,' said Twinkle, a serious look in her eye, 'I dislike the idea of going over as much as you do, but everything's a mess and we need to put it right. So over we go.' She looked behind her to check where Salor was; he was talking to Sid, she lowered her voice. 'As for Salor, I doubt he knows any more than we do. We will just have to play it by ear.'

'You don't think this magus he was talking about exists?'

'I don't know so it's not for me to say, so the jury is out on that one.' She let go of his arm and stared deeper into his eyes. 'As is whether you're the real deal in so far as heroes are concerned.' She took another glance over her shoulder; the others were heading for the door. 'But it is written, so for the moment, like it or not, you are. Therefore I promise I will do my best to keep you safe.'

Something in the way Twinkle spoke told Danrite she would look after him, hero or not. 'So not that dangerous then?' said Danrite.

Twinkle couldn't help but smile, but said nothing more; it was time to go.

'You coming?' said Salor, as he stepped over the door's threshold.

'Right behind you,' said Twinkle. She pushed Danrite ahead of her and together they went through the doorway after the others, and straight into the back of a stationary Vlad, nearly knocking him over.

'Problem?' asked Twinkle.

'He doesn't know which way to go,' said Vlad.

'I do, I do,' said Salor, 'it's just been a little while since I was last here. Things have changed.'

'Can't you remember anything?' said Twinkle.

'It's been over a hundred years or more,' said Salor.

'Wow!' said Danrite. 'A hundred years ago?'

'Don't be taken in Danrite, that's no time at all to an immortal,' said Twinkle. 'It's just a feeble excuse.'

'You're immortal!?' said Danrite.

'We're magical,' said Twinkle.

'Can't you remember anything?' said Vlad, eager to get on and out of the Otherside as soon as.

'A little I suppose,' said Salor, looking this way and that, 'but it's that tree, I don't remember that.' He gestured towards a huge grizzled oak tree. 'It shouldn't be there. It's throwing everything out.'

'He always has to blame someone, or something,' said Twinkle, winking at Danrite.

'Perhaps it's grown since the last time you were here,' said Danrite, trying to be helpful.

'Perhaps it's because he's never been here before,' said Twinkle, glowering at Salor.

'Perhaps it's because the tree isn't a tree.'

'Precisely,' agreed Salor. 'Perhaps it's because it isn't a tre- what! Who said that?'

'I did.'

Everyone, except Danrite, was looking here and there; he was looking at the tree. 'I think the tree did,' said Danrite.

'The tree?' said Salor.

'For goodness' sake, I am not a tree,' said the tree, gathering its lower branches together in indignation at such an idea.

'What are you then?' said Twinkle, pushing her way to the front.

'Shoo,' said the not a tree. Jose had wondered over for a closer look and had started to sniff around the base of its trunk. He started to cock a leg. 'No!' yelled the not a tree. But it was too late. Jose made a show of scratching at the ground, grass flicking up at the bark, and then went back to the others, a satisfied look on his face.

'It is smelling like a tree,' Jose announced on his return.

The not a tree started to cry.

'Blimey,' said Danrite.

'Bad dog,' said Salor, wagging a finger at Jose.

'It is what I do,' said Jose, scratching at an ear.

Vlad sniggered behind an invisible hand.

'Right, umm… there-there,' said Twinkle, for want of something better to say to a sobbing oak tree; sobbing not a tree.

'It's not fair,' wailed the not a tree. 'I didn't ask to stand here.' The not a tree wailed again and rubbed a branch near the top of its trunk, where two small knots sat above and either side of a larger, more bulbous knot. Below these was a hole; one a woodpecker might be associated with. Together, they looked remarkably like a face. And as most of the wailing appeared to be emanating from the hole it wouldn't prove to be too much in the way of a stretch of the imagination to assume that that was exactly what it was; a face; eyes, nose and a mouth.

'Who did then?' said Twinkle.

'Who did then what?' said the not a tree, sniffling.

Twinkle sighed. 'Who asked you to stand there?'

The not a tree stopped its sniffling and stared suspiciously at Twinkle with knotty eyes, that looked a tad puffy around the edges. 'How did you know someone asked me to stand here?' The question was guarded.

'Call it an educated guess,' said Twinkle, hands going to hips. She turned to Danrite and whispered to him. 'As two short planks,' she said, raising her eyebrows.

Danrite grinned.

'I heard that,' said the not a tree. Who would have guessed that its hearing was as good as Danrite's was.

'Ah,' said Twinkle, not wishing to get embroiled in something she didn't want to get embroiled in. 'I was talking about Rosie here,' she said, quickly.

Rosie rattled her flaps at the indignity of it.

The not a tree's lower branches were lowered again. 'Well, hello there,' said the not a tree, noticing Rosie for the first time. Leaves were fluttered.

'She's a wood nymph,' said Vlad, in way of a strange introduction.

'You don't say,' said the not a tree, seemingly now forgetting its earlier distress. 'So am I.'

'You're a wood nymph?' questioned Twinkle.

'Of course I am,' said the not a tree. 'My name's Leif.'

'No way,' said Jose.

'Way,' said Leif, blinking his knotty eyes, 'and don't you go tinkling on my feet ever again.'

As Jose couldn't promise such a thing, he wondered off to have a sniff at things, one of which eyed him suspiciously.

'So,' said Twinkle, 'who was it?'

'Who was what?' said Leif.

Twinkle scowled at the tree. It was trying her patience. 'I hear oak burns well,' she threatened.

'Twinkle!' exclaimed Salor.

'You wouldn't?' said Leif, leaves suddenly all a tremble.

'She wouldn't,' said Salor, appalled by the idea.

'She would,' said Vlad, imagining her capable of anything.

'Try me,' said Twinkle, menacingly.

'You wouldn't, would you?' whispered Danrite.

'Sssch!' Twinkle whispered back.

Leif decided to err on the side of she would. 'The F-Font,' he spluttered reluctantly. 'The Font sent me.'

'Well I'll be,' said Salor.

'What?' said Leif.

'What?' said Salor.

'What will you be?' said Leif.

'Oh for goodness' sake,' said Twinkle, 'enough!' She glared at Leif. She would glare at Salor later. Leif shut up and looked oaken – the equivalent to looking ashen – and did some more leaf trembling. Now surrounded by relative silence – she could hear Jose licking himself – Twinkle asked a sensible question. 'Now,' she said, still glaring, 'why did the Font ask you to stand there?'

Leif didn't answer straight away, he just stared straight ahead, intensity in his knotty stare. He had been told what to say if such a question was asked. He had to say the answer exactly as it had been told to him. He would say it in his own time, regardless of hostile staring. Finally he spoke. 'To wait for those that come,' he said.

'Anyone in particular?' asked Twinkle.

Leif's knots took on a glassy look as he spoke again in a slow and deliberate way. 'Those that look for the Font, that look for the book, that look for what is written, that look for the answer, that wear the most garish of make-up combinations, that-'

'Okay-okay,' said Salor quickly, 'I think we get the idea.'

'That's us, isn't it?' said Vlad.

'Would appear so,' said Twinkle, grinning at Salor's discomfort.

'Why are you waiting for us?' said Salor, ignoring the sniggers.

'You?' said Leif. He bent forward and looked at Salor, studying him. It was as if seeing him for the first time. How could he have not noticed? The blue eye shadow, pink blusher, purple lipstick, all put on with the finesse of a giddy plasterer. They were the ones he was waiting for. 'This way,' he said, forming his roots into makeshift legs, 'but stay close. To stray from the path is dangerous.' Leif started to move.

Salor looked at Twinkle, who shrugged. 'I guess he wants us to follow him,' she said.

'But how did the Font know?' said Salor, picking up his feet. It's amazing how fast trees can move when they want to.

'She's the Font isn't she?' said Twinkle.

CHAPTER 22

Mister Power had unscrambled the lock to his office door as he had left, and was just about to turn off the monitor linked to the secret cameras in his office, when he noticed the office door opening. Hand in mid-air, finger poised over the off switch, Mister Power watched as Miss Manager entered the office. She nosed about for a moment, appearing to sniff the air as she did then, shrugging her shoulders, left the room.

'Hmm?' said Mister Power, as he flicked the monitor's off switch. He wondered if he should be worried by what he had just seen. Miss Manager hadn't actually done anything wrong or suspicious, but she should have been away from the office by now. But then again, he had put her in charge; there was nothing wrong with putting in a bit of unpaid overtime. Still though, something niggled at him, but now wasn't the time, he had things to do. Miss Manager and her nosing would have to wait; he had other staff members to round up; the cannon fodder kind.

It didn't take Mister Power long to find what he was looking for. Rogi and Ergo were lounging in the lounge of a gentleman's club. They were wearing suits, therefore they were gentlemen. No one at the club was going to argue with them. They stood when they saw Mister Power approach.

'Gentlemen,' said Mister Power, in no mood to rock any boats, 'please be seated.' They sat, and Mister Power wondered how long the seats they were sitting in would last. One of the chair legs below Ergo was already bowing dangerously.

Drinks were ordered. Mister Power had a brandy, Rogi a martini; shaken to an inch of its life, not stirred, and Ergo a leek and spring onion smoothie. They all took a sip and then Mister Power divulged what he wanted of his two minions/muscle/cannon fodder. They listened. They nodded. There was no argument; there never was.

Mister Power sat back and allowed himself a moment of relaxation, there was no hurry, not when one had a fine brandy in one's hand. He studied his minions.

Rogi was the most handsome creature anyone could lay eyes on. A head turner. Tall. Straight of back. A living example of the classical male form. Suave. Urbane.

Ergo on the other hand was not. Slightly taller, burlier, Ergo was so something else. The demise of myth had not been kind to him. Human-ish in form, but many features he had been originally endowed with were still lurking beneath the surface. Those that weren't gave him the look of an alleyway ruffian; cauliflower ears, small eyes, rounded shoulders, greenish around the gills. He actually didn't have gills; it just looked like he did. Even so, Mister Power leaned forward and secretly gave the area a closer inspection. Perhaps it was a sign of deterioration? A reason for concern? No, no gills and the greenish colour appeared to be caused by the play of the light in the room. But he would have to keep an eye on them; on this side anyway. On the Otherside such concerns could be ignored, they could deteriorate all they wanted, and when they came back – because he was sure they would – it wouldn't matter then either; he wouldn't need them anymore, but until that day…

'Right gentlemen, finish up, we have work to do.' Mister Power finished his brandy and stood up just as the room echoed with the sound of splintering wood. 'Help him up Rogi, there's a good fellow.'

CHAPTER 23

Leif led the way. Salor strode purposely by his side. The others were following a few paces behind in a gaggle.

'Twinkle?' said Danrite, when he was sure Salor couldn't hear him.

'Yes,' said Twinkle.

'When did Salor change the colour of his lipstick?' said Danrite. He could have sworn the wizard's lips were blue when they had stepped into the Otherside.

Twinkle shrugged. 'Who knows?' she said, 'Who cares?'

The gaggle fell into silence.

It didn't last long.

'Twinkle?'

'Yes Danrite?'

'How far is it?'

'To the centre?'

'Yes.'

'You'll know when you get there.'

Deciding he wasn't going to get any sense from Twinkle on the how far score, and because he didn't like the silence that had fallen on them earlier, it was kind of unnerving, Danrite decided to turn his attention to Leif. An answer was needed where the not a tree was concerned. 'He's not a wood nymph, is he? Leif, I mean.'

'No.'

Twinkle appeared to be going through a quiet phase; Danrite persisted. 'Can we trust him then? If he's lying about what he is, surely he could be lying about other things.'

'Oh, I think so,' said Twinkle, turning her head to look at Danrite. 'He's just a little mixed up that's all. We've all gone through it sometime or other.'

'Have we?' said Danrite.

'It's called an identity crisis.'

‘An identity crisis?’ said Danrite, mulling over the meaning. ‘I don’t think I have,’ he decided.

‘You sure about that?’ said Twinkle. ‘Perhaps you’re right in the middle of one now.’

‘I…’ Danrite had to think about this. He hadn’t, had he, was he? He wasn’t sure. Maybe thinking what he was thinking meant he was? And then… oh, he thought. He was, right in the middle of one, but with one subtle difference; he wasn’t the one having it, everyone else about him was. ‘Oh,’ he said. He looked at Twinkle, she was smiling at him.

‘A tree, I suspect,’ said Twinkle.

‘Sorry?’ said Danrite, a little lost.

‘Leif. I think perhaps he was just a tree before he learned to walk and talk.’

‘A tree?’

‘And that is enough with the questions for now; they’re bad for the brain you know.’

Danrite didn’t think that was right, and was just about to say so when Twinkle brought the gaggle to a sharp halt. Salor and Leif had stopped some twenty paces ahead; Salor appeared to be examining thin air. ‘It appears we have arrived at the first of the lands.’

‘What lands?’ said Danrite, who had been expecting the path they were following to lead them straight to the Font. No one had mentioned there being lands; then again, he supposed, no one had bothered to tell him a whole lot about anything about the Otherside and what to expect thus far, except for it being dangerous that is.

Twinkle explained.

The lands were not lands in the sense of one looking from one county to another, or country to the other, but rather pages like in a book, going from one to the other, but not like a book, more a toilet roll. Imagine looking down on the toilet roll from above, the centre is where the Font lives, the layers of tissue paper the lands. They needed to pass through all the layers/lands, before they could reach the Font. Obviously there are not as many lands as there are layers of tissue on your common or garden toilet roll, but suffice it to say, there are many. But each layer, when stepped into, does become a land as we know it; perhaps a landscape with rolling hills, flat plains, forests, spreading out before you; a trek waiting to be embarked on to the next land; layer of tissue.

'I didn't know that,' said Vlad, who had been eavesdropping on Twinkle's explanation. 'Are they two or three ply?'

Twinkle swung a mighty backhand at him, but he dodged it.

'I was only asking!' Vlad complained.

'Enough of this nonsense,' snapped Salor, who had re-joined them. 'It appears we have bigger problems at hand than the quality of toilet paper.' Salor went on to explain.

It appeared all was not as it used to be with the Otherside. Before the waning of myth, magic, and make-believe, the layers were stable, would stay put, now they were shifting, swopping places, no one now knew which layer/land they would step into next; you might travel forever and never find your way out again.

'Crikey,' said Twinkle.

'Sí,' Jose agreed, 'it is crikey.'

'Double crikey,' said Vlad, not wanting to be left out.

'What do we do now?' said Danrite.

'Only one thing to do,' said Salor.

'Go home?' said Vlad, hopefully.

'No,' said Salor. 'We continue following Leif until journey's end.'

It transpired that Leif had some sort of sixth sense that enabled him to travel through the shifting lands without getting lost; it was why the Font had chosen him for the mission. So, with fingers crossed, with bated breath, with Leif leading the way and with the greatest of reservations, they warily stepped through thin air, into the land beyond.

CHAPTER 24

The room Miss Manager had been renting was spartan, bordering on empty. Just four pieces of furniture; a table with a single chair pushed under it stood against one wall, a single bed against another. The only other piece of furniture in the room was a chest that sat at the foot of the bed. It was to this that Miss Manager headed after she had closed the room's door behind her.

Miss Manager lifted the lid and started to rummage within, not frantically, but with measured urgency. She removed four suits, four shirts and four pairs of shoes, all identical to the clothes she was wearing. She placed them all neatly upon the bed. She then reached into the chest and removed a whip. For a moment she was tempted to lash out with it, but let the idea slip and placed that too on the bed. There followed, each of which she placed on the bed, a bowie knife and sheath, a length of rope, a leather belt, a pair of sturdy walking boots, walking socks, a suit that could loosely be described as safari, that was made up of shorts, not skimpy, shirt, not showy, and a jacket. Lastly she removed a vest, the type of which was bullet and knife resistant. All was placed on the bed.

Happy that all was in order Miss Manager then proceeded to undress. High heel shoes removed, dropped in trunk. She was now at least five inches shorter. Suit removed, dropped in trunk. Showy blouse removed, dropped in trunk. She then, with a certain amount of glee, removed her glasses with their plain glass and threw them in the trunk. Next into the trunk was the wig she was wearing; revealing short cropped, blonde hair, and finally she removed the coloured contact lenses she was wearing, revealing grey as the true colour of her eyes. She ran a hand through her short locks, went to the bed and got dressed.

Whip and rope attached to her belt, knife sheathed, vest neatly hidden beneath her jacket, Miss Manager was ready. She headed for the door.

CHAPTER 25

Mister Power had had a concern. With the loss of El Yograg he was sorely lacking in the tracking department. But imagine his delight when he discovered the late El Yograg had a brother. A brother who, according to Rogi, was every bit the tracker El Yograg had been; perhaps even better. Why Mister Power had never heard of him before, with the many eyes and ears at his command, was beyond him, but he was not one to look a gift tracker in the mouth; especially one of the ilk of El Yograg, who would have bitten your face off if you looked too closely. Still, he would ask questions when all was resolved, and undoubtedly some of those ears and eyes would be removed; literally. Mister Power did not like being in the dark; which wasn't literally as he had had some of his finer moments in the dark.

Rogi called a halt at the mouth of a large cave. Mister Power peered at it from between his two massive minions. 'He's in there?'

'Yes.'

'Then what are you waiting for, go get him'.

'He is dangerous and to be approached with caution,' Rogi explained.

'So?'

'I'll need to use the whistle.' Rogi put a huge hand into an equally huge pocket, and pulled from it something resembling a panpipe. He put it to his mouth and started to blow into it.

'What's wrong with it?' said Mister Power, when the noise he was expecting failed to materialise.

'Nothing, sir,' said Rogi, 'it's silent.' Mister Power frowned. 'Sorry, I should have explained, it is akin to the dog whistle, sir.'

'Ah,' said Mister Power. He looked at the cave entrance; nothing had appeared. He had his doubts about the whistle, silent or not. 'Try it again.'

Rogi blew into the whistle.

‘There,’ said Ergo, suddenly. He was pointing to a large clump of shaking bushes to the side of the cave entrance.

Something appeared from their depths. Something big. Something grotesque. Something that was staggering somewhat awkwardly along on its hind legs as if in a trance. It swayed and tippy-toed first this way and then that and then tippy-toed and swayed that way and then this. It was as if drawn by a mysterious force. Closer it came. Then fell over.

‘Now!’ ordered Rogi.

With all the speed of a minion fearing for its life, Ergo dashed to the something on the ground and attached a collar and leash to its neck. Job accomplished, Ergo dashed back at the double with the other end of the leash in his hand; stopping only when it became apparent the leash wasn’t as long as he thought it was. It was his turn to fall over.

‘He will be fine now,’ said Rogi.

‘You sure?’ said Mister Power, nervously eyeing the leashed creature. It appeared to be asleep, but Mister Power trusted nothing and no one.

‘Watch,’ said Rogi. He blew on the whistle again. The something creature stirred. It opened an eye. It opened another one. It started to blink, as if stepping from dark into the light.

‘So you reckon it’s safe to use?’

‘Yes,’ said Rogi. ‘Ergo, bring him here.’

Ergo scrambled to his feet and tugged on the leash. The something creature responded by getting to its feet. Ergo pulled at the leash. The something creature started to walk towards Rogi and Mister Power.

For all his power, Mister Power took a precautionary step back. He had seen this creature’s brother, El Yograg, in savage mode and it wasn’t for the faint-hearted, and this one had bigger teeth.

‘There,’ said Rogi, as the something creature ambled over as docile as a lamb, ‘like a lamb.’ Rogi reached down and patted the something creature on the head. In turn, the something creature gently nuzzled said hand, and then bit it off. Blood spurted from Rogi’s arm, just below the wrist, splattering Ergo.

‘Good grief!’ exclaimed Mister Power, dodging spatters of blood.

‘Just as I said,’ said Rogi, attempting to stem the flow of blood, ‘like a lamb. It no doubt would have ripped me apart if I had not used the whistle.’

‘Well done you,’ said Mister Power with more than a touch of sarcasm. He made a note to not get anywhere near the creature. Happily though, the thing would soon cease to exist along with the rest of them, as soon as he stopped the boy from doing whatever it was he was supposed to do. Until then… ‘What’s the little fellow’s name?’ he asked.

‘Euqsetorg,’ said Rogi, managing to not twist his tongue in a knot as he said it.

‘U-what?’ said Mister Power, not even trying to pronounce it; he had people for that.

‘But we call him Hewie,’ said Rogi.

Mister Power didn’t see the connection, but whatever. ‘Hi there, Hewie,’ he said, keeping his distance as he did.

Hewie gave Mister Power a suspicious look then spat out one of Rogi’s fingers.

‘I believe he likes you, sir,’ said Rogi, making no attempt at retrieving his drool-covered digit.

‘I’m glad to hear it,’ said Mister Power, giving Hewie and the digit an equal look of disgust, ‘but perhaps we can now get on with finding that boy.’

‘Right away, sir,’ said Rogi, standing to attention and saluting, his bloody stump thumping against the side of his face with no hand to stop it.

He’s never done that before, thought Mister Power, shock setting in no doubt. ‘Perhaps you should put something on that,’ he said. He didn’t really care, but Rogi was still useful at the moment; a lot of good he would be fainting all over the place. ‘Get it stitched up.’

‘No need,’ said Rogi cheerfully, ‘I have plenty more hands at home ready to replace it.’

Of course you have, thought Mister Power with a shake of his head, Rogi was a Rogi after all. ‘Good-good,’ he said. ‘You… er… go do that.’ And now for the portal, he thought, smiling grimly, now for the portal.

CHAPTER 26

With apprehension in abundance, Danrite stepped into the first land. A second later he gasped the gasp of the surprised.

The land was beautiful, nothing like the scenario he had been preparing himself for; which was becoming a bit of a habit. The sun was shining. The sky was blue, dotted with small white fluffy clouds, like so many crisp white woolly lambs gambolling across a gigantic azure field. The scene framed by the most wonderful rainbow. Each end disappearing behind the greenest of hills. Meadows, so much lusher than the staging area they had left behind, spread before him, filled with every wild flower imaginable. Trees, golden and silver, their bows straining under an abundance of fruit, dotted the fields, their foliage as green as the hills. And in the distance, nestled between those greenest of hills, was a village, so quaint it could easily grace the front of the very best of picture postcards.

Danrite was awestruck. 'It's beautiful,' he said.

'It's dangerous,' said Twinkle.

'But how?' asked Danrite, hardly able to believe what he was seeing. It was something from a fairy-tale.

'Because Leif said it was,' said Twinkle, seeing the scene before them in a totally different light. 'Stay close.'

They stepped towards the nearest meadow of wild flowers; Leif was leading the way, heading for the village. Everyone's eyes peeled for the unexpected, but they never expected it to come from within their little group.

The scent that rose from the gently swaying flowers, caught on a faint warm breeze, was heady. It caressed the senses. Lulled the senses. Lulled Danrite's senses.

'Danrite?' said Twinkle, alarmed at what she saw.

He was blinking; trying to stay awake. 'Sorry,' said Danrite, 'I'm feeling awfully sleepy.' His eyes closed again, but this time they didn't flicker open again. Instead his knees buckled under him and slumped forward.

Twinkle just managed to catch him before he hit the ground. 'Salor!' she shouted. Salor came running.

'What happened?' said Salor, concern etched on his face.

'He said he was feeling sleepy, then this.'

'Sleepy?' Salor looked at Danrite, and then their surroundings. The concern showing on his face quickly changed to realisation and dismay. He started to fumble in his pocket and removed something from one of them. 'Quick,' he said, handing Twinkle something, 'put this over his face.'

Gently laying Danrite on the grass, Twinkle placed something that looked remarkably like a pig's snout over his mouth and nose; two straps positioned over the back of his head kept it in place. 'What is it?' she asked, looking at the thing on Danrite's face.

'It's an oxygen mask,' said Salor, reddening slightly.

'It's not like any I've ever seen before; looks more like a pig mask.'

'Okay, it is a pig mask, but with an added touch of magic. It's all I could think of.'

Twinkle gave him a funny look. 'And you just happened to have it in your pocket?'

Salor shrugged and looked sheepish. 'What can I say; fancy dress party.'

Takes all sorts, thought Twinkle.

'What's going on?' said Vlad; his hood appearing over Salor's left shoulder. The others gathered around.

'He's coming round,' said Twinkle.

'Eh?' said Danrite, his voice muffled by the pig mask. 'What's going on?' He raised a hand and went to remove it.

'Ah-ah!' said Twinkle, slapping his hand away. 'You need to keep that on until we work out what happened; its oxygen.'

'You fainted,' said Salor.

'Why?'

'We don't know,' said Twinkle, momentarily making eye contact with Salor, who quickly glanced away. He didn't have to say he was thinking the same as Twinkle was. Danrite went to remove the mask again. 'No, is what I said, and no, is what I meant.' He decided to try and get up instead. 'Whoa there,' said Twinkle, stopping him again, 'you need to take a moment.'

Vlad, who wasn't always as stupid as everyone had decided he was, had noticed the look Twinkle had given Salor and the way he had furtively looked away, and as Salor was still with the furtiveness, he decided to tackle Twinkle. 'What really happened?' he whispered.

Twinkle frowned at Vlad, and after making sure Danrite was doing as he was told, she stood up and took Vlad to one side. She returned his whispering with some of her own. 'It was the flowers,' she said.

'The flowers?' said Vlad. It took a moment for the true meaning of what Twinkle was saying to sink in. 'Oh, the flowers. Drat.'

It was a well-known fact in the land of Myth, Magic and Make-believe, that the scent of some flowers in the Otherside had a somewhat peculiar effect on those that did not live in its realms; namely the non-magical, non-mythical or non-make-believical. At least, it would send them to sleep; to wake later with a rather nasty headache, or at worst it could induce a coma that would need the kiss of a member of a royal family to rouse them; something that was very unlikely to happen if you were your common or garden Joe Bloggs; no disrespect. But it wasn't only your run of the mill humankind that could be affected. No, there was the odd case documented right there in the Otherside of people succumbing to the flowers' effects, but the symptoms were different, no sleepiness involved; more doolallyness. There was that poor girl that kept losing her sheep for one. It was rumoured she would often sniff the flowers on purpose. The boy whose sheep were in the meadow and cows were in the corn was another. At first the powers that be had looked into a possible ovine connection, but this idea was discarded when it was found that the boy often slept in the fields, amongst the flowers quite frequently; he was a sort of shepherd for goodness' sake. A warning was promptly issued, and the dallying with the wrong sort of flower was deeply frowned upon.

Which meant Danrite was human. Which meant a meeting was called for. Which meant a meeting was called; about Danrite being human.

'So what do we do now?' said Vlad.

'Carry on as planned,' said Salor.

'But he's not magical, mythical, or make-believicle,' said Vlad.

'See, I told you,' said Twinkle.

'Is make-believicle even a word?' said Salor.

'I think so,' said Vlad. 'I think some writers use it.'

'Neigh–whiney,' laughed Sid, which was most unlike him; especially in the circumstances.

Rosie rattled her flaps in disapproval.

'But if he's not magical etcetera, he can't be our hero,' argued Twinkle, 'which means we might as well give up right now.'

'No one said the hero had to be magical etcetera,' said Salor.

'That's true,' said Vlad.

Twinkle looked fit to burst. 'But no one has seen what's written.'

'That's why we're going to see the Font,' said Salor.

A silence fell on the group. It appeared they had argued themselves into a circle.

'We go on then?' said a deflated Twinkle.

'Regardless,' said Salor.

'No matter what he is,' said Vlad.

'Exactly,' said Salor.

'Even if we think it's a waste of time?' said Twinkle.

'Precisely,' said Salor.

There followed, a polite cough.

They all now turned as one as they suddenly remembered Danrite. He was still on the floor, awake and staring daggers at them.

'Eh, did you hear any of that?' said Salor.

'Der!' said Danrite, through his mask. 'I'm laying less than a foot away from you.'

Red faces all round, they shuffled over to him; it only took a second.

'How're you feeling?' said Twinkle, giving him a weak smile.

'How do you think?' said Danrite.

'Still woozy eh?' said Salor.

'A little,' said Danrite. He started to get to his feet.

'Here, let me help you,' said Twinkle, offering him her hand.

'If you're sure I won't be too much of a burden for you,' said Danrite, testily.

Twinkle helped him up. 'Look, sorry about all that, it's just you know.'

Danrite stood before them and dusted himself down. He then gave them a look that would have withered a patch of grass. 'If you remember, it was you lot that said I was the hero, not me.' He wobbled for a second. Twinkle went to steady him. 'I'm okay, I just need a moment.' He brushed her hand away. 'And yes, before anyone else says anything else, I do understand the pressure you're all under, but just for a moment give a thought to what I might be feeling.'

There followed general murmuring and head nodding and shaking. This was followed by several sheepish looks of the variety woody, horsey, invisible, garish, and sparkly. Those who were perhaps expecting doggy would be disappointed.

'Where's Jose?' said Vlad, suddenly realising he hadn't seen the little werechihuahua for a while now.

'He was here a moment ago wasn't he?' said Twinkle, not really recalling if that was true or not.

'I haven't seen him for a while,' admitted Salor.

And just like that the lingering animosity suddenly disappeared. One of them was missing and they were in a dangerous place.

'Leif,' said Salor, 'you haven't seen Jose have you?'

Leif had been standing a little way away from everyone else. 'The pain in the-'

'Yes.'

Leif did a one-eighty degree turn and pointed towards the village. 'I believe he went that way.'

All eyes turned towards the village.

Dum-de-dum-dum!

CHAPTER 27

Finding another portal wasn't easy. Well, it was, for those in the know.

Mister Power gazed at the portal with respectful suspicion even though his sources had advised him that with magic failing, this one out of all of them was the most vulnerable and therefore the safest one to try. Advice he was equally suspicious of; he trusted no one, hence the use of the cannon fodder or test subject, as he liked to think of him, which was being brought to him. He could have used one of the cannon fodder he already had at hand, but he felt they may be put to better use later on; muscle and keeping Hewie under control.

The portal was one of a number no longer used as the need for travelling from one world to the other gradually diminished, so under less scrutiny security wise, but that didn't mean it was open for just anyone to wander through; you still needed the password. It consisted of a basic shield, a brick archway housing a rusty wrought iron gate, which looked real enough, but wasn't, with a high brick wall going on for a hundred feet or so either side of it; which was real. On the gate hung a sign "KEEP OUT" under which hung another "PLEASE" and under that was another reading "DANGER OF DEATH OR WORSE". Mister Power had smiled at that, but he had been disappointed he hadn't been able to see his heart's desire, unless of course he was into derelict brick archways; that or he didn't have a heart to have one. Most people who knew him would have plumped for the second option.

When he had first seen the rusty old gate, Mister Power had had the urge to just walk up to it and push, but he managed to keep the idea in check; he hadn't got where he was by being stupid. The thing might look harmless, but the bottom sign meant what it said. Instead he had decided to stay his hand and wait for the test subject to arrive. He arrived.

‘Sir?’ said a small, bespectacled young man, of the *ever so humble* mould. He had arrived at the hurry and had stopped just as quick when the enormity of the situation he was in finally arrived a second after he had.

‘Ah, Mister Scribe,’ said Mister Power, all smiles and greeting the young man as warmly as he could pretend, ‘so prompt.’

‘Master, sir,’ said the humble young man, correcting Mister Power’s mistake and instantly regretting it; rumours. ‘If it so pleases you.’ The young man even managed a quick nervous hand wring. ‘Sir.’

‘What? Not yet a Mister?’ said Mister Power, trying hard not to show the contempt he was feeling for the horrible little man. ‘Unbelievable, something shall have to be done with you.’ He hadn’t thought what yet, but it would come to him later.

Master Scribe’s eyes widened. Whatever could Mister Power mean by that? He didn’t know whether to click his heels together, or run for the hills. For the moment though, neither was an option as Rogi had a firm grip on his shoulder. Instead he settled for further hand wringing. ‘Thank you, sir,’ he said, most humbly.

‘But for now I have a little job for you,’ said Mister Power, ‘something to show me what you’re made of.’ He had the sneaking feeling that that could soon be dust.

Master Scribe immediately pulled a notebook from a pocket, a pen from another. He licked the tip of it in anticipation.

‘No-no,’ said Mister Power, giving the young scribe’s ink-stained tongue a look of disgust. He waved the pen and paper away. ‘I want you to open that gate over there.’ He pointed to the archway.

‘That gate?’ said Master Scribe, pointing and wondering.

‘Brilliant,’ said Mister Power, also wondering – how such an idiot could be in his employ. ‘We’ll make something of you yet.’ He didn’t know what, but parts were always handy.

Master Scribe blushed, forgetting how dangerous a man Power was. There would be some serious heel kicking and perhaps even a whoop back at the humble, but comfortable room. With a serious lack of hesitation, he headed for the gate. It caught both Power and Rogi on the hop.

‘Wait,’ said Mister Power. He grabbed at the scribe’s sleeve, stopping him in his tracks. ‘You have to…’ Grief, thought Mister

Power, I've hesitated. But how should he put it? He couldn't say he wanted him to say a silly magic rhyme to open the gate. The man might spook and run or faint or worse. He didn't have the time or patience to wait for another halfwit. 'Ah-ha!'

'Sir?' said Master Scribe, spectacles slightly askew. He straightened them.

'Right,' said Mister Power, regaining his composure, 'I need a sound check, just before you open the gate.'

'Sir?'

'I want you to read this out loud.' Mister Power handed Master Scribe, a sheet of paper. The scribe gave it a dubious look, which didn't go unnoticed, but didn't take it. 'It's for an advert I'm toying with,' said Mister Power, lying on the hoof. 'Who knows, if all goes well you could be in it. Think of it as an audition.' Master Scribe finally took it. If Mister Power was relieved he didn't show it.

'For an advert?' said Master Scribe. If he thought the idea of him being called in the middle of the night – he was usually in bed by half past eight – to open a gate and read something out loud for an advert he may or may not be in, a little strange, *he* didn't show it.

'Yes,' said Mister Power, so wanting to bodily push the horrible little geek towards the gate, and perhaps through it. Instead he amiably pointed the way.

'And I might be in it?' said Master Scribe, suddenly dazzled by bidding footlights.

'If you're good enough.'

Now in the thrall of his coming role, the rumours about Mister Power completely forgotten, Master Scribe cleared his throat. 'Oh-'

'Not now,' said Mister Power. 'Just before you open the gate.' He gave the young man a helpful nudge in the right direction.

'Should I be dramatic?'

'If you think it will help.'

'Just before I open the gate?'

'Clever man,' said Mister Power, patting Master Scribe on the shoulder. 'Rogi, make a note; Master Scribe here, promoted to Mister as soon as I get back to the office.'

Rogi patted his pockets. His missing hand now replaced.

'I didn't mean…'

'Here,' said Master Scribe, offering Rogi pen and pad.

'Oh, good grief.'

Rogi took them, wrote heavily on a page; there was a snapping sound, then tore the page from the pad. He then handed pen and pad back to Master Scribe. He handed the page to Mister Power.

An incredulous Mister Power took the page and stuffed it in a pocket. Inwardly he seethed and sighed. Outwardly he managed to smile at the scribe. 'Shall we?' he said, once more pointing to the gate.

Master Scribe beamed and started for the gate, which he reached in several quick strides. Behind him Mister Power took several quick strides in the opposite direction. Putting his now broken pen and crumpled notepad away, Master Scribe prepared for the sound check with a couple of throat clearing coughs, then began to recite, in a fairly dramatic way for one so humble, from the sheet of paper Mister Power had given him. He finished with a flourish and went to open the gate, but to his surprise found the gate was already open, as if it had opened by itself.

Expecting the inevitable, Mister Power, tensed with expectation, nearly fell over backwards when the inevitable failed to materialise. There was no dust producing flash. The horrible little man was still in one piece. The gate was open. *The gate was open!*

'How was that?' shouted Master Scribe, all smiles as he pointed at the gate.

'Perfect,' replied Mister Power, himself all smiles; the tension draining from him like water down a plug hole. 'Now off you go, and be all the earlier tomorrow.' He waved his hand dismissively.

Master Scribe took a step and then hesitated. Should he say something? He hadn't actually opened the gate. No, it was done. What about Mister Power's promise? Why not, things were going well for a change. Surely it wouldn't hurt to ask? 'I'll be sure to,' he said nervously. He steeled himself. 'And the Mistership, sir?' He thought asking about the advert was perhaps chancing his arm a bit; baby steps.

The smile on Mister Power's face faltered a little, but not enough to be noticed by anyone else. 'Of course, of course,' he said, through gritted teeth; the urge to get going through the gate and beyond was near unbearable. 'Come to my office in the morning and I'll deal with you then. Now off you go.' Mister Power made shooing motions with his hands.

Not wanting to press the question, it was Mister Power he was talking to after all, Master Scribe slipped back into ever so humble mode, and with head bowed, scuttled off in the direction of his ever so humble, but comfortable room. As he did he attempted to smile, the sort associated with success, but every time he tried, the words "I'll deal with you" popped into his mind to worry him. What had Mister Power meant? Surely it wasn't anything sinister. But it was Mister Power who had said them. Could you meet anyone any more sinister? Master Scribe's shoulders slumped, perhaps there wouldn't be any heel clicking when he got back to his room. Perhaps he shouldn't go back to his room. He had heard that Australia was nice this time of year. Now, where was his passport?

Watching him go, Mister Power took the crumpled page Rogi had given him from his pocket and tore it into tiny pieces. He threw the pieces on the ground.

'Not a Mister then, sir,' said Rogi, watching the pieces fall.

'Not while I'm breathing,' muttered Mister Power. He turned his attention to the gate. At last, he thought. With eager steps he started walking towards it.

CHAPTER 28

Having had the foresight to attach tracking devices to Mister Power's leading minions was reaping its reward for Miss Manager. She had thought of attaching one to the man himself, but decided in the end that that might just be a dangerous step too far. There had been one blip, or rather the sudden lack of blips, when the tracking device she had placed on Nomed suddenly stopped working. Something she would attempt to rectify when she had the chance, but for now that was by the by as she had her sights on the main prize; Mister Power. Hidden from view, she settled down to watch, listen and wait, and then follow him wherever he went.

The gang, apart from Nomed, were all there, but they had brought something with them, something she hadn't seen before. It was on a leash and was huge, hairless and appeared to be a cross between a dog and a pig, with other ugly bits and pieces thrown in for good measure. It slavered furiously. It also looked very, very dangerous. She was glad she was nowhere near it. Then someone else appeared.

Eyebrows raised, Miss Manager watched as this new character to the plot walked, no, sidled up to Mister Manager. She didn't know him, a young man, but from the way he was dressed he had to be one of Mister Power's employees. He looked humble, perhaps too humble, trying too hard to please. He spoke to Mister Power, they chatted for a moment or two, and then Mister Power pointed at something. Was he pointing at that old gate? What was going on? Miss Manager frowned, and even more deeply when it appeared the new arrival went to go towards the gate, but was pulled back by Mister Power. More chat. Now Rogi was writing something. He then gave whatever he had written to Mister Power who stuffed it in a pocket without even looking at it. Curious, thought Miss Manager. Mister Power pointed again, and again the young man headed for the gate, but this time he was allowed to go on his way.

Several quick strides and he arrived at the gate. Mister Power had also taken several quick strides, but in the opposite direction, her direction. For a moment she thought she had been discovered, but he stopped well short of her and took up the position of someone expecting something bad to happen. Meanwhile, the young man now seemed to be talking to the gate; rather dramatically; all arms and such. Miss Manager couldn't quite make out what he was saying. The young man at last finished what it was he was reciting and shouted to Mister Power. He pointed at the gate. The gate was open. Had the young man opened it? Miss Manager wasn't sure. Mister Power, now smiling a very dangerous looking smile, looked to be ushering the young man away. There followed a moment of hesitation and muted conversation, but in the end the humble young man seemed to get whatever message Mister Power was putting across and quickly scuttled from the scene. While this was going on Miss Manager slipped forward amongst the shadows to get a better view of what would happen next. She watched intrigued as Mister Power took from his pocket the piece paper that Rogi had given him earlier, and then puzzled as he immediately tore it into pieces and threw them to the ground. Litter bug, thought Miss Manager. Mister Power now turned his attention to the gate and headed for it. Maintaining a safe distance, Miss Manager quietly followed.

But just as he reached it, it closed with a loud click. Mister Power looked far from happy, his smiley façade dropping for once. He appeared to hesitate a moment before calling Rogi over to him. Mister Power said something to him and Rogi nodded. Next moment Rogi was bellowing what sounded to Miss Manager the lines from some nursery rhyme she had never heard of.

Rogi finished his bellowing, and the second he did the gate opened again. Mister Power gestured for Rogi to open it further as he took a couple of steps backwards. Rogi did as he was asked and the smile returned to Mister Power's lips as the gate opened further. The smile then grew into a grin as he, Ergo and the thing on the leash followed Rogi through the gate. This couldn't be good, thought Miss Manager, a horrible feeling rising in her gut.

After waiting for what Miss Manager felt was a safe amount of time to wait for any sudden returning by Mister Power or his minions she slipped from her hiding place and cautiously made her way over to the gate.

At the gate Miss Manager took out her tracking console and went to check how far on the other side Rogi and Ergo had travelled; brilliant tracking that would be, to go blundering through the gate only to find they were standing just behind the wall. But to her dismay the blips that should have been flashing their position were dull and lifeless.

'What the…?' she said to herself, as she shook it. It didn't make any sense; it was working a moment ago. She shook it again. Still nothing, it was as if they had just disappeared. She thought about the light going out on Nōmed. One going on the blink could perhaps be explained, but two, together, just like that? But it wasn't one, or two, it was three. Three blips had disappeared. Something was wrong. Her tummy did another turn as she realised that if she wanted to continue following them she would have to do it blind, until she had a visual that is.

With a deep breath, Miss Manager stepped up to the gate and went to push it open, or would have done if something in the back of her mind hadn't handed out a niggling warning not to. She stopped; her fingertips a layer of atoms away from touching it. Why had she stopped? She couldn't understand. She thought hard, and then after a moment realised something; neither the young man nor Mister Power had stepped up to the gate and physically pushed it open; not until that silly rhyme was said first. Did the rhyme have to be spoken before you could enter, like some version of open sesame? The idea sounded stupid, but Miss Manager wasn't. It was always better to be safe than sorry. With that in mind she gave her surroundings a furtive once over, just in case someone was around. She didn't want anyone to witness what she was about to do. She thought hard and recalled what Rogi had bellowed. Should she bellow it too? No, the young man had just said it. She decided to whisper it.

'Oh doorway of fae so old
allow me free passage so bold.'

There followed another line that Miss Manager uttered in an even quieter voice. Once she had done another quick sweep of the area that is.

'And a ninny nanny noo too.'

The gate opened. A slightly embarrassed Miss Manager gave it a tentative push. It easily opened wider. She took a cautious step forward, took another quick look around, and then, happy all had gone unseen and better still unheard, but not happy that she was stepping blindly into who knew what, she, still with caution, stepped through the open gateway.

CHAPTER 29

The village, for want of a better word, was quiet, and for the want of two words, was eerily quiet.

They stopped at the village boundary, scanning it and the area around it for a glimpse of their little friend.

'What do you think has happened to him?' said Danrite through his pig mask. It was making him itch; that or the smudges of blusher smeared on it.

'I think you'll be able to take it off soon,' said Twinkle, noticing, and not sure if that was true.

'With magic the way it is, anything could have happened,' said Salor. 'He may have even slipped into another land.'

'Or worse,' said Vlad.

'Worse?' said Danrite.

'Don't listen to him,' said Twinkle, 'he always thinks the worst.'

'Do not.'

'Do.'

'Stop it you two,' snapped Salor. 'I think we'll have to split up. Some of us circle the village while the rest go in.'

'Go in?' said Vlad, clearly not liking the sound of that idea.

'Any other suggestions?' said Salor.

'We should pick straws,' said Twinkle.

'Straws?' said Salor.

'To see who does what,' explained Twinkle.

'Oh,' said Salor, who in his mind had been the leader of the group skirting the village. 'Well, yes,' he was suddenly having second thoughts about his idea, 'unless anyone has a better idea that is?' He was now clutching at different straws.

Leif narrowed his knotty eyes. 'I don't like this,' he said, waving a couple of branches in the direction of the village. 'It's too quiet.'

'He's right you know,' said Salor, happy to agree to something that might delay a sortie into straw picking.

‘It is,’ said Vlad, also more than happy to agree. ‘Very quiet.’

‘Wussies,’ said Twinkle.

‘It does seem spooky though,’ said Danrite.

‘Sí,’ said Jose, ‘I am not liking it also; it is giving me the heebie-jeebies.’

‘Wo!’ said everyone, jumping back as one, as Jose made a sudden appearance in the middle of them; apart from Leif that is, who was too busy still branch waving to notice the return of the missing pooch.

‘Where the heck did you come from?’ said Twinkle, not sure whether to be angry or happy with the little werechihuahua.

There formed a puzzled look on Jose’s cute little face. ‘Qué?’ he said.

‘We were worried,’ said Danrite.

‘Qué?’ said Jose.

‘Where have you been?’ said Vlad.

‘Qué?’ said Jose.

‘Why does he keep saying K?’ said Salor, wondering if Jose had taken a knock to the head.

‘What?’ said Jose.

‘You disappeared,’ said Twinkle. ‘We thought something had happened to you.’ She then frowned at the little dog. ‘Leif said he saw you heading for the village.’

‘Ah, sí,’ said Jose, ‘I look for somewhere.’

‘Somewhere?’ said Twinkle.

‘Sí,’ said Jose, cocking a leg. ‘I look for the post with the lamp.’

‘Qué?’ said Salor. He knew not why.

Twinkle pursed her lips and placed her hands on hips. ‘You mean to tell me that while we were all worrying our socks off wondering what had happened to you, you had gone off for a bit of light relief?’ She now sided with angry.

‘Better them than me,’ said Leif, who had finished his branch waving, but who then suddenly started doing it again. ‘Away with you!’ he chided. Jose hopped away quickly on three legs. Leif then brought everyone’s mind back to the village. ‘It’s much too quiet. Where are the children?’

‘Children?’ said Salor.

‘The ones from the town, they should be out playing.’

‘Town?’ said Danrite. ‘I thought it was a village.’ He thought it much too small for a town.

‘That’s because it’s a town the size of a village. It’s Nursery Town,’ said Twinkle. ‘And Leif has a point, where are the children?’

Danrite, who was starting to feel a lot better now, was puzzled. A nursery town? Maybe that’s what the people in this land called large villages. Perhaps a large town that wasn’t quite a city was called a nursery city. Who knew? He should ask. Perhaps not. Did it really matter? But curiosity got the better of him. ‘Nursery Town?’ he asked.

Twinkle explained. ‘It’s where the majority of nursery rhyme folk live. Others like Jack and Jill live on the outskirts, they have a farm up by that hill, yonder.’ She pointed out a hill. ‘For some reason, only known to them, they decided to dig a well up there. A well on top of a hill?’ She shook her head. ‘I ask you.’

‘Nursery rhyme characters?’ said Danrite, trying to get his head around this latest piece of news.

‘This is Nursery Rhyme land,’ said Twinkle, realising Danrite had no idea where they were, ‘but don’t let them hear you call them characters, here they are as real as you and I.’

Danrite was agog. But when he came to think about it, why should he be surprised to find out Jack and Jill actually existed, here at least, on the Otherside, where the lands of Myth, Magic and Make-believe were as real as the lands of the world he had come from. Of course they existed in their own land, as he expected the likes of Odin would in a mythical land, and Unicorns in a magical land. He suddenly remembered that Sid was really a unicorn and was about to ask him about his land when Leif interrupted with a warning.

‘Someone’s coming,’ hissed Leif.

Everyone looked to see that indeed someone was heading in their direction; running in their direction in fact.

‘This doesn’t look good,’ whispered Twinkle to whoever was in earshot. ‘Ready everyone.’

What they needed to be ready for no one knew, but they readied themselves for it anyway.

As the figure got closer, Danrite saw that it was a man, tall, thin, well-dressed if a bit old fashioned, morning suit, cravat, but rather dishevelled. He was pasty faced, with a bald head that was oval in shape, and when the man got closer still, Danrite realised that the man wasn't just hairless on top, he was hairless all over his head; no eyebrows, no eyelashes, no facial hair at all. He also had a rather nasty cut on top of his shiny bald bonce that oozed a yellow substance.

'Good grief!' said Salor, as the man reached them. 'Humpty, is that you?' Salor looked horrified.

Danrite looked at Twinkle. 'Did he just say what I thought he said?' he said.

'Uh-huh,' said Twinkle.

'No way,' said Danrite, who had always thought Humpty more egg than man.

'Sí way,' said Jose, who, for the moment, had lost interest in Leif's roots. 'It is he, the man who should not be sitting on walls.' Jose cocked his head, appraising the scene. 'Ha, he has the egg on the face again.'

Egg? thought Danrite; had Humpty done something wrong? 'Egg on his face?' said Danrite, seeking clarification. 'Have I missed something?'

'Sí, egg,' said Jose, 'like in the shell.'

'He means yolk,' said Twinkle.

'Sí, yolk,' said Jose. 'The yolk is on him.'

Danrite gave the cut on Humpty's head closer scrutiny. The yellow stuff oozing from it did have a yolkish look to it. Ugh, he thought.

'You're hurt,' said Salor, going to Humpty's aid, 'what happened?'

Humpty took a quick look behind him before fixing Salor with fear filled eyes. 'The unthinkable has happened that's what,' he said, his body shaking. 'May the Font help us.' He then slumped moaning to the ground, landing heavily on his bottom.

'Quickly, Twinkle, help me with him,' said Salor, stooping and gripping Humpty's arm.

Twinkle stepped forward, as did everyone.

'For goodness' sake,' said Salor, ushering everyone but Twinkle away, 'give the man some room.'

Danrite decided this was the opportunity to get a third opinion on what Twinkle and Jose had said.

'Vlad,' said Danrite.

'Yes?'

'Is that *really* Humpty Dumpty from the nursery rhyme?'

'Yes.'

'But I thought he-'

'Was more egg shaped?'

'Well, yeah.'

'He was,' said Vlad, 'but as you know, things are changing.'

'Cripes.'

'Mind you, it looks like walls are still out of bounds for him,' said Vlad, nodding at the cut on Humpty's head.

'You think that's what happened to him? He fell off a wall?'

'Seems likely with his track record.'

But Danrite thought Humpty looked scared. Surely falling off a wall wouldn't have that effect on him, especially if he was used to doing it? Perhaps it was the unthinkable that he had spoken about that had something to do with it? He asked Vlad if he knew what he meant.

'No idea,' said Vlad, shrugging shoulders, 'could mean anything. Look, he's back on his feet. Perhaps we'll find out.'

'How many fingers am I holding up?' said Salor, sticking two fingers up in front of Humpty's face.

'I'm dazed, not stupid,' snapped Humpty, who instantly regretted it as it made his head hurt worse than it already was. But serve him right, he thought, for being so rude. 'Sorry,' said Humpty, 'I'm not feeling too well. Two.'

'Two?' said Salor, forgetting his question.

'Fingers,' said Humpty.

'Oh, yes,' said Salor, 'very good.'

'But I'd be careful old fellow which two you use in future.' Humpty managed a weak smile; which also hurt.

'Eh?' said Salor. He looked at the fingers he was still holding up. 'Oh, right.' He quickly put his digits away. 'Now, what in the world is going on Humpty?'

'I told you, the unthinkable has happened.'

'Which is?' said Twinkle, who had just finished sticking a plaster to Humpty's shell-like. That would be his head, not his ear.

Appearing to ignore her, Humpty turned and started staring at the village, his eyes glazing over as he appeared to enter his own little world.

'Humpty,' said Salor, not quite snapping, but his tone hinting at impatience. 'For goodness' sake, what is it?'

Humpty turned around, the fearful look back. He met Salor's stare and held it, he opened his mouth. At first he said nothing, as if he was afraid to speak; to say what had frightened him so. But then, while slowly lowering his head as if to inspect the ground at his feet, he managed to find his voice again, it coming out in a whisper. 'I'm afraid they've got out old fellow.'

'Who has?' said Salor.

Humpty looked up, his lips trembling. 'The nightmares have, old fellow; the nightmares have.'

'The nightmares?' said Salor, ashen-faced; which was quite a feat considering how much rouge he was wearing. 'Good grief.'

'What did he say?' asked Leif, towering over them.

A shaken Salor turned to the group. 'It would appear our journey to seek out the Font has just become slightly more dangerous.' He then told them what Humpty had just told him.

CHAPTER 30

'So,' said Mister Power, blinking in the sunlight that had greeted him, 'I take it this is the Otherside?'

'No,' said Rogi, who had said the same thing when Mister Power had uttered the same question when they had stepped into a corridor after passing through the gate.

'No?' said Mister Power, wondering when the heck it was they *were* going to get to the Otherside.

'We have to wait,' said Rogi. At his feet, Hewie growled for no reason in particular.

'For what?' said Mister Power, growing just a tad impatient. 'And what's the matter with the pooch?'

Rogi looked down at Hewie. 'I don't know, sir, hungry perhaps. I wouldn't get too close just in case.

Mister Power narrowed his eyes at Hewie and took a step back. 'So?' he said. 'What is it we are waiting for?'

'A doorway, sir.'

'A doorway?' Mister Power scanned the surroundings, but all he could see were daisies, green fields, blue skies, and yet more daisies.

'It will appear when it is ready for us.'

Mister Power didn't understand, and was about to say so, in a way that didn't make him out to be an imbecile, when a shimmering door suddenly appeared to his left, hovering in mid-air.

'It appears,' said Ergo, gripping Hewie's leash and tugging him back as he went to make a move towards it.

Giving Ergo and Hewie a wide berth, Mister Power went over and stood in front of the door. 'What do we do now?' he said, hating himself for having to ask, but better safe than sorry.

'We step through,' said Rogi, lumbering forward.

Just like that, thought Mister Power. It seemed a little too easy. 'Perhaps Ergo and the pooch would like to go first?' said Mister Power, remembering Mister Fix's dusty ending. So sticking with the better safe than sorry approach, he stepped out of the way. It hurt him to do so of course, a leader should always lead, but what was the point of having cannon fodder if you didn't use them in times of uncertainty?

Hewie, fairly pulling Ergo's arms from his sockets, eagerly leaped through the doorway when urged on. Ergo, who had a fond attachment to his arms, quickly followed. Mister Power on the other hand, stayed just where he was, waiting.

When Mister Power neither saw nor heard the bluish flashes and the sound of sonic booms he had been half expecting as Ergo and the pooch had entered the doorway, he decided that it was safe for him to proceed, so he stepped forward and in. It was only when he was halfway through did the thought occur to him that maybe blue flashes or sonic booms from the Otherside might somehow be shielded from him on the side he had waited. Drat, he thought. But it was too late now.

CHAPTER 31

The spells used to bind the boundary walls that surrounded the land of Nightmares, put there to keep its inhabitants from seeping into other lands, had weakened and finally broken. They were now free to invade other lands and do their worst, and at the moment, according to Humpty, they were in the town; he had seen them.

'Ay caramba!' exclaimed Jose on hearing Salor's bad news. 'I was just being there.' His eyes grew wide at the thought, but then went back to normal. 'But I see nothing.' He wandered away to have a sniff at Leif's roots.

Leif shook his leaves at the news and his lower branches at Jose.

'Creepy castles!' muttered Vlad, hardly able to believe what he was hearing.

'Shimmering glitter balls!' uttered a shocked Twinkle.

'Neigh-neigh, whinny!' whinnied Sid.

Clap-clap went Rosie's flaps.

'Who are the nightmares?' said Danrite.

'Who… who are the nightmares?' stammered Humpty, hardly believing his, not unlike a bird's, ears.

'He's new here,' said Twinkle, coming to Danrite's defence. She took Danrite by the arm and led him away to explain.

'Flipping 'eck!' said Danrite, when she had.

'Better,' said Twinkle.

Now they were all on the same page they gathered together to discuss what to do next.

'Humpty says that he saw some of them in the town,' said Salor.

'That's when I fell off the wall,' said Humpty, 'so afeared was I by the sight.'

'So what do we do?' asked Vlad.

'Hightail it outta town as soon as, I reckon,' said Twinkle. Her suggestion was met by a hundred percent approval rating.

Salor turned to Humpty and placed a reassuring hand on his shoulder. 'You can come with us if you like. Help us seek out the Font.'

'But what about the others?' said Humpty. He looked sideways at Danrite. 'And why is he wearing a pig mask?'

'The others?' said Twinkle. She looked at Danrite and rolled her eyes skyward. 'Long story.'

Danrite, embarrassed, touched his mask.

'The townsfolk; they went to Old McDonald's farm and holed up in his barn. I was the last one to arrive, because of my fall, loss of consciousness and all that, but when I tried to get in they thought I was a nightmare trying to trick them and wouldn't open the door.' Humpty looked wild-eyed. He was frightened. What had he seen? Was it his own nightmares in the flesh, or had he seen those of others? He spoke again, his voice barely a whisper. 'What if they're trapped in there, or worse?'

Everyone looked at each other.

'What now?' said Vlad.

'Well, we can't just leave them,' said Twinkle.

'We can't take that many people with us to the Font,' said Salor.

'Leif could help us lead them to another land,' said Danrite, 'a safer one.'

'But we don't know if there is a safer one,' Salor pointed out.

They were in a quandary and no mistake, but something had to be done.

'We'll have to try,' said Twinkle.

'But what if the nightmares are at the barn?' said Humpty. 'Or they've taken them away?'

'One thing at a time,' said Salor, 'if they can be rescued, we'll try. If not…'

'One of us could go on a recino… recunnoit… reconoi… go look,' said Vlad, butting in and rescuing Salor from having to finish his sentence.

'Good idea,' said a relieved Salor enthusiastically, in the process pouring water on, and flushing away, the poo-pooing Twinkle had been about to unleash on Vlad's idea.

'Really?' said Vlad, who was used to people poo-pooing his ideas.

'Yes,' said Salor, 'and you're just the chap to do it.'

Vlad's chest had barely had the chance to swell. 'Me?' he said.

'Who better?' said Salor. 'You being invisible like you are.'

'He has a valid point,' said Twinkle.

'But…'

But it was decided. Vlad begrudgingly disrobed and prepared to set off on his reconnoitre of the barn.

Danrite furrowed his brow; he had a question; he whispered it to Twinkle. 'Why doesn't Vlad wear any clothes under his cloak?' he asked.

'Good question,' she answered. 'But one I doubt we should dwell on.'

'Oh,' said Danrite.

'Good luck, Vlad,' wished Twinkle, waving at nothing in the distance as Vlad set off.

'I haven't gone yet,' said a voice beside her.

'Oh, right,' said Twinkle.

'But I'm going now.'

'Good luck.'

There followed a heavy silence as everyone stared at where they thought Vlad was; everyone but Twinkle. 'You're still here, aren't you?' she whispered.

'Do you think I should take a weapon?'

'No,' said Twinkle, imagining a club dancing along in mid-air. No, no one would notice that.

'Just a thought.'

'Off you go then.'

'Going.'

One minute passed. Two minutes. Feet began to shuffle. The waiting game had started. People huddled, began to talk in hushed voices about what might be.

Twinkle on the other hand looked with suspicion at the empty space beside her. 'Vlad?'

'Yes?'

'Thought so,' said Twinkle, hands on hips.

Nearby there was the sudden sound of wood on wood. Rosie had heard Twinkle and Vlad talking. She was trying to say something.

‘Sorry, Rosie, I don’t understand,’ said Twinkle. ‘Salor.’ She called Salor over as he was, apart from Sid, the only other one amongst them that spoke table. Salor could also talk horse, which was handy on the occasion Rosie wouldn’t talk to him.

‘Yes?’ said Salor, ambling over.

‘Rosie’s trying to tell me something.’

‘Ah,’ said Salor, ‘what is it Rosie?’

Rosie rattled her flaps at him.

‘But he’s already gone,’ said Salor, looking bemused.

‘What did she say?’ asked Twinkle.

‘She says she’ll go if Vlad won’t.’

Drat, thought Vlad, she knows I’m here.

‘Oh, Rosie,’ said Twinkle, patting her, ‘that is very brave of you, but I think you’d be noticed.’

Rosie clapped her flaps again, and Twinkle looked at Salor.

‘She says she’ll zigzag,’ said Salor, even more bemused than before. He looked at the little table and smiled. ‘Whatever are you going on about?’ he said, knowing Vlad must be well on his way by now. But Rosie kept quiet, saying nothing about Vlad’s immediate whereabouts.

‘Ha,’ said a voice from on below, ‘a table that is zigging and zagging, that I would like to be seeing.’ It was Jose, who had been sniffing around close by and had overheard what Salor had said.

Double drat, thought Vlad, as he realised there was the real chance that everyone might soon find out that he had been dragging his feet and was still there, and worse still that a table, a girl table at that, was way braver than he was. He was going to look a right wuss in a minute if he didn’t do something quick.

Twinkle, who had noticed Rosie had kept shtum about Vlad, and had then realised what it was Rosie was doing, smiled and patted her again before kneeling down beside her. ‘That’s a good idea Rosie, but this isn’t a job for a wee slip of a girl now, is it?’ she said. ‘Besides, Vlad must be ***miles away by now***.’ Twinkle then leaned closer. ‘Clever girl,’ she whispered. Rosie raised her flaps slightly and stared in the direction she thought Vlad was standing.

Vlad, who had heard enough, but not Twinkle’s last comment, sidled up to Twinkle and whispered, in a voice that Rosie could hear, that as he had, at last, finished planning his moves, which weren’t a thing to be hurried in such perilous times, he was now ready to hit the road. If it was a choice between danger and being made to look silly in front of everyone by a young slip of a girl table, Vlad knew which one he would choose.

Twenty or so metres later, as Vlad arrived at a hill that would take everyone out of sight, after travelling to it at the slowest pace he could possibly muster, no point rushing to his demise, he suddenly stopped in his tracks, looked back, and frowned. Nah, he thought, that's not possible; tables can't smile; especially a little sly, knowing smile like the one he thought Rosie had aimed at him. No, not possible he decided. Shaking his head at the very idea of such a thing, but not totally convinced he hadn't seen what he had seen, Vlad picked up his feet again and continued on his merry, but oh so slow, way.

CHAPTER 32

After stumbling for a moment or two in pitch blackness, and then being bathed in sudden light, as if someone had flicked a switch, Miss Manager found to her surprise that the other side of the gate wasn't anything like she had been expecting. She had thought perhaps a garden, overgrown, with a ramshackle house in the middle of it, or a deserted courtyard, with old and weathered statues, a defunct fountain and maybe a broken sundial in the centre of it, a field even. Instead, she found herself standing in a corridor. Never in her wildest dreams had she expected to find a corridor on the other side of the gate, but here it was, and what a corridor. Lined on either side with doors it, at first glance, appeared to go on forever. It didn't though. Once Miss Manager's eyes had recovered from the sudden light that had engulfed her, she could just make out, some thirty, forty, fifty metres away, another door at the far end of it; this one though, was facing her.

Staring at the corridor with something akin to wonder, Miss Manager took a couple of wary steps along it. She stopped at the first door and listened. Even though the place was as quiet as a church mouse who had taken to wearing crêpe-soled slippers, and she had been ultra-careful while tailing them, and doubted they knew she was following them, she knew she still had to be careful. Mister Power and his boys could be lurking anywhere; waiting for a chance to pounce on her unsuspecting person from behind any one of the many doors; doors she suddenly realised, that would have to be checked. A despairing thought for Miss Manager as she looked down the length of the corridor; so many doors; so many places Mister Power and his minions could have disappeared into. A despairing thought that led to another, as she wondered what the people who had hired her to keep an eye on him would say if she was to lose track of him so soon? Nothing good she suspected. With heavy heart and defeatist sigh, she reached down to try a tentative turn of that first door's handle, but as she went to grab hold of it she noticed something that gave her pause for thought, something that was about to brighten her day a little. The door had a large padlock on it; a large, locked padlock. She instantly realised what this meant, there was no way Mister Power would be leaping out from behind this door.

With a lighter step, Miss Manager looked at the next, and then the next. Both were locked as tight as the first door. She moved on. Door after door after door was padlocked shut. All the doors, along each side of the corridor, were locked tight. Until finally she came to the last door, the door that had been facing her when the light had come on. She stopped, but didn't look down. A thought had occurred to her as she'd approached it; a terrible thought; what if this too was locked? With her heart beating a little faster than it was a moment ago, she plucked up the courage to look.

CHAPTER 33

And on the farm there was a Vlad…

A very cautious, slow-moving, foot-dragging, would rather be somewhere else, Vlad. The barn was now in sight and, to Vlad's relief, no sign as yet of the nightmares Humpty had warned them about. He slowed even further, and then had to speed up again when he realised he had actually stopped. He moved closer, but not too close.

The barn was massive, as was its double doors. He stopped on purpose this time. There was no way he was going to be able to open one of those and take a peek inside without someone noticing. So what did he do now? Wait and see what happened? Scout around a bit more? Go back? Go back; Vlad liked the idea of that, nothing more he could do here. He would go back and tell the others that the coast was clear; what he could see of it anyway. It wasn't a lie, he had a clear conscience. And that was what he was just about to do when he noticed movement. A small door had opened at the bottom of one of the large ones and then quickly closed again. Drat, thought Vlad, who hadn't noticed the door before; so well did it blend in with its surroundings. Just another second and… but there was no point dwelling; Vlad knew what he had to do. He might be a bit of a scaredy-cat vampire, but he was an honest one with a conscience. He made for the small door.

He reached it. Now what? Perhaps he should knock. No, no, a stupid idea, he thought. He would have to try and gently open it a smidgeon. That was what he would do. He steeled himself. He steeled himself some more. Unless, he thought, there was another door somewhere, or a window. He hadn't seen one yet, but if there was one, problem solved. He decided that that was what he was going to do. He quickly scurried away to look.

A minute or five later, he was back. The mission a failure, there were no other doors or windows. Vlad started to think about doing another circle of the barn just to make sure he hadn't missed anything, but before he could finish his thought, the small door opened again. Vlad instinctively flattened himself against the barn; against the roughly-sawn wooden planks that walled the barn. Oh why do I still feel pain? thought Vlad, on becoming Vlad the Impaled; in several places at once about his person; mainly in the posterior area. He gritted his fangs and hoped that whoever or whatever was opening the door wouldn't keep it open for long.

'Hello?' said a small nervous voice from behind the door.

Vlad's eyes crossed as he pressed his body tighter against the barn wall. The voice sounded innocent enough, but it could be a trap; a lulling into of false security.

The door slowly inched further open until a white shape could be seen emerging from the top of the doorway.

Please don't be a ghost, thought Vlad, eyeing the emergence with trepidation. Please don't be a ghost. Vlad wasn't happy around ghosts. He was also very unhappy around nightmares; or felt he would be should the occasion arise. Please don't be a nightmare, thought Vlad. Please don't be a nightmare.

'Hello?' repeated the voice, its owner now pushing the door open wide enough for it to be within an inch of Vlad's nose.

This was more than close enough for Vlad who decided it was time to make a run for it; splinters or no splinters. Or he would have done had he not spotted the ribbon. A red ribbon that he now saw was wrapped around a white bonnet. It wasn't a ghost. It could still be a nightmare though, but something stopped him from fleeing; curiosity perhaps?

'Is there anybody there, Bo?' yelled a deep voice from deep inside the barn.

A young girl cautiously stepped from the doorway and looked this way and that. 'I can't see anyone,' said the young girl called Bo.

What did he do now? Vlad was in a quandary. The young girl looked as innocent as she sounded, but some nightmares start out like that; all innocent like and then WHAMMO something nightmarish occurs; hence the name. But if she really was just a young girl, then he should say something. She might be able to tell him what was going on; where the nightmares were? What they wanted? But if he spoke, invisible as he was, he would surely scare the bonnet off her. Oh what should he do? What he did, after a second of agonising, was to stay as quiet as the splinters would allow and see what happened next.

‘Can you see them?’ questioned the deep voice from deep within.

‘No,’ said Bo, with a certain amount of relief.

‘You sure?’

‘I know how to peep,’ said Bo.

‘You sure, you’re sure?’ said a different voice to the one she had been talking too; this one old and creaky. ‘Because you know what happened with the sheep.’

What happened next had Vlad pressing himself even tighter to the wall in terror. Bo’s demure little face had gone from creamy white to snarling angry purple in an instant. She had then let out such a stream of expletives that all the soap in the world would have had trouble cleaning her mouth out.

Vlad was mortified. Potty mouth, he thought, and here in Nursery Land. But the sudden tirade had given Vlad an opportunity. In her anger, Bo had spun and swished her way back into the barn, leaving the door wide open. If Vlad wanted to see inside, this was his chance. Quick as a flash he made for the door and peered in.

Inside, an old man of crooked stature, supported by a crooked stick, with a crooked cat sitting between his crooked feet, was cowering defensively in front of the outraged Bo. ‘I was only saying,’ said the old man.

‘Yeah, he was only saying,’ said a thin young man, coming to the old man’s defence.

‘And you can shut the heck up Pratt!’ shouted Bo, turning on the young man.

‘Sprat,’ said the young man, taking umbrage, ‘my name’s Sprat.’

‘Whatever,’ said Bo, waving a dismissive hand his way.

‘The door,’ said the deep voice, ignoring the minor spat and reminding Bo she as yet hadn’t closed it behind her.

With a swish of her petticoats, Bo swung around and, with a touch of venom, slammed the door shut; or would have done if it were not for Vlad’s trailing foot.

Vlad howled the howl of the dead; which was apt. In fact, so good was it, Vlad may well have taken considerable pride in it in different circumstances.

The barn, which was filled to the rafters with nursery rhyme folk, instantly erupted into mayhem. Bodies went this way. Bodies went that way. Vlad's went to the floor; a heavy weight on his back.

'I HAVE HIM!' roared a triumphant voice. 'I HAVE THE NIGHTMARE SNEAK.'

The air had been knocked out of Vlad and it was doubtful he would have been able to get to his feet even if he wasn't pinned to the floor by a huge big toe. The pressure on his back suddenly eased and he was hoisted into the air.

'Where?' shouted someone, as the mayhem started to abate on the realisation that the barn wasn't being invaded by hordes of nightmares after all.

'HERE!' bellowed the voice that belonged to the big toe that belonged to the person that held Vlad between finger and thumb. Vlad was lowered to just above floor level.

'Where?' said someone else.

'You been drinking Jack?' asked someone else.

'HERE!' said Jack, shoving Vlad forward.

'Jack,' said someone else, 'what have I told you about indoor voice?'

Jack looked abashed. 'Sorry Mum,' he said in a somewhat quieter voice.

'Now,' said Jack's mum, 'what is it you think you have?' She gave him a stern look, the so called magic beans and loss of her only cow still burned in her memory; even though, as it happened, all turned out well in the end; almost.

Jack now pushed Vlad towards his mum. 'This,' said Jack, and gave Vlad a squeeze.

'Ow!' yelled Vlad, as one of his ribs shifted awkwardly in his chest. Jack's mum took a rapid step back.

'There is something there,' said an amazed voice from within the throng of nursery folk.

'Told you,' said Jack, beaming.

'Let me through!' demanded a deep voice; the one that had earlier been deep in the barn.

Vlad looked up and saw the reassembled Nursery Land characters, part and make way for something black and shiny which walked on two spindly hose covered legs. It made its way over to where Vlad hung. It also had two spindly arms that were in sleeves of the finest silk, one of which reached up to straighten the crown it was wearing.

It couldn't be, thought Vlad as the black shiny thing approached, could it? Could the Otherside be in that much trouble?

The black shiny thing stopped in front of where he thought Vlad was. 'Who are you?' it demanded in the most regal of voices.

Blimey, thought Vlad, it is.

'Well!' demanded the shiny black thing when Vlad failed to answer straight away.

When Vlad had been caught, he had thought for a moment that he had somehow become visible, but now, as he watched the black shiny thing talking to thin air a foot or so to his left, he realised it had been down to just dumb bad luck. But, just to confirm this, he held out his hands. No, he was still invisible. This was good; he could still make a stealthy, unseen, escape; or could have if he wasn't being held firm between a giant's thumb and forefinger. Only one thing for it then… but then again he doubted screaming for help at the top of his voice was going to achieve anything. Only one thing for it then…

'Vlad,' said Vlad. 'I'm-'

'Ah-ha!' said the black shiny thing, cutting Vlad off in mid-sentence. It was now looking in the right direction. It now raised one of its spindly arms and pointed a spindly finger in Vlad's face. 'And what manner of thing secretes itself in a barn when no one is looking? Tell me that Vlad?' it said.

Interrogation, thought Vlad totally missing the point, but why riddles? It didn't help that he was rubbish at them; but he decided to play along anyway. He had a think. Mice creep into barns; or rats, he thought. Better not mention rats though he decided. 'A mouse?' he chanced.

This was greeted by a chorus of "ah's" from around the barn.

The black shiny thing took a step back, he had never heard of such a thing; a talking mouse? Or had he? No, he doubted it but decided to play along. 'A black one or a white one,' the black shiny thing asked.

Vlad's stupid answer had been trumped by an equally stupid question. Did it matter? thought Vlad. He decided to keep playing along, but couldn't help but think the question was in some way loaded. He would have to be careful with his answer. He decided to play it safe. 'A black and white one,' he said.

The black shiny thing immediately shouted for his guards. 'Surround it!' he shouted. 'Surround the two-headed mouse!' He hadn't finished. 'Surround the two-headed thing of nightmares!' He still hadn't. 'Surround the two-headed, black and white, mousey, nightmare spy!'

A score or so of sharp-looking weapons surrounded Vlad, who at first hadn't noticed them as he was frantically trying to see where this two-headed nightmare the black shiny thing was shouting about was hiding. Only when he failed to see it did he notice the weapons pointed at him. This had a most sobering effect, to the point where Vlad now realised what the black shiny had been going on about.

'Me?' said Vlad, suddenly becoming fearful. He furrowed his invisible brow. 'I'm not a nightmare spy.' He just knew that question had been loaded.

'He says he's not a nightmare spy,' said a chorus of voices.

'And if it moves, stick it,' said the black shiny thing, ignoring Vlad's protestations and the chorus of voices.

Charming, thought Vlad, going cross-eyed as the point of a pike waved perilously close to his nose. He decided he was going to have to come clean before he became a vampire pin cushion. 'I'm not a two-headed mouse either,' said Vlad.

'He says he's not a two-headed mouse,' said roughly the same chorus of voices.

The black shiny thing took no notice and started to walk away.

'Wait,' said Vlad, now getting a tad desperate. He would have to come clean. He was sure the others would understand. How many of them would have withstood the interrogation he had been put through? 'Humpty sent me,' he said.

'Humpty sent him,' said the old man of crooked stature. Who then looked embarrassed when he realised he had been the only one to speak this time. All around him a chorus of surprised faces were staring at the space the weapons were pointed at.

The black shiny thing stopped in its tracks and then turned. 'Humpty?' it said.

'Yes,' said Vlad.

The black shiny thing stroked a non-existent beard and shook its head. 'So,' it said, 'Humpty has turned on us.'

A murmur of voices suddenly rose from the nursery folk. 'Humpty's a traitor,' was muttered.

'What?' said Vlad. 'No, you don't understand, he sent me to spy out the land.' And as soon as he had said it he knew he was in trouble. You idiot Vlad, thought Vlad, silly silly idiot.

'He admits it,' said the chorus of voices that had earlier embarrassed the old man of crooked stature.

'He admits it,' said the old man of crooked stature a couple of seconds out of sync. Everyone looked at him. He slunk away and hid at the back of the barn.

'Off with his head,' said the shiny black thing suddenly, pointing to the space that held the invisible Vlad. 'And when the time comes, we'll deal with that traitor Humpty in the same way.' But only if he remained in his present form, if Humpty went back to how he normally looked it would be a bit of a problem; being normally all head that is. Could be messy, thought the black shiny thing. Something he would have to deal with when the time came.

'Off with his head,' agreed the chorus of voices, but with a little less conviction than earlier times. Nursery Land wasn't a place of violence, but as the king had spoken… a lot of the chorus now put a hand to their throat and gulped.

'But I came to save you,' said Vlad, realising the shiny black thing might be serious.

'But he came to save us,' said the chorus of voices, some still with their hands at their throats.

'And why would a two-headed thing of nightmares try to save us?' said the black shiny thing.

'But I haven't got two heads,' said Vlad.

'Take him away,' said the black shiny thing, ignoring Vlad's pleas. 'There's a chopping block at the back of the barn.' Two of the guards walked towards Vlad.

At the back of the barn, the rather crooked elderly man, upon realising on what it was he was sitting on, gulped and made a hasty, if crooked, retreat to somewhere as far away from it as possible.

But just as the two guards reached for Vlad, who was starting to realise that the black thing might be really going to go through with what it said and have him actually taken to the chopping block, a voice from the doorway bellowed for them to stop.

'Stop!' bellowed the voice, a voice Vlad had seriously begun to think he would never hear again.

All in the barn turned. Salor was stood in the small doorway, his staff held aloft its nub a brilliant, yet not so brilliant, more ember-like, slightly ember-like, glow.

A hush now fell on the barn as Salor stepped through the door. Weapons were lowered. Salor moved those weapons aside and stood by the giant's hand, offering one of his own to Vlad.

'Ow,' said Vlad, as one of Salor's fingers inadvertently poked him in the eye – something you would think he would be used to by now, it having happened many times before.

'Sorry,' said Salor, keeping one eye on the barn's occupants, especially the black shiny thing.

'It's okay,' said Vlad rubbing his eye. He couldn't really complain seeing as Salor may just have saved his life, death, whatever. He took Salor's outstretched hand and stepped away from the giant and the sharp pointy weapons. As he did, someone else appeared at the doorway.

Twinkle, having just a little problem negotiating the small door, squeezed into the barn. She was carrying Vlad's cloak, which she gave to him. He quickly slipped it on.

'Now,' demanded Salor, using his sternest of stern voices, 'what is going on here?'

The black shiny thing took a haughty step forward, but before he had the chance to speak a voice piped up beating him to it.

'He was going to cut his head off, he was,' said a crooked voice from somewhere in the barn.

Salor looked aghast. 'Shame on you,' he said, glaring at the black shiny thing, 'and you such a merry old soul.'

The haughtiness the black shiny thing had been wearing suddenly slipped from him and he became as sad-looking as a black shiny thing could look. 'Was,' he said waving his little stick arms and pointing at his body. 'Would you be, if you looked like this? I used to be king, now I'm just a piece of coal.' He was a far from merry shiny black thing. 'I can't even smoke my pipe, I'm smokeless!'

Salor harrumphed, nodded, and then put a consoling arm around old King Cole's shoulders. With the other, he ushered Twinkle and Vlad from the barn.

'Hold on a mo,' said Vlad, as Twinkle started to bundle him through the small door. He looked back.

'What?' said Twinkle.

'The giant, he said his name was Jack.'

'So,' said Twinkle, eager for them to be on their way.

'But wasn't Jack the giant killer not the giant?'

'Tomato, tomahto,' said Twinkle, shrugging and not that interested. 'Besides, he lives in Fairy Story Land, not here.'

Suppose, thought Vlad, deciding that strange things were happening on the Otherside right now, so who knew. He shrugged his shoulders and followed Twinkle out of the barn.

CHAPTER 34

'Are we on the Otherside now?' said Mister Power, as he checked himself over to make sure all was as it should be.

'Yes,' said Rogi.

And now it can begin, thought Mister Power, eagerly eyeing his surroundings. Everything would soon be just as he wanted it; as soon as he caught the boy and stopped him from saving myth, magic and make-believe, that is. The nonsense would all cease to exist and reality would reign supreme; a world of reality that he would be king of. He saw it in his mind's eye; hour upon hour of mind-numbing reality television, the publication of the most noxious, boring, repetitive non-fiction. He would own it all. He would dull the minds of the world and bend their will to his. And it had already started. Bookshelves, shops and online, were filling with biographies. Mister Power laughed out loud at the thought of yet another biography of some boring minor celeb or other, eager to tell the world of their boring little lives again and again and again; the early years, the later years, the college years; their years in the womb! And the shows he would produce; one after another, after another, of reality television, filled with those same minor celebs and others. Imagination and individuality would soon be things of the past. Yes, oh yes! Mister Power cackled and wrung his hands enthusiastically.

'Sir?' said Rogi, giving his boss a concerned look.

'What? You say? Yes?' said Mister Power, landing back in the world of here and now with a bump.

'Are you well?' asked Rogi.

'Well?' said Mister Power, casting a quizzical glance in Rogi's direction. 'Why wouldn't I be?'

'The strange noises, sir,' said Rogi.

'Strange noises?'

'Sort of cackles, sir.'

'Cack…? Ah.' Mister Power looked slightly perturbed for a moment as he realised the cackling hadn't just been inside his head. But Mister Power, being Mister Power, threw back his shoulders, steadied the happy ship he had been sailing in, and regained his composure. He couldn't have the minions seeing him happy; it was a weakness. 'Just a cough,' he said, cackle-coughing into his hand to prove it. 'Nothing to worry about.' But there was. He was on the Otherside now. He shouldn't be careless, couldn't be careless. He should be ever vigilant. Everyone here was his enemy, even his minions if they but knew it; no one wants to become extinct. He put on his best stony face. 'Set the… thing, to work.' He waved a hand at Hewie.

Ergo let out Hewie's lead a little, and Hewie set about sniffing and snuffling at the surrounding area.

Mister Power waited, perhaps not patiently, but he waited. He also watched. He watched Hewie sniff this way and that way, and he watched Hewie snuffle that way and this way, one time a little too close for comfort; Mister Power had done a nifty, yet stern, skip and hop out of harm's way. He watched and waited, and at last, just as he was about to enquire as to the usefulness of Hewie, Hewie suddenly stopped his sniffing and snuffling.

'He's found something,' announced Rogi.

About time, thought Mister Power. 'Anything in particular?' he enquired, rather testily.

'The boy's scent I believe,' said Rogi, getting Ergo to move Hewie out of the way so he could get a better look. 'Trouble is, everything appears to be covered in chihuahua urine.'

This brought a look of disgust to Mister Power's face. Chihuahua's urine? He wasn't going to ask. 'But you have the boy's scent?'

'It would seem so, sir; it matches the scent on the item of clothes we took from the boy's house,' said Rogi, sniffing first the clothing, then the ground. 'Definitely so, I'd say.' Rogi stood up and offered the item of clothing to Mister Power, who instantly recoiled.

'I'll take your word for it thank you,' said Mister Power, grimacing. 'So, does this mean we are on the right track at last?'

'Yes, sir,' said Rogi.

'Then what are we standing here for, let's get moving.' Mister Power ushered his minions forward, carefully sidestepping a small yellow puddle as he did. He shuddered. The sooner he had the boy, the better.

CHAPTER 35

The last door had been unlocked; a relief, but now Miss Manager was faced with what she had been half expecting after walking through the gate.

Miss Manager had been approached, employed, trained and then put in the field, not like the one she was now looking at, but the field as in Mister Power's company. The path had been laid out for her to be his private secretary. She was to infiltrate; lay low; listen. But as time passed and when no further contact was made for the longest of time she had begun to think she had been forgotten. What was going on? What was the plan? Why was she there? And then, out of the blue, just when she thought the plan was that she would be Mister Power's private secretary for the rest of her days, she had received further orders. "Follow Mister Power should he decide to go on holiday." Short, sharp, just that, nothing else. Miss Manager would have laughed had she not been so depressed. Mister Power going on holiday, she should be so lucky; he had never even taken so much as a day off, including sickies, since she had been there and that was nearly two years now! She felt let down; felt she was going nowhere. And then POW, he had decided to take a holiday, just like that, and she was now standing in a field of daisies. A field sadly devoid of Mister Power though. What now?

A sudden noise; low beeping, drew her attention away from the field and the problem of what to do next. Looking puzzled, she reached inside her jacket to the pocket within, from where the noise was emanating, and found the beeping was coming from a mobile phone, which puzzled her even further as it wasn't hers. Frowning, she took it out and put it to her ear.

'Hello?' said Miss Manager, wondering.

A voice she didn't recognise responded. 'Look for a distortion in the air around you, it will be vaguely door-shaped. Walk through it.'

'Who-' said Miss Manager, but before she could say anything else the connection was cut. She held the phone away from her ear and stared at it. Who and what was that all about?

With a deeply puzzled look on her face, Miss Manager put the phone back in her pocket. It had to have been her real employers, but the voice on the other end was different to the one that had told her about Power's impending holiday, this voice had been a woman's. Things were getting stranger and stranger. How did the phone get in her pocket? Where was she? What had the voice meant; look for a door-shaped distortion in the air? She could sort of understand the corridor, the field; places on the other side of the gate. Okay, maybe not what she had been expecting, but they were normal enough; if you forgot about all the locked doors. But looking for a door-shaped distortion that she was supposed to step through? Weird or what? She had wanted adventure. She had wanted her mission to pick up speed, but she couldn't remember wanting weird. Then on the other hand, she was here, so she might as well get on with it. She could always go back if things got weirder; she didn't have to walk through the distortion if she didn't want to. With that in mind, Miss Manager stepped further into the field of daisies.

It was over half an hour before the distorted doorway deemed to make an appearance. It was like a mirage in the desert when it did, a shimmer in mid-air. When it arrived Miss Manager, who after ten minutes of futile searching for it had given up because she didn't want to wander too far from the corridor door, was sat cross-legged on the grass making daisychains, something she hadn't done since a child. She had looked up instantly. She didn't know why, she had just sort of felt its presence; which was another serving of weird. Calmly putting her latest chain with the others; five in all, she got to her feet and stepped towards it.

It was like nothing she had ever seen. It was most certainly door shaped. It most certainly distorted the air. But did she want to step into it? She wasn't sure. She was also unsure as to the how's and why's of it. She had always been of the mind that all could be explained scientifically, logically, if you just put your mind to it. This though, the hovering shimmering door, she had her doubts about. Something about it did not strike her as being scientific. Logical thought was not going to help. She peered around it; walked round it a couple of times. It was just there, suspended in thin air, surrounded by a field of daisies. She had real doubts about stepping into it. Perhaps she should throw her knife into it, see what happened? But what that would accomplish she didn't know, apart from a lost knife or her having to go in any way to retrieve it.

Five minutes later Miss Manager was still umming and ahhing. One minute after that she noticed the doorway seemed to be fading a little. Two seconds after that she decided it *was* fading. Another second later and she realised the doorway wasn't going to be around much longer. What did she do? Did she stay or did she go? She had a job to do, but… it faded a little more. It wasn't shimmering so much. She took out her knife and gingerly dipped its point into the distortion. She quickly pulled it back. It still had a point. Her heart was now thumping in her chest; decision time. But it was *weird*. The doorway continued to fade. Oh dear, she thought. Shoot-shoot-shoot, she thought. Okay, she thought. She had made a decision. Deep breath Frida old girl, she told herself. She breathed deep, moved forward. She did it; had done it. She had stepped into it. She was on the other side of it; *wasn't she?* She was still in one piece; *wasn't she?* Only one way to find out she supposed. Miss Manager, Frida, slowly opened her eyes.

CHAPTER 36

What had happened, whilst Vlad had been gallivanting in Old McDonald's barn, was that the nightmares had converged on and surrounded Danrite and his pals. It had looked pretty dire for a while as the nightmares closed in, but thankfully no malice had been afoot, instead they had sent a pair of the less nightmarish amongst them ahead to parley. It transpired the nightmares weren't that keen on the idea of extinction either. Things of nightmares they might be, but they still had feelings. They themselves were mere products of one's imagination, scary yes, but just the result of peoples' minds trying to find answers and make sense of the world. The meeting had gone like this:

'Yah!!' said Salor, as the first of the nightmares appeared.

'Woa!' said Twinkle.

'Brrrrah!' said Sid.

'Ay caramba!' said Jose.

'Cripes!' said Danrite.

Rustle went Leif's leaves.

Flap went Rosie's flaps.

Humpty fainted.

'Quickly,' said Salor, regaining some composure, 'form a circle!'

They did, around Leif, propping Humpty against him as they did, but what good it would do them was anyone's guess, it wasn't as if they had any covered wagons to hide behind.

The lesser nightmares approached, one was carrying a white flag.

'They've got a white flag,' said Twinkle.

'Do you think they're surrendering?' said Danrite.

'Could be a trap,' said Salor, knuckles white around his staff.

'Ay caramba,' said Jose.

Sid said nothing.

The approaching lesser nightmares stopped and the one without the white flag spoke. 'We want to talk,' it said.

‘He doesn’t look too scary,’ said Danrite.

‘As long as his towel doesn’t drop,’ said Twinkle.

‘I too, for one, would not be liking that,’ said Jose.

The nightmare that had spoken, a man, who appeared to have just stepped from a bathroom, wore nothing but a towel around his waist and a tall hat on his head with writing on it which read “Do it again and woe betide thee”, took another step forward.

What the writing meant, or why the nightmare was as it was, no one in the circle knew or was eager to find out. Salor took a step from it, and brandishing his staff, warned the nightmare to venture no closer.

‘We mean no harm,’ said the nightmare, holding up a placating hand. ‘My name is Dorothy,’ it added.

This caused a ripple of whispers amongst the circle, and one doggy snigger.

‘Yeah-yeah,’ said Dorothy, pursing his lips. ‘Laugh all you want, but we don’t choose our names you now, they’re dreamt up for us.’

‘Must be a bit of a nightmare,’ said Twinkle, wishing Vlad was there for a high five.

Another doggy snigger.

The nightmare rolled his eyes.

Salor called for hush, he knew all about ridicule, and spoke to the nightmare again, his staff at the ready. ‘If you mean us no harm, then set the nursery rhyme folk free.’

‘I don’t think that would be wise,’ said Dorothy.

‘Ah-ha,’ said Salor, pushing his staff forward.

Dorothy sighed. ‘But enough of them; I was sent to talk to your leader.’

Salor scowled and drew himself up to full height. ‘I *am* the leader,’ he bellowed.

‘The half and half,’ said Dorothy.

All eyes turned to Danrite.

‘He calls him half and half also,’ whispered Jose, remembering what Vlad had called him.

‘Shush,’ said Twinkle, gently pushing Danrite forward. Salor now scowled at Twinkle.

‘Me?’ said Danrite.

‘Yes,’ said Dorothy.

'Oh,' said Danrite.

'Ask him what he meant about the nursery rhyme folk,' Twinkle whispered, as Danrite faltered in the limelight.

Salor dropped his scowling and adopted a sulkier look.

A nudge from Twinkle prompted Danrite into finding his tongue. 'Er,' he said, a tad nervously as the nudge had moved him closer to the nightmare, 'why wouldn't it be wise? I mean, about the nursery folk?' Danrite, having said his piece, took the opportunity to take a step back towards the ring, away from the nightmare.

'Because they'll only hurt themselves,' said the nightmare.

'Enough,' said sulky Salor, he wasn't going to let Twinkle undermine him. 'I am the leader of our band, and you talk to me.' He held his staff out before him, but in a more slightly threatening manner this time.

The nightmare called Dorothy frowned and then whispered over his shoulder. The nightmare holding the white flag, who had until that moment stayed quietly hidden in the shadows caused by Leif, stepped forward and stood beside Dorothy.

A sudden scream came from… no, more a wail came from… no, it was a scream, a girly one! All looked at Salor.

The scream *then* trailed off to become a wail. 'Nooo!' wailed Salor. 'Not you!' He fell to his knees in the most dramatic of ways.

'Salor?' said Twinkle, raising her eyebrows at the sight before her. 'You okay?'

'I know him,' sobbed Salor.

'Do you?' said Twinkle, looking from Salor to the nightmare with the white flag.

'Only in his worst dreams,' said the white flag-toting nightmare.

'That's your nightmare?' said Twinkle, suddenly realising why Salor was acting the way he was. She courageously held back a titter.

Jose on the other hand was a little more forthcoming. 'You have the nightmares about the putting on of the make-up badly?' He gave a doggy laugh and rolled onto his back in hysterics.

It appeared Salor did. The nightmare holding the flag was the spitting image of Salor; a doppelganger; a twin, complete with makeup. But the makeup on the nightmare was smeared and smudged. Its mascara was running, its foundation orange and not blended in, its blusher making its face look like a story book apple;

all red and rosy, but orangey, and when it smiled, and it was doing so now, red lipstick could be seen smeared across its teeth. Its makeup was the cheapest; its smile was the most hideous; it was Salor's worst nightmare, and it had come to life.

'Sorry about that,' said Dorothy, 'but it had to be done. We haven't time to argue who is or isn't in charge. We need to talk to Danrite Willocky now, without interruptions.'

It had been a cruel thing to do, to divulge someone's worst nightmare like that, but the nightmares were desperate. People on the other side of the Otherside had started to dream less, some had stopped altogether so bland had their lives become, and because of it nightmares were ceasing to exist on an almost daily basis. To some people this might sound a good thing, but nightmares are as important as dreams.

This though wasn't helpful to Salor who was beside himself on the ground. Dorothy noticed and called for Sailor to leave Salor alone; Salor was called Sailor in his nightmare for some reason.

'I was just trying to console him,' said Sailor, looking a little put out as he hurried over to Dorothy.

'And was it working?' said Dorothy.

'No, not really,' Sailor admitted.

'I wonder why,' said Dorothy, ushering Sailor back into the shadows. He then spoke to Danrite again. 'So Danrite, will you hear what I have to say?'

As Danrite was standing a little over three feet away and so could hear quite clearly, he didn't think it a problem. There was a nudge in his ribs. 'I suppose,' he said, especially if it meant Twinkle stopping poking him. But if he was going to be the leader, if only until Salor found his wits again, he was going to do it properly. 'But first you must answer my question about the nursery folk.'

'I did,' said Dorothy. 'They were put in the barn for their own good, and there is an example of why, right there.' He pointed away to his right. Everyone looked to their left to see Humpty, who had just come round, running away as fast as he could and heading straight for a rather high wall. 'He did that the first time he saw us.'

They watched as he reached it. They watched him climb it. They then watched as he fell off it, backwards. There was a sickening thud, followed by a very eggy-sounding wail.

‘I better go see how he is,’ said Twinkle.

‘I go too,’ said Jose.

‘Oh no you don’t,’ said Twinkle, who knew how much the little chihuahua loved his eggs, especially if they were scrambled. ‘You stay here.’ Instead she headed to the wall with Sid and Rosie who had first aid training in the field, and the trees, and everywhere else a wood nymph might have been needed when she hadn’t been a table.

A sullen Jose decided what he needed was a tree, and as Leif was the nearest one, walked over to him. Leif, on seeing where Jose was headed, walked away. Salor, not himself at the moment had wandered off in no particular direction when everyone else had. This left Danrite alone with the nightmares.

‘You are very brave facing us alone,’ said Dorothy.

‘You’d think so,’ said Danrite, knowing full well that if he had had his wits about him, he too would have been a wandering.

‘We know so,’ said Dorothy, bowing slightly. ‘Even in our land, cut off from the rest of the Otherside, we have heard of the famous half giant - half dwarf who would be the saviour of us all. I have to say though; I didn’t expect our saviour to be wearing a pig mask.’ Dorothy made a face. Danrite shrugged. Dorothy continued. ‘And that is why we had to talk to you, to give you something, to help you with your quest.’ He beckoned to Sailor to come forward.

Sailor carefully, so that he didn’t drop the white flag, held out something wrapped in a large oil cloth.

‘Take it,’ said Dorothy.

‘What is it?’ said Danrite, not looking too sure about it.

‘Armour,’ said Dorothy, taking it from Sailor and handing it to Danrite, ‘every hero needs armour.’

‘Armour?’ said Danrite, putting the bundle on the ground. He was puzzled; shouldn’t armour weigh a ton? He knelt down and undid the oil cloth.

‘Put it on,’ said Sailor, when the armour was revealed.

‘You can wear it over your t-shirt,’ said Dorothy, ‘like a jacket.’

But Danrite wasn’t sure, and he most definitely wasn’t going to wear the miniskirt, or the sandals. ‘I don’t know,’ said Danrite.

‘You don’t have to wear the skirt thingy,’ said Dorothy, as if he had read Danrite’s mind, ‘and the sandals are so passé.’ He smiled.

Danrite still wasn't sure, did he need armour? But then he remembered the solicitor and his gun; perhaps it wasn't such a bad idea after all, and it hardly weighed anything. He made a decision and picked up the breastplate. He studied it. Was it some sort of metal? It could be leather. It was hard to tell. And what was going on with the colour? He was sure it was golden when he had picked it up, now it looked more like brown. Weird, he thought. He wasn't too sure about the dangly things at the bottom of it either, but decided it must be some sort of decoration; Romans liked that sort of thing didn't they? 'Okay, I suppose,' he said, attempting to put it on backwards.

'Here, let me,' said Dorothy. He took but a second. 'There,' he said when he had finished buckling it in place, 'a true hero.'

A true plonker more like, thought Danrite, trying to see what it looked like on. But it was no good, he couldn't see properly, he would have to ask Vlad for a loan of his mirror next time he saw him. 'Does it fit?' he asked.

'Like a glove,' said Sailor.

'Like a proper Roman soldier,' said Dorothy.

Danrite liked the sound of that; a soldier. He had wanted to be a soldier when he was little, but Percy had taken away his broomstick gun and potato peeler bayonet and had told him that little boys should have other things occupying their minds at such a young age. And that had been that, until now. He couldn't wait to show the others.

'And now that our job is done we must say goodbye,' said Dorothy.

'Your job?' said Danrite, puzzled by what Dorothy had said. 'But I thought you had escaped?'

'Maybe we did, maybe we didn't,' smiled Dorothy. 'Good luck, Danrite.' Dorothy turned to go, but an urgent word from Sailor had him turning back. 'Oh yes, Sailor just reminded me, there is something else I have to tell you, there's a short cut to where you're heading.'

'A short cut?' said Danrite, beginning to wonder if he would ever stop asking questions.

'Yes.' Dorothy explained. He also told Danrite that Leif wouldn't like it.

The last bit had been just a little bit cryptic, but as Danrite was determined not to ask another question, he didn't ask Dorothy to elaborate.

'And now we really must be on our way,' said Dorothy, and he and Sailor went to walk away.

'Wait!' said Danrite, before he could stop himself. He did have one more question. One he really shouldn't ask, but he did. 'Is mine with you?' he asked, meaning his own personal nightmare.

'Which one?' said Dorothy.

For a moment Danrite looked shocked. How did he know there were two? But then realised, of course he would. 'The really bad one,' said Danrite.

'No,' said Dorothy.

'Oh,' said Danrite, who didn't know himself if the "oh" was relief or disappointment.

'But she is waiting for you.'

Again with the cryptic, but Danrite assumed Dorothy meant in his dreams.

'But the other one is with us, if you want to meet?'

'Could I?' said Danrite, still not sure if he should or not.

'But just a quick peep,' said Dorothy, who clicked his fingers.

'Aghhh!' said Danrite.

Another click followed less than a second later. It wasn't good to meet your nightmares face to face, but Dorothy felt Danrite would be able to handle a small dose.

'Enough?' said Dorothy.

'Enough,' said Danrite, who's complexion had lightened somewhat. 'The cheese, it… it looked so real.'

Dorothy smiled. 'Farewell, Danrite, I hope we never meet.' The remark caused Danrite to frown. 'In your sleep, I mean.'

'Ah,' said Danrite, 'me too.'

And then, just like that, the nightmares disappeared.

Danrite, who had been about to wave, gingerly lowered his hand. They had gone, he was all alone; but wearing cool Roman armour. Danrite turned, and eager to show his friends, set off apace to find them.

And it only took but a pace to do just that, as Danrite promptly tripped over a prostrate Salor, who had been lying on the ground just behind him.

'Grief,' said Danrite, as he pushed up onto his knees. He thought Salor had wandered off.

He was right, Salor had indeed wandered off, but he had wandered back again unnoticed, draped in the daze he had existed in after meeting his nightmare, and finally coming to rest on the ground behind Danrite.

As Danrite attempted to rise amid thoughts of how he could help Salor, a disembodied head suddenly materialised above his own.

'Wah!' went Danrite, cowering.

'Ooh!' said Dorothy, whose head it was. 'Oops, sorry, slight miscalculation there.'

'What's up?' said Danrite, sitting up and expecting something along the lines of the worst.

'Nothing,' said Dorothy, 'just forgot to do this.' A hand suddenly appeared that clicked its fingers, instantly wiping from everyone's memory their meeting with Salor's nightmare. It wasn't really the done thing; to divulge one's dreams and nightmares to others without permission. Both hand and head then blinked once more from sight.

'Yikes!' said Danrite, as they did. He frowned and wondered what that had been about.

And then they appeared again.

'Wah!' said Danrite.

'Sorry,' said Dorothy, looking suitably embarrassed, 'forgot to give you this, but be careful with it, it's sharp. Best to keep it in its scabbard until needed.' He handed Danrite a Roman sword called a gladius. And then he was gone again.

Danrite's eyes were wide as he looked at the sword, and then grew even wider when he realised what Dorothy had said; until needed. But he only had time for a moment of wondering about the remark as Salor had come to with a groan.

And that was what had happened; while Vlad had been away.

After Salor had released the nursery rhyme folk from the barn, a young girl by the name of Jill checked Humpty over and had praised Rosie on her medical know-how, but had advised and provided extra treatment. Humpty would smell like a fish and chip shop for a while, but he would mend. The nightmares had returned to their own land as they had achieved what they had set out to do; talk to the half and half and bestow on him a gift of armour. Which everyone had admired, with words such as "dashing" and "quite the hero" and "watch that thing it's sharp" being bandied about, causing Danrite no end of embarrassment and secret pride, especially when he saw the armour in Vlad's mirror; it fitted so well. And the nursery rhyme folk, having survived their ordeal in the barn, were well on their way to getting back to normal; in the loosest sense of the word. So it was all's well that ends well and everyone was happy. Well, with the exception of a fellow called Jack, who was looking a tad peeved over all the attention Jill was giving Humpty. And why not, it was his brown paper and vinegar she had used. But apart from him all was as well as could be expected. Although it was still a mystery as to why Salor had been lying senseless on the ground, but hey, it was Salor, he's a wizard; they do strange things.

And so now it was time for Danrite and the others to resume their search for the Font. Farewells were bid, and goodbyes were waved and they left Nursery Town behind.

'So,' whispered Twinkle to Danrite, as Nursery Town grew smaller with distance, 'what else did Dorothy say to you?' Danrite had been thus far a little vague on the substance of his meeting with the nightmares. 'You can tell me.'

'Not much really,' said Danrite, which was true, 'like I already said, I'm supposed to tell everyone something when we reach the border of the next land.' He wanted to keep what Dorothy had said about Leif to himself for the moment.

'There must have been something else,' said Twinkle, 'you were with them for ages.' It was true, but Danrite couldn't really remember much about it; there were blanks he couldn't explain.

'Yeah, ages,' said Vlad, whom Twinkle hadn't noticed was hobbling along closer than she realised. Not that he knew how long Danrite had been with the nightmares, he being in the barn at the time.

'Unless it is all quiet-quiet,' said Jose, who no one had noticed, as he quietly meandered between their feet.

'You mean hush-hush,' said Vlad.

'Sí,' said Jose, 'hush-hush.'

'Is it hush-hush?' Vlad asked eagerly.

'Very hush-hush,' said Danrite, happy to play along. He then left them wondering as he went to join Salor who was with Leif at the head of their little party.

CHAPTER 37

With Ergo and Hewie on Danrite's scent, Mister Power was happy to tag along behind talking to Rogi.

'Many,' said Rogi, answering Mister Power's question as to how often he had visited the Otherside.

It was small talk, idle chit-chat, Mister Power wasn't interested, but it offered him the chance to get a closer check on his cannon fodder without causing suspicion. He had noticed, since they had arrived in the Otherside, a marked improvement in their health, though that meant they had reverted a little to their original state. He hoped the change wouldn't go too far, but on the bright side it did mean that they might last long enough to find the boy and get out of there. He couldn't bank on that though, if Miss Manager was doing her job properly and getting those biographies on the shelves as he had ordered, the Otherside's inhabitants, or indeed the Otherside itself, might suddenly cease to exist. He hoped not; well at least not while he was in it, so the sooner he was out of there the better.

'Sir?' said Rogi, for the second time.

'Yes, what is it?' said Mister Power, his mind returning from the thoughts that had been running through it.

'Ergo appears to have found something.'

Ergo and Hewie had stopped some ten paces ahead. Ergo was looking up and down, Hewie was scratching at an ear.

'What is it?' asked Mister Power.

Rogi went to find out and returned a moment later. 'We have reached the border of another land,' he reported.

'Do we know which one?'

'We believe so, sir,' said Rogi.

'Good, lead on then.' Mister Power waved Ergo and Hewie forward and watched as they disappeared from sight into the next land, but as Rogi went to follow, Mister Power grabbed his arm. 'Is it dangerous, this next land?'

'Not really, sir,' said Rogi.

'Not really?'

'No, sir. I'd say about as dangerous as walking down a dark alley in the dead of night in an undesirable neighbourhood, sir.'

'Ah,' said Mister Power. And with that reassurance ringing in his ears Mister Power followed Rogi to the next land.

CHAPTER 38

It was only when they got to the border with the next land did anyone notice Danrite was no longer wearing his pig mask.

'It must have fallen off when I tripped over Salor,' said Danrite, licking a finger to remove a bit of blusher that Vlad had pointed out was still stuck to his cheek.

'All gone,' said Vlad, offering up his mirror for Danrite to see, as Jose, Sid and Rosie looked on.

Salor had taken Twinkle aside. 'It would seem our Danrite is all right,' he said.

'So it would seem,' said Twinkle.

'No coma,' whispered Salor.

'Just the headache type,' said Twinkle, 'lucky boy.'

'Did he have a headache?' said Salor.

'He didn't say,' said Twinkle.

'Hmm,' said Salor.

'Hmm?' said Twinkle.

'I was just thinking that if he didn't have a headache, perhaps he isn't human after all,' said Salor.

'Really,' said Twinkle, 'we going down that old route again?'

'Just a thought,' said Salor.

'Well I for one suggest we wait for the Font to work that one out for us, and until then I say we should be thankful he isn't lying in a coma waiting for some out of work prince to come along and plant a smacker on him.'

Salor nodded sagely. 'Amen to that,' he said.

And then Danrite was calling them over. It was time for him to tell everyone what the nightmares had told him.

CHAPTER 39

Some used an orb. Some used a cauldron with murky waters that cleared when you waved your hand across it. Some preferred a magic mirror. Some plumped for the less traditional method. The Font used the latter. The Font was mythical, magical, the pinnacle of make-believical. The Font wasn't a witch or an ice queen, or for that matter a wizard. The Font was above all that. Leave the seeing orb to the wizards. Leave the cauldron to witches. Leave the mirrors to queens. The Font was different. The Font was non-traditional. The Font was modern; forward thinking. The Font shied from gimmicks. When the Font wanted to see how the land was lying, the Font used the *seeing machine*.

'Oh!' said a little chap dressed in white, as befitting a servant of the Font, as the remote control he had been holding was snatched from his grasp.

'What have I told you?' said the Font, angrily.

'No seeing until I've finished my homework?' said the little chap, with more than a little sarcasm.

'Try again,' said the Font, scowling.

'Only when I've eaten all my greens?' The little chap was now wandering onto very thin ice.

The Font glared at the little chap. 'What I told you, as well you know, is that the seeing machine is for seeing, *not* watching.'

'But it's a television,' said the little chap.

The Font glared all the harder. 'It is a seeing machine, and a seeing machine is all it is.'

The little chap looked glum. 'But I bought a TV guide.'

'That's your problem not mine.'

'But…'

'Enough!' said the Font, on the verge of temper losing. 'Your room awaits.' The Font pointed towards a door.

'But it's not my bedtime.'

'I didn't say it was.'

The little chap knew when he was beaten, but he had a stubborn streak that asked for trouble. 'Wouldn't happen if I had one in my room,' he said, as he started for the door.

'Wouldn't *happen* if I didn't have an awkward one hundred and forty year old to deal with twenty-four seven.' The Font just didn't know what was wrong with the youth of today.

'I didn't ask to be created,' said the little chap.

'Out!' shouted the Font.

The little chap wrinkled his nose and scurried quickly through the door.

'And close it behind you!'

The door slammed shut, nearly shaking the hinges from it.

Asked for that I suppose, thought the Font. But servants had to be put in their place. The Font looked at the remote control. It was time to see.

CHAPTER 40

Just as Frida felt the relief that stepping through the door-shaped shimmer in one piece had given her, the phone rang again. With the exaggerated care that sometimes comes with the unknown, she took it from her pocket. She stared at it and let it ring for a moment longer. Frida had questions. The most important of them, could she trust whoever it was on the other end of the phone? She decided, for the moment anyway, that she had no real reason not to; they had after all seen her safely through the shimmering doorway. She answered.

It was the same female voice as before. 'Follow the path before you; it will lead you to another doorway. Step through it.'

'Okay, but-.' The phone cut off. 'Drat!' said Frida, glaring at the phone. 'Double drat!' She shoved the phone back into her pocket. Frida had wanted to know where the heck she was. She had wanted to get some bearings. Was she even in the same county? And what the heck were those doorways about? She had never seen anything like them. Well, she thought, not quite true, there was that film, the creepy sci-fi one she'd watched while crouched behind some cushions. She gave an involuntary shiver and looked about. But that was just a film, something made up. This was real. This was the here and now; wherever that may be. She had a job to do. The phone rang again.

Snapped from her obsessing Frida grabbed for the phone. This time they would answer her questions. It wasn't right to be blindly going on. 'Right,' she snapped.

'The path waits,' said the female voice, talking over Frida.

'Agh!' said Frida, as the phone went dead again, leaving her frustrated. She slammed the phone back into her pocket, but this time she was a little wiser; she had learned something; she was being watched. Somewhat warily, Frida headed for the path and the next waiting doorway.

CHAPTER 41

'Okay I admit it, I was leading you astray, but what could I do?' whimpered Leif, finally breaking under Twinkle's questioning and dagger-like stare. Leif's leaves had gone a pale green when Danrite had mentioned the short cut, and had almost turned white when asked why the nightmares had said they didn't think he would like the idea. 'They have my family.'

'Who has?' said Twinkle.

'I don't know,' wailed Leif, leaves all a tremble. 'I went home to tell them what I was doing and all I found was a note telling me to do this or else.'

'So the Font didn't send you?' said Salor, appalled that he had been taken in so easily, and by a tree of all things.

'But the Font did send me,' said Leif, leaves now doing a tremble that threatened to throw them from their branches, as the thought of what the Font might do to him hit home. 'Oh woe is me.'

'The Font did send you?' said Salor, doubly appalled.

'Yes, but didn't know what I was doing,' said Leif.

'So you deceived the Font as well?' said Salor, darkly.

'I know, I know,' said Leif, his leaves all a tremble again. 'I'm so doomed.' He began to cry.

Ignoring Leif's wailing Salor, his face like thunder, continued with his grilling. 'So where were you taking us, eh? Some place where a hideous trap awaited no doubt.' Leif did a lip tremble. 'Well!' Salor demanded.

'Nowhere,' Leif managed to say between sobs.

'Nowhere?' snapped Salor.

'In circles,' sobbed Leif. 'Slow circles.'

'But why?' said Vlad.

Leif sniffed and gave Vlad a pathetic, tearful look. 'I don't know,' he said. He managed to take a deep breath. 'It's what the note said I should do if I ever wanted to see my family again.'

'Why didn't you tell the Font?' said Twinkle.

'The note said I shouldn't,' said Leif. He sniffed. 'What was I supposed to do?'

'Well I for one don't believe you,' growled Salor, waving his staff threateningly. It brought another tremble to Leif's lips.

'Now hang about,' said Twinkle, stepping between Leif and Salor before he did something stupid. She had a mind to believe Leif was telling the truth and being mean to him wasn't going to help the situation. She looked up at the knots Leif called eyes and saw that they were filled with tears; remorseful ones she thought. He looked so sad. Twinkle suddenly felt sorry for him, a lump came to her throat, and it wasn't one of the doughnuts she'd had for breakfast. 'There, there,' said Twinkle, speaking as softly as she could, 'how about you tell us all about it?'

But there wasn't much more to tell. There had been the mysterious note that had greeted him when he'd gone home, telling him what to do if he wanted to see his family again, and that was about it. He had no idea who had sent it, and he had no idea why.

'You're not a wood nymph either, are you?' said Twinkle.

The patch on Leif's bark that was his face, darkened somewhat. 'No,' he said, 'I don't know why I said that. The oak thing I suppose.' He looked at Twinkle. 'How did you know?'

'Der,' said Twinkle, 'wood nymphs are female.'

Leif's face darkened again.

'So what are you?' said Vlad.

'I'm a wood elf,' Leif confessed.

This surprised Twinkle a little as she had him down as a common or garden tree.

'Cool,' said Danrite.

'Thank you,' said Leif, brightening up a little. 'But I'm not a very good one. I have no craft you see.'

Danrite didn't. 'No craft?' he said, puzzled.

'Wood craft,' Twinkle explained. 'Very important if you're a wood elf. It's what makes them what they are.'

'Right,' said Danrite.

Twinkle saw that Danrite still didn't quite get it, so she simplified things for him. 'He's rubbish at being a wood elf.'

'Ah,' said Danrite.

Twinkle gave Leif a searching look. 'But you weren't made an outcast?' In the world of the wood elf, if you had no craft you were banished from the woods.

'No,' said Leif.

'This is getting us nowhere,' said Salor, his anger still festering.

Twinkle ignored him. 'Why?' she asked Leif.

'The bit I told you about me having a sort of sixth sense is true. The Font found out and decreed I had a craft after all, albeit not technically a wood one. The rest is history.' Leif sniffed and his eyes started to well up again. 'The Font introduced me to my wife you know.'

Twinkle held out a hand and gently touched one of Leif's lower branches. 'And you'll see her again.' Leif brightened a little. 'But first you have to take us to the short cut.' The short cut the nightmares had told Danrite about was a glade in the centre of a gigantic forest called the Enchanted Forest. The glade acted as a sort of magical conduit that could take someone to any land on the Otherside, including the Font's. They had all heard of the Enchanted Forest, apart from Danrite, but only Leif, because of his sixth sense, knew where to find it.

'But I can't,' said Leif, suddenly looking terrified.

'Aha!' said Salor.

'But it's the only way to put everything right,' said Twinkle. 'We need to get to the Font as soon as possible.'

'He can't be trusted,' said Salor, not about to let things go.

'The Font trusted him,' said Twinkle, glaring at Salor, 'and that's good enough for me.'

'And me,' said Vlad.

'Me too,' said Danrite.

'Sí, I too trust the tree,' said Jose, who might have had an ulterior motive for his decision; liking all trees as he did.

And after Sid and Rosie had also agreed, Salor found he had been seriously outvoted.

'Pah!' said a disgruntled Salor, folding his arms.

'But you don't understand,' said Leif, 'the Enchanted Forest, it's not safe. It's said the magic has become unstable, bad even. Even the wood elves give it a wide berth these days.' Leif's words caused a stir amongst the friends. Things were worse than they thought if the Enchanted Forest was being affected. 'That's why the Font never asked me to lead you there.'

'Then we make the tree take us the way the Font intended,' said Salor, giving Leif the darkest look he could muster.

'But my family,' said Leif.

'Either way is going to be dangerous,' said Twinkle, 'but as we need to get to the Font as soon as possible, the Enchanted Forest could be the quickest option,'

'It's a trap,' said Salor. 'He wants us to go that way.'

'It was the nightmares that told us about the short cut, not Leif,' Twinkle pointed out.

'And who's to say they're not in cahoots,' said Salor, desperate not to lose his argument.

'It was them that said he wouldn't like it,' said Vlad, taking a turn with the pointing out.

'We should take a vote,' suggested Danrite.

'Good idea,' said Twinkle. 'Okay, hands up those who think we should chance the Enchanted Forest.'

A small wood of nervous hands, hooves, paws and flaps went up. Salor's stayed firmly by his side.

'Decided,' said Twinkle, 'the Enchanted Forest it is.'

'Over my dead body,' said Salor, standing firm.

CHAPTER 42

'And where are we exactly?' enquired Mister Power, eyeing the new surroundings suspiciously. It smacked of sugar and spice and all things he hated. There were fluffy clouds over an idyllic countryside scene, and even a perfect rainbow framing it. Not exactly the dangerous dark alley at midnight he had been led to expect.

Rogi was scratching at his perfectly coiffed hair. 'Not where I expected,' he confessed.

Great, thought Mister Power. 'And what does that mean?' he asked.

'It means, sir, that the lands are shuffling. It was rumoured to be on the cards the last time I was here.' Rogi shielded his eyes from the sun. 'And judging by the village up ahead I believe we are in Nursery Rhyme Land.'

'And you never thought to tell me this?' said Mister Power, raising an eyebrow.

'It was only rumour, sir. Besides I know where we are and Hewie still has the boy's scent. It appears he headed towards the village.'

Mister Power's eyebrow lowered. All, it appeared, was in order, but he wasn't enamoured with Rogi's attitude. It was a good thing for Rogi that he still needed his cannon fodder or else he would be on the ground pushing down daisies this very minute.

Narrowing his eyes, Mister Power scanned the village that stood in the distance. 'Are the natives friendly?' he asked, thinking the question a stupid one considering the name of the land, but also thinking one could never be too careful.

'That depends on who you are, sir. I myself was chased by a group of villagers carrying torches and pitchforks the last time I was here.'

'What did you do?' asked an intrigued Mister Power.

'Nothing really, sir,' said Rogi, frowning at the memory. 'Wrong company I guess.'

‘Fell in with a bad lot eh?’ said Mister Power, thinking nothing new there then. He afforded himself a small chuckle.

‘I suggest we proceed with caution, sir,’ said Rogi, with his last visit still to mind.

‘Proceed away then.’

‘To the village, Ergo,’ said Rogi.

Ergo, whose arms were struggling to stay in their sockets as Hewie, eager to follow his prey, slavered and pulled on his leash, was more than happy to.

Rogi took a couple of steps before realising Mister Power wasn’t following. ‘Sir?’ he said, stopping and turning.

Mister Power had decided it might be better perhaps if he distanced himself from the others, at least until they were past the village, if indeed the boy had travelled through it. ‘Thought I would take the scenic route and meet you at the other end,’ he said, smiling. He would lay low and skirt the village, that way he could dodge any trouble should it arise; he wasn’t keen on the idea of torches and pitchforks.

‘And if the boy is still in the village, sir?’

‘I’ll wait until you arrive with him.’

‘As you wish, sir, but don’t wander too far.’

‘I won’t,’ said Mister Power, wondering at the concern. He started for a long, low hill to his right that ran parallel with the village. With luck, it would shelter him for most of the way.

He had gone but a couple of steps when Rogi called after him. ‘Sir?’

‘Yes?’ said Mister Power, not breaking pace.

‘Are you feeling sleepy at all?’

Strange question, thought Mister Power, but as he didn’t and he was making good time, he decided he wasn’t going to waste time asking. ‘Do I look sleepy?’ He suspected a little bit of deterioration was in progress, which in turn could explain the way Rogi was acting; the sudden concern. The sooner they had the boy the better. He picked up his pace.

‘No, sir,’ said Rogi, frowning. He had thought he would have to be carrying Mister Power by now, him being human and all. But as Ergo and Hewie were almost at the village he didn’t have to time to dwell on things. Instead he shrugged his shoulders and started to run to catch up with them.

CHAPTER 43

Luckily for Salor it was his unconscious body they went over. Not that they actually went over it, more stepped around it as Twinkle picked it up and slung him over her shoulder. Time was running, and as Salor was going to be awkward, as was his wont sometimes, Twinkle had taken things into her own hands, or *fist* as was the case. A perfect left hook; Salor hadn't seen it coming. She would lie about it later.

'Are we getting there yet?' asked Jose, for only the first time since they had set out; a small miracle considering the amount of trees awaiting him. Those that knew him had been worrying he was coming down with something.

'Soon,' said Leif, his knotty face a picture of concentration.

Jose, who was walking beside Leif, now noticed. 'Your face, it is constipated,' he said. 'Are you having straining?'

'It's the forest,' said Leif, 'it's having an effect on me. The closer we get the worse it's getting. It's because I'm a tree, the forest wants me. I can feel it in my sap.'

'Why didn't you say?' said Twinkle, who was walking just behind.

'Because I didn't want to let you down again,' said Leif, his face changing from a look of concentration to one of fear. 'I'm afraid I may have come too close. The Enchanted Forest wants me and I don't think I'm strong enough to fight it.' Tears started to well up in his eyes.

'Another dodge no doubt,' said Salor, nursing a bruised cheek, put there by the low flying pigeon everyone but he had seen.

'I think not,' said Jose who had, for all their arguments regarding Leif's roots, become friends with the tree, 'I am thinking he does not look too good.'

Everyone crowded round, and the general consensus was that Jose was right; Leif was looking proper poorly.

'What do we do?' said Vlad.

'Can't we leave Leif here?' suggested Danrite. 'He could point the way to the forest, we can't be too far from it?'

'Perhaps that's what he wants us to do,' said Salor, still with the suspicions.

Just then Rosie began to flap her flaps.

'What's she saying?' said Danrite.

Salor suddenly looked a tad embarrassed. 'She says she can also feel it, the pull from the forest, but maybe not as much as the tree.'

'That's decided then,' said Twinkle. 'We go on, Leif is going back and Rosie is going with him.'

Rosie flapped again.

'She doesn't want to leave us,' Salor interpreted.

Twinkle put a hand on Rosie's top and patted her. 'I know you don't, but I think it's for the best. Besides, we need someone to look after Leif here.'

Rosie turned and looked at Leif, and seeing his big sad wet eyes, she flapped again. She was reluctant to go, but would if everyone promised her that they'd be careful.

'Of course we will,' said Twinkle.

It was agreed, Danrite, Twinkle, Jose, Vlad, Salor and Sid would continue on and Leif and Rosie would go back and lay low until they got word to them that all was well. All settled. Or was it?

'But you don't understand,' wailed Leif, 'I'm too close to go back, the forest won't let me!' His knotty eyes were wide, almost wild.

'Try,' said Twinkle.

'I am.'

Up stepped Jose, who walked over to Leif and cocked a leg.

'Hey!' said Leif, waving a branch at him. 'I thought we were friends.'

'Sí, we are, but a dog has to do what a dog has to do.' Jose had another go at leg-cocking.

Leif backed away and waved his branch again.

'Jose!' said Twinkle. 'Stop it.'

It was no good, Jose wasn't for stopping. 'How will I be knowing when I am seeing another?' he said. Onwards he went. Backwards went Leif.

Everyone looked on in horror. Even Salor was thinking Jose was taking things a little too far; Rosie's admission perhaps softening him towards Leif a little. A murmur of protests sprang up.

But Jose continued with his pursuit, his leg-cocking and dodging branches, until Leif could take no more. Leif started to run, Jose followed.

'Enough!' wailed Leif. 'I've had enough.' And just like that Jose stopped, set his cocking leg to idle, and headed back to the others. Leif looked on in confusion, but at least his roots were dry.

Jose was met by an angry looking Twinkle. 'Jose, what the heck do you think you were playing at?'

But Jose wasn't concerned; he had done what he had set out to do, namely get Leif out of harm's way. He gave Twinkle a smug doggy smile as he jogged past her. 'My job here is done I am thinking.'

Twinkle gave him a bemused look, then looked at Leif, and then realised what the clever little doggy had just done. She shook her head, Jose never ceased to amaze her, or annoy her for that matter. 'Yes, well,' she said, 'well done I suppose, but next time let the rest of us in on your little plans.' She went to wink at him, but Jose was already gone, scouring the horizon for somewhere to spend a penny.

Twinkle explained to the others what Jose had been up to, then went over to Leif to tell him. There were amazed looks all round, but not as amazed as the one on Leif's face.

'He did that for me?' he said, feeling slightly guilty for all the things he had been wishing on the little dog while he was being chased.

'He did,' said Twinkle. But had Jose's plan worked? 'How are you feeling?'

Leif thought for a moment. His sap was his again. There were still echoes of the Enchanted Forest's pull, but he no longer felt compelled by it. 'I think I'm okay,' he smiled.

As the others gathered round, Twinkle spoke to Rosie. 'I think it's time to go our different ways.'

Rosie wasn't happy, but goodbyes were said. Sid nuzzled Rosie.

'He'll miss her,' said Twinkle.

'I think I will too,' said Danrite.

'We all will,' said Vlad, 'but we'll see her again.'

One last nuzzle, then Sid trotted back to the others to watch Rosie and Leif wander to safety. Then there were six.

'Right,' said Twinkle, when the pair were distant specks, 'shall we do this?'

Danrite's hand went to his sword, something he had been doing more and more the further they went; a comfort thing. 'Ready when you are,' he said, with more confidence than he was feeling.

With varying degrees of tummy flutters and forebodings, they set off once more to find the Enchanted Forest.

CHAPTER 44

The Font flicked another button on the remote. The seeing machine's picture was abuzz with interference.

'Drat,' said the Font, rising from the grand chair. The Font walked over to the seeing machine and gently tapped the top of it. When this had no effect, the Font twiddled with the knobs on the front. It made no difference. The Font tapped it again; a little harder. Still no change. The Font called for the little chap dressed in white. 'Sage!'

In an adjoining room, the little chap sighed. 'What now?' he mumbled under his breath. He put his copy of the latest television guide to one side and got up out of his chair. 'Coming!' he shouted. 'Oh wise one,' he whispered.

'I've a job for you,' said the Font, as the little chap entered the room.

'Oh good.'

'Sorry?'

'Nothing.'

'Good, I need you up on the roof; the seeing machine is on the blink.'

The little chap blinked, he didn't like the sound of that. Had the Font seen what the weather was doing out there? He would be blown to some American state and no mistake. He hoped he didn't have to wear red shoes. 'But it's blowing a Hooley out there,' he protested.

The Font's castle was built on the top of a mountain, so it was usually windy, but since things on the Otherside had started to deteriorate, it had gradually become worse. Blowing a Hooley may be an understatement.

'Use a harness,' said the Font, with a total lack of sympathy. 'I have to see what is going on. It is of utmost importance.'

'Yeah-yeah,' grumbled the little chap, resigned to his fate, 'it always is.'

'What did you say?' said the Font.

'Harnesses,' said the little chap.

The Font's eyes narrowed. Something would have to be done; Sage's attitude was getting beyond. But that something would have to wait. 'Here, take this.' The Font handed the little chap a talkie-walkie. It was the same as a walkie-talkie but said the other way round. 'I'll be able to keep an ear on you.' The little chap sullenly took it. 'Off you go then.' The Font did a shooing motion. 'Good Sage.'

The little chap walked to the door that led outside in a huff, but turned around as he got there. 'It's Basil,' he said. 'My name is Basil.' But it fell on deaf ears; the Font was preoccupied with the seeing machine, banging a fist hard on the top of it. Basil sighed and left the room.

CHAPTER 45

It had been a little disorientating to say the least for Frida. One moment she had been stepping purposely along the path she had been told to follow, and the next she found she was standing in a field of green, blinking in the sunshine of a blue, fluffy-clouded sky that was framed by the most marvellous of rainbows. She hadn't even noticed the doorway.

After a couple of seconds of eye-blinking, Frida regained her senses and noticed for the first time that a village, nestling among a spattering of hills, stood not far from where she was standing. All looked peaceful enough, but she was in the open. The situation was not ideal for one playing the covert game. It was time to move. Frida saw a small copse nestling at the foot of one of the hills a little distance away; somewhere to hide perhaps until she decided what to do next. It would mean a dash across open ground, but better than just standing there waiting to be seen. She quickly made for it.

Hoping no one had seen her make her suspicious-looking sprint for cover, Frida stood for a moment behind a tree trying to catch her breath. She had been half expecting the phone to go off as she ran, but it hadn't.

Breath caught, Frida took the phone from her pocket. Why hadn't it? If she was being watched as she thought she was, why hadn't the voice on the other end made contact? Perhaps they were waiting for her to get out of the open? Would make sense, she thought. And now she was? She waited. No call. She waited some more, casting a wary glance here and there as she did, but still nothing. But did she want it to ring? Did she like the idea of being spied on? Maybe not, but as invasive and annoying as it was, it would be a good time for whomever it was that was watching, to phone. Frida had no idea where she was, or even if she was where she was supposed to be. She waited a little longer then, when it seemed doubtful anyone was going to call, she put the phone back in her pocket.

Frida weighed up her options. Wait until someone called. Wait until someone found her. Neither to her mind, a particularly viable option. Start moving. That was a better idea, because she would soon have to, but to where?' Frida peered around the tree trunk. She could make a dash to the village perhaps? But to what end? It was hopeless, she hadn't the faintest idea where she was, she couldn't just wander willy-nilly, she was supposed to be following Mister Power. But how, in all that was weird, was she supposed to do that? She had to know where he was to follow him. Frida slumped back against the tree trunk and closed her eyes. It was all going wrong. She stood like that for a moment or two then decided to have another look at the phone. Why? She didn't really know. She took it out and looked at it, and then looked at it again, and only then did it register that it wasn't the phone she was holding. In her growing despair Frida had gone to the wrong pocket. She was holding the tracking console. She had forgotten all about it, fat use it was now. It had stopped working back at the gate where she had said that stupid rhyme, the two blips that had been telling her where Mister Power's minions were, just blinking out as if they had just ceased to exist. Two blips just like the ones on the console now.

Frida jerked upright. Blips! Grief, she thought, the console's working again. This changed everything. With a small modicum of excitement, which was all she would allow herself for the moment, she realised the minions weren't far away. Someway ahead yes, but if she was reading the console right, they were somewhere in the village. At last she was back on track.

With a wary eye, Frida made her way to the edge of the village and hid in the shadow of a cottage. Now, did she chance going through the village or along the edge of it?

'There, there!' someone shouted off to Frida's left, as she decided on the latter.

For a horrific moment Frida thought she had been seen, but she hadn't. The shout had come from someone in a small group of excited people wearing what she assumed was fancy dress, heading away from her, down what looked like the main village street. She waited for them to move a safe distance away then carefully looked around the corner of the cottage. Strange, she thought, as she watched them go; they all appeared to be carrying a garden implement of one kind or another.

Ducking back, Frida again looked at the tracking console. The blips were still burning bright, but how to get close to them without them becoming aware of her. Her change of appearance would help, but she couldn't totally rely on that. She then had an idea. Peeping back around the corner of the cottage, she scanned the street. The boisterous group that had made her heart skip a beat earlier had stopped as others joined them. The newcomers were also carrying hoes and pitchforks and the like, and some had burning torches. If she could somehow join them and blend in, perhaps she could get a chance to see if she could see Mister Power.

It wasn't the greatest of plans, but if it got Frida what she wanted, so be it. She left the relative safety of the cottage's shadows and headed for the group that had passed her. Walk don't run, she told herself. No need to draw any undue attention. Along the way other people appeared from alleyways and cottages and Frida found she couldn't help but stare. There were bows and bonnets everywhere, but she was sure it wasn't Easter. There were also plenty of frills; mostly worn by the men. And there were bells, lots of them. And seashells. One young woman, Mary someone had called her, appeared to have an unnatural bent towards them, as the garden of the cottage she had come from was literally covered in them; cockle and mussel shells by the thousand. And the more she saw, the more Frida had the strange feeling that she somehow had seen some of these people before somewhere. But she put it down to a case of déjà-vu. Something she had seen on television, maybe? Perhaps, she decided.

As Frida got closer to the crowds that were rapidly forming in front and around her, the more she realised just how out of place she looked amongst them. Not that anyone was taking any notice of her, they all appeared to be much too excited by what was going on ahead of them for that, but she felt she needed that extra bit of security all the same; the need to blend in. And when the opportunity arose to do so, she took it. A bonnet from a washing line, and a rake someone had left against a wall. Not the greatest of disguises, but it was something. Time to find Mister Power.

CHAPTER 46

Leif, to everyone's relief, hadn't been lying; the Enchanted Forest at last loomed large in the distance. To get a better look, Danrite and the others climbed a ridge that was too small to claim to be a hill, but high enough for everyone to be able to gaze on a sight that fair took their breath away.

The Enchanted Forest was huge, spreading from east to west, as far as the eye could see. A sea of green that's depth spread far into a hazy distance.

'Blimey,' said Danrite, fingering his pommel nervously.

'Ay caramba!' said Jose, eyes wide. 'So many trees.'

'Dangerous trees,' said Salor, darkly.

'Dangerous place,' said Vlad.

'Neigh,' said Sid, agreeing with all.

'But a way to the Font,' said Twinkle.

'So many trees,' said Jose.

'Yes,' said Twinkle, managing a smile at the little chihuahua despite the general mood, 'lots of trees.'

They stood for a while in silence taking in the sight, wondering what lay ahead for them. Then, with Salor taking the lead, they slowly headed down the ridge towards the Enchanted Forest.

They stopped just before the shadow of the closest tree; the forest even more daunting close up.

'Hug me,' said Vlad, to anyone who was listening. No one did.

Sid pawed the ground nervously.

'Grief,' said Danrite, as he twiddled with his pommel.

Salor scowled and fiddled with his staff.

'It doesn't look friendly,' said Twinkle, clenching and unclenching her fists.

Only Jose seemed unfazed as he stared with saucer-sized eyes. He had never seen such trees. From his low vantage point the trees seemed to reach to the sky. He couldn't wait to get in amongst them. 'We go?' he said.

Everyone else looked at everyone else. This venture; step into the unknown, couldn't be taken lightly. Courage needed to be plucked. Deep breaths needed to be taken. Considerations needed to be considered.

And while they were busy doing that, Jose went and cocked a leg.

CHAPTER 47

Basil was holding on for dear life as the wind buffeted him against the west turret where the seeing machine's receiver was. Things weren't going well; the wind was making things as difficult as Basil had imagined it would, the talkie-walkie was proving hard to keep hold of, the receiver still wouldn't receive, and the safety harness strapped about his waist, was straining and making alarming noises.

'Try the other way,' crackled the Font's voice from the talkie-walkie.

'But I've tried that way already,' wailed a grimacing Basil, as he tried to hold on with one hand, hold the talkie-walkie with the other, and blow upwards at the wet leaf that had landed on and stuck to his forehead, all at the same time.

'Then try it again,' demanded the Font.

Basil made a face at the talkie-walkie and tried again. 'Anything?' he said, not really expecting any improvement.

'A little,' said the Font, 'try a little further.'

He couldn't believe it, it had been in the exact same place but a moment ago, and was now not that far from where it had started. Basil rolled his eyes and then crossed them at the talkie-walkie before turning the receiver a little bit more. 'How about now?' he asked, his misery increasing as it had now started to rain.

'Just a little more,' said the Font. The screen was beginning to clear at last.

Basil scowled and attempted to turn the receiver back to where it had started. But that little bit more he was trying to achieve was proving difficult. The pole the receiver was on was becoming more and more slippery; greasy even. He would need both hands. How he wished he had brought his all-weather gloves now. Putting the talkie-walkie in a pocket, Basil gripped the pole with both his hands. He grunted. The receiver turned the tiniest bit of little, but not enough. He tried to wipe his wet hands on his coat, but to no avail;

his coat was as wet as his hands. He gripped the pole and tried again. He grunted. His hands slipped. He grunted again. His hands slipped again, but this time his grip went with them. He screamed. He fell. The safety harness twisted. Basil went sideways. The edge of the turret suddenly loomed large. The rocky ground below loomed closer. Basil tried to twist away from the edge, slipped again, span towards another edge, grabbed at the parapet, missed, screamed again, and finally went over the edge.

The rocky ground now not only loomed, but now zoomed as he headed for it, but today was not the day Basil would get more than his hopes dashed. The rope the harness was attached to, which if Basil hadn't had his mind on more urgent matters, would have wondered why it had let him fall at all; perhaps the rain had got into the breaking mechanism; perhaps it had failed because the harness was older than he was; had unfurled to its full length. Basil should have come to a shuddering halt no more than a few feet from that rocky ground, but instead of Basil suffering the indignity of being left hanging low and wet, the rope decided to act like a bungee cord, and just as his nose scraped the tallest alpine flower, he sprang back again towards the turret.

Needless to say Basil screamed the scream of the terrified as he suddenly flew skyward. Up he went. Up. Up. The turret loomed. The sky beckoned, but Basil, not wanting to spend the rest of the day being jerked this way and that; something he was used to in the service of the Font, managed to twist in mid-air and make a grab at the receiver as he passed by. He missed. He screamed again. The rope caught on his feet causing it to twist and in turn catch on the edge of the receiver. The rope, now wedged between the receiver and pole, changed Basil's trajectory from vertical to horizontal. Round and round he went as the rope coiled round the pole at speed. Basil felt sick. The rope shortened. Basil felt even sicker. There was a crunch. Basil had become introduced to the pole again, but he had no time to celebrate his good fortune as the rope now started to unwind. There followed another crunch as Basil landed on the turret's floor with a bump; a bump that knocked the talkie-walkie from his pocket. It crackled into life.

'That's it,' said the Font. 'Perfect!'

Basil, resisting the urge to celebrate, threw up all over the talkie-walkie instead.

CHAPTER 48

Much to his annoyance, Mister Power had let himself dwell on Rogi's remark of asking him if he was feeling sleepy, but in the end, after a stern internal dressing-down, he decided it was just Rogi being the dolt he was. Sleepy indeed! But that had been a while back, he was now more concerned with the shouting he could hear in the near distance.

Mister Power carefully skirted the last hill, which he felt should have him just past the last of the village's hovels, when the shouting suddenly intensified. He instinctively hid behind a handy tree. Was that Rogi's voice he could hear? He listened. It was! What the heck was going on? He peered round the tree just in time to catch the eye of the fast-approaching Rogi. He stepped from behind the tree. 'What the-'

'Quick, sir, this way,' said Rogi, drawing beside Mister Power. 'Ergo and Hewie are holding them off, but I don't know for how much longer. They've got a giant.'

'What?' said Mister Power, looking beyond Rogi. 'Who has?'

'Sorry, sir, no time to explain, we have to go,' he said, as he passed.

Rogi it appeared was not for stopping, and if Rogi was running, then there had to be a very good reason for him doing so. Mister Power, deciding any further questions could wait a moment, picked up his knees and quickly followed in Rogi's slipstream.

Behind the fleeing duo, the shouting had reached fever pitch, which suddenly morphed into a triumphant cheer.

'I think that's Ergo and Hewie making a dash for it, sir,' said Rogi.

Mister Power wasn't for looking back again so took Rogi's word for it. 'What happened?' he puffed.

'I don't rightly know, sir,' said Rogi. 'One minute we were minding our own business, sir, skulking in the shadows and the like, and the next someone shouts, "he's back".

'"He's back"?' panted Mister Power.

'Yes, sir, and then all heck breaks loose and everyone's chasing us with garden and farm implements.'

As they ran, a question formed in Mister Power's mind, or rather a suspicion. 'Did they mean you?' he puffed. He was also thinking he should perhaps have spent a little time in the company gym.

'Sir?' said Rogi.

'Back there, when they shouted, "he's back",' said Mister Power, his lungs feeling like they were going to burst soon.

'Can't see why, sir,' said Rogi, who wasn't even puffing.

'You said it had happened before,' puffed Mister Power.

'Yes, sir, but I'm wearing different clothes this time.'

Mister Power cast Rogi an incredulous glance. Not the different-looking body then? thought Mister Power, but Mister Power, his lungs fair to bursting, decided he didn't want to waste his ebbing energy on pointing that out, or indeed pressing any further with his suspicions. Better to just concentrate on not letting his lungs erupt from his chest. But before he could do that there was something a little more important on Mister Power's mind that needed clarifying, and he had to ask, because he didn't know how much further he would be able to run. 'Where are we going?' he managed.

'The next land, sir. Hewie picked up the boy's scent in the village before the crowd attacked, and it appeared he was headed that way.' Rogi stole a glance Mister Power's way. 'Are you okay, sir? Would you like me to carry you?'

Mister Power was mortified. 'Of course not,' he replied sternly, between pants, as he gamely upped his pace. His body though was going *please-please-please!* 'How far?' he wheezed, hoping the answer would be in the region of *we're there.*

'Not far, sir,' said Rogi.

Good, thought Mister Power, *not far*, good. He just hoped his lungs would last as long as *not far*.

CHAPTER 49

As far as Frida could make out, from snatches of conversation she caught here and there, the crowd was after someone. The pursuit though wasn't a running sort of one, more a controlled surge; odd. But she had the idea the crowd were well-versed in what they were doing, and had done it before. Frida tried to see above the crowd, to try and get a glimpse of who they were pursuing, perhaps the crowd and she were after the same prey, but she wasn't able to; being near the back as she was.

More people joined the throng; one in particular, with a slightly larger than normal egg-shaped bald head with what looked like brown paper covering the top of it, had climbed on a wall and was shouting support. Frida, the surge pushing her closer to the wall, saw that a young woman was trying to get the bald man to climb down, while a young man carrying a pail of water was telling her it was none of her business. Suddenly the bald man, his arms wind-milling, toppled backwards and fell. The young man, on seeing this, laughed so hard he spilled half the water he had in his pail onto the ground. The young lady, obviously not in the least bit amused by the laughing and spilling, scowled fiercely at the young man. The crowd then suddenly picked up a bit of speed and Frida, pulled away by the crowd's rising tide, was left wondering as to how that particular little drama would end. Onwards the crowd surged. Faster the pace gathered. Louder the shouting became. Excitement was building. Leaving Frida in no doubt that whomever it was the crowd was after; they were closing in on them.

Things were hotting up and Frida, not wanting to be in its midst, if and when they caught whomever it was they were chasing, decided it was time to leave the cover of the crowd and dodge back into the shadows of the side streets and cottages. From there she might be better able to see Mister Power, and if by chance it was the man himself the crowd were chasing, then better to be hidden than recognised by the man and then hunted by association. As gently as she could, Frida, head down, trying not to draw attention, started to elbow her way through the crowd.

It was not easy, the crowd was dense and moving fast, making any headway slow; it would take time. But she persevered, and suddenly, quicker than she had expected and to her utmost relief, she found the space she was looking for. Only it wasn't. With her head down she had failed to notice she had veered from the direction she had been heading, and in doing so had accidently forced her way to the front of the crowd.

And there she stopped and stared, dumbfounded by what she saw. Her mind trying to somehow rationalise what it was her eyes were seeing. People were complaining; moaning at her for stopping as they passed. But Frida didn't care. She had to get away from there. She started again with the elbows, but with more purpose this time, moving as quickly as she could away from the front.

Frida elbowed and pushed her way through the crowd, ignoring the complaints and odd curse aimed her way, all the time hoping no one would stop her. But the people weren't interested in her; they moaned and cursed yes, but were more focused on their pursuit than a rude young woman pushing her way past them without even an "excuse me".

Finally, slightly bruised and battered, she managed to escape the throng; staggering gratefully into the shadows of an alleyway. She slumped against the wall of a cottage, her mind a whirr. What the heck was that thing? she wondered. But it could only have been one thing. But that thing didn't exist. Did it? Her head suddenly jerked sideways towards the entrance of the alleyway she had just entered, but there was nothing there. She closed her eyes. She knew she needed to keep moving, but she needed a moment to think. She had seen it with her own eyes, she knew that, but how was that possible? Eyes could play tricks. The mind could play tricks. But she doubted they had. Then what? She had of course heard of them; even seen some, but only in books; childrens' story books. But they didn't exist in real life. Not grown-up real life. But she had seen one, at the front of the crowd, as large as life; real life; a giant as real as she was. And then she wondered about the people in the crowd; the couple with the pail; the bald man on the wall; the girl in the frills holding a shepherds' crook. No, surely not? What the heck was happening?

But as surreal as her life had suddenly become, she couldn't stay in the alleyway. She knew that. She had to focus, even if all around her was chipping away at her sanity. Frida decided she needed something to concentrate her mind on; something she knew was real. She took the phone from her pocket. Where were they when she needed them? She tried to focus on it, but it didn't help; perhaps because she felt it was part of the insanity. Frida put it back, then remembered the tracking console and took that out; she stared at it, the two glowing blips were still there. She stared harder. She stared even harder. Frida concentrated her mind. It was working. Not a lot, but she was now standing. She was now walking. She started to run towards the other end of the alleyway.

CHAPTER 50

The Font stared at the seeing machine in disbelief. How had this happened? The Font shouted for Basil. 'THYME!!'

Basil had only just finished throwing up when the Font's not so dulcet tones reached his ears. He thought for a moment he was going to throw up again, but he didn't. Instead he reached for the talkie-walkie, wiped the mouthpiece, and said he was on his way. With a limp and a hobble, and the occasional groan, Basil, in his not so white anymore attire, made his painful way to the waiting Font.

'At last,' said the Font, as Basil shuffled into the seeing room. The Font was standing in front of the seeing machine in quite a huff, and didn't seem to notice the state Basil was in. 'Where have you been?' the Font said, without looking from the screen of the seeing machine.

Basil thought about making some funny remark in reply, but didn't as he thought he might snigger, and that was surely going to hurt something on his person. Instead he said, 'Here and there.' Which was quite funny when he thought about it, which in turn made him snigger, which in turn proved his theory regarding his feeling pain.

'Well you're here now I suppose,' said the Font, huffing. 'Look at this.'

Basil looked. His eyes widened. 'How did they get there?' he said.

'A good question,' said the Font. 'And look at this.' The Font pressed a button on the remote. The screen flickered.

'What's he doing?' said Basil, eyes still wide.

'Another good question,' said the Font. 'And there's this.' The Font pressed another button.

'Oh,' said Basil, his eyes now narrowing.

'And it doesn't stop there, look.' Another button was pressed.

'Oh dear,' said Basil, frowning.

‘Oh dear indeed,’ said the Font. ‘Get me the speaking machine.’

‘Right away,’ said Basil. He turned to limp away and get it.

‘Oh, and Mint.’

‘Yes?’ said Basil, screwing his face up in frustration.

‘Get me a cuppa will you, there’s a good chap.’

A cuppa! He would have thrown his hands up in despair if he hadn’t thought it would hurt. He knew what he would really like to give the Font, and it wasn’t a cup of Rosie Lee. A tongue biting, scowling Basil limped and hobbled from the room.

CHAPTER 51

The Enchanted Forest was daunting from a distance, more daunting close up, and even more daunting on the inside. There were ancient forests. There were primeval forests. This one was older still. Its trees, gnarled with age, twisted this way and that, looked angry. Shadows played on them, giving them faces, giving them the appearance of movement. Danrite shivered, but not from any cold. He suddenly wanted to get a move on. Get to the centre as quickly as possible. His hand moved to the hilt of his sword and rested on it, but this time the reassurance he was seeking wasn't there.

'Not as dark in here as I thought it would be,' said Vlad, his voice so close to Danrite's shoulder it made Danrite jump.

'Whaa!' said Danrite, his skin managing to keep hold of him. He pulled himself together. 'Don't do that.'

'Sorry,' said Vlad, who had been seeking reassurance of his own, 'just saying.'

The Enchanted Forest was indeed not as dark inside as everyone had been expecting. Salor (after Jose had emerged from it none the worst) had bravely led the way inside using the crystal on his staff to cast a light with which to see by. He now let it fade.

'What now?' said Twinkle, casting worried glances hither and thither.

'We find the centre,' said Salor, bravely taking a step forward, and then stopping, as the realisation that he had no idea where it might be kicked in.

'Now what?' said Twinkle.

'I…er…'said Salor, now doing his own hithering and thithering.

'Ahem,' said Jose, getting everyone's attention. Everyone looked down. 'Perhaps I am being of service with the finding of the centre,' he said.

'You?' said Salor, frowning at the little chihuahua.

‘Sí,’ said Jose. ‘I will sniff it.’ He then turned and headed to the closest tree. This he sniffed. He then went to a second, a third, a fourth, a fifth; sniffing each in turn. At the sixth he stopped and turned to find no one was following him. ‘Why is it you no follow?’ he said, looking puzzled.

‘Why do you think?’ said Twinkle, raising an eyebrow.

Jose, not known to be big on the thinking front, gave the question some thought anyway. It took only a second. ‘Ah,’ he said, unknotting his forehead which had looked in danger of falling in on itself. ‘I am knowing this. I am being too fast. I slow down.’ He took a few slow steps to the next tree, but stopped when again no one made any attempt to follow. ‘Ay caramba,’ he said, ‘if I am moving any slower I am thinking I will be doing the falling over sideways.’

Twinkle sighed. ‘You’re going in a circle.’

‘I am?’ said Jose.

‘Yes,’ said Salor.

Jose looked behind him, the small puddles he had deposited as a means of identifying where he had been told its story. ‘Ay caramba! It is true, I am in circles.’ Jose gave the trees a suspicious look. ‘I am thinking there is tree mischief afoot.’ He wandered off to sniff at the puddles to make sure they were his.

‘So,’ said Twinkle, as she watched Jose creep up to one of the puddles, ‘plan A or B or C?’

‘A or B or C?’ said Salor, who hadn’t realised there were any plans.

‘Yeah,’ said Twinkle, ‘left, right, or straight on?’

‘Oh,’ said Salor. ‘Well…’ He looked left, right, and then straight ahead. They all looked the same.

‘I’ve a coin we can toss,’ said Vlad, helpfully. He delved in a pocket and produced something that looked like it had seen much better days. ‘It’s my lucky one.’

‘It doesn’t have a head or tails,’ said Danrite, looking closely at the coin floating in front of his face.

‘I’ve had it a long time,’ Vlad explained.

‘Fat lot of good that is then,’ said Twinkle.

Vlad popped it back into his pocket.

They were no closer to finding the centre of the Enchanted Forest, and perhaps never would have been, if they hadn’t had the most magical of creatures with them. Sid, once a unicorn, but now just a horse, but retaining a modicum of magic, nuzzled at Salor's back, gently pushing him toward plan C.

It transpired that Sid, who had been the most magical of creatures, could somehow feel the centre pulling him. The feeling wasn't strong, but it was something; a start. So Sid now led the way, pulled by remnants of his magical force. He headed straight on, closely accompanied by Salor, Twinkle, Vlad, and Danrite. The first real steps into the Enchanted Forest, to its centre, were being taken.

'So many trees,' said Jose, so in awe of the Enchanted Forest, so oblivious to the events of a few minutes ago. He was still sniffing at his puddles. 'I am thinking I will be coming here on my holidays. What you think?' He stopped his sniffing when no one answered him. He turned from the puddle he had been inspecting. 'I say I…' But no one was listening. No one was there. Jose was alone. Alone in the middle of his wee-riddled trees. Wee-riddled trees that now seemed much closer than they had a second or so ago. 'Amigos?'

Then there were five.

CHAPTER 52

By the time a shattered Mister Power and a barely ruffled Rogi reached the edge of the next land, which wasn't far as it happened, Hewie and Ergo, more Hewie really, Ergo had just held on for dear life, had managed to lead the chasing villagers, less the giant, who it turned out was surprisingly slow and had been left well behind, on a merry dance before losing them by leading them into a certain barn, darting back out again as the last one stepped through the door, then closing that door behind them. It appeared Hewie wasn't all just claws and slaver; he also possessed a survival instinct that bordered on thinking. They now rushed headlong in the general direction of Mister Power and Rogi.

They appeared on the horizon as Mister Power, hands on knees, got his breath back. Rogi drew Mister Power's attention to them. They drew closer. Mister Power stood up. They drew level. The trailing, dragged-along Ergo, still hanging on, was trying to say something, but the dirt and grass in his mouth was making that difficult. They weren't stopping.

'Quick,' said Mister Power, as Hewie sped past them, 'grab it.'

Rogi dived headlong at the speeding Hewie, missed, rolled, but managed to grab hold of one of Ergo's trailing legs. But still Hewie kept on. Mister Power, with no choice but to chase after them, as Hewie didn't look like stopping anytime soon, did just that.

CHAPTER 53

The Font put the speaking machine back in its place, sipped at the tea Basil had made, and then reached for the remote control. The images on the seeing machine did not make for good viewing. A button was pressed. Another one pressed. Something had to be done. Something had been done. All the Font could do now was wait.

CHAPTER 54

The phone had rung just before Frida reached the end of the alley, startling her, causing her to drop the tracking console. Thankfully it hadn't broken.

She looked at it now, the two blips burning bright, but it was no longer needed, a change of plan the voice on the other end of the phone had said. She ran a hand through her hair. She was frustrated; edgy. She had seen things that didn't make sense, and now she was being told that the only thing that did, the one thing of reality she was clinging to, didn't matter anymore.

Frida pressed herself deeper into alleyway's shadows. She was still being watched. How else would the voice on the other end of the phone know she was in an alley? But now wasn't the time for paranoia. The voice had told her to go to the end of the alley and then to keep moving, straight as the crow flies. Someone would meet her. Who would? The voice had gone dead before she could ask. She was in the dark. She was in the dark of the alleyway. But she would go. The sooner she put the village behind her the better; the quicker the better. Frida started to run again.

CHAPTER 55

'Whoa,' said Leif, suddenly stopping. He and Rosie were well on their way to Nursery Town when his sixth sense suddenly kicked in. 'Something's coming.'

A puzzled Rosie flapped her flaps.

'I don't know,' said Leif, answering Rosie's question as to what did he mean, *something*? But whatever it was, his sixth sense was telling him it should be avoided. He lowered a branch and ushered Rosie behind him.

Rosie didn't need telling twice and tucked in behind Leif's trunk as tight as she could. She gave a little flap to let him know she was hidden.

'Good,' said Leif, as the something he had been sensing came into sight. He made like a tree.

The something was moving at pace, slaver all over its face. It looked like a dog crossed with a pig. It reached Leif and passed him. Leif saw that it was towing something covered in grass and dirt, which in turn was towing the most handsome man Leif had ever seen. None of them looked at him. The something, the grass, the dirt, and the handsome man, started to disappear into the distance. Rosie gave a flap; she wanted to know if it was safe to come out yet.

'Not yet,' said Leif, as this time a *someone* rather than a *something* appeared on the horizon. It was a man in a sharp-looking suit. A dangerous man said Leif's sixth sense. A man nearing exhaustion, Leif's eyes told him.

The man had been running, but on seeing a tree, rather than Leif, he had slowed to a walk and was now approaching it.

Leif watched nervously as the man walked up to him and then leaned on his trunk. The man then sat down. The man then spoke to himself. 'Flipping cannon fodder,' said the man, who was obviously not happy about something.

The man rested a few minutes under the shade of Leif's branches then got to his feet. He was breathing heavily, but not as heavily as he had been. He slowly walked over to a shallow rut left in the ground by the something that had passed by. He then looked in the direction the something had taken and started to follow. Leif thought the man had decided to track rather than chase; a good idea he felt, considering the state of him.

Leif watched him go. Waited until he was the tiniest of dots in the distance; then and only then did he think it safe to give Rosie the all clear. Rosie flapped her flaps as she noticed the shallow rut in the ground.

'I don't know,' said Leif, admitting he didn't have the faintest idea what it was that had made the rut or who the man in the sharp suit was. 'And I don't think I want to,' he said, with a slight shiver. He felt they were bad news whoever they were, and the further they were from them the better. 'You ready to go?' he asked.

But Rosie wasn't listening; she was too busy staring at the large white thing that was falling from the sky, directly above them.

Too late, Leif's sixth sense, letting him down for once, kicked in, but there wasn't anything he could really do, not when the Font was involved.

There was a scream, followed by a thump, followed by a lot of billowing whiteness that tangled in Leif's branches.

'Well, don't just stand there like the doofus you are, get me down,' demanded a voice Leif knew only too well. It was Basil, the Font's rude little sidekick.

Doofus indeed, thought Leif. He shook his branches a little harder than he would normally have done in such a situation. Basil dropped through the air like a stone, taking most of his parachute with him.

'Oof,' said Basil, as he landed.

Rosie flapped her flaps.

'Don't ask,' said Leif, looking at the parachute, as beneath it Basil tried to get free.

Basil's head finally appeared. He looked up at Leif and scowled at him. 'The Font's not happy with you, you know,' he said. And nor am I, he thought.

CHAPTER 56

Sid stopped, pricked his ears, and listened.

'What's he doing?' said Danrite.

'He's listening,' said Salor.

'What for?'

'I don't know.'

Sid trotted on.

'I don't like this,' said Twinkle, as the forest brooded menacingly about them.

'Nor me,' said Vlad, pulling his robe tighter round him. They had been walking for nearly ten minutes, moving deeper and deeper into the forest. 'What about you Jose, still enjoying the trees?' Jose didn't answer. 'Jose?'

When Jose didn't answer a second time, which wasn't that unusual, but because of where they were, heads faced down to see where he was.

'Hold up,' said Twinkle, realising Jose wasn't in sight, 'I think we've lost the dog.'

They all stopped and looked. Twinkle was right, they were chihuahua-less.

'What do we do?' said Danrite, worried for the little dog. His hand clamped and unclamped the hilt of his sword. He wanted to unsheathe it. Why, he didn't know. What would he do with it if he did? Probably hurt someone; himself. He let go of the sword.

Sid suddenly snorted, his ears pointing forward. Something was rustling in the undergrowth. Everyone huddled closer.

'Jose? Is that you?' said Twinkle, as the rustling grew closer. Twinkle was going to give that dog a piece of her mind if he had worried them all for nothing.

The rustling stopped.

'This isn't funny,' said Salor, expecting Jose to burst into the open with a silly doggy grin all over his face.

The rustling started again, then stopped as a small creature burst from the undergrowth to stand before them.

'That's not Jose,' said Vlad, stating the obvious.

'The vampire wins a coconut,' said Twinkle.

It wasn't Jose, it was a small fellow akin to the garden variety, and it wasn't a fishing rod he had in his hand.

'Is that what I think it is?' whispered Twinkle, referring to the thing in the gnome's hand.

'It is,' said Salor, verifying her fear.

'Good grief,' she said.

'It's rude to whisper,' said the gnome, glaring at Twinkle.

Salor stepped forward. 'My name is-'

'I know who you are,' said the gnome, sharply. 'You are to come with us.'

'Us?' said Salor, seeing no one else. The undergrowth suddenly parted to reveal a score of fearsome-looking gnomes. Salor stepped back. All of them had something nasty in their hands. 'Why?' he asked.

'We are to escort you to our king,' said the chief gnome.

Salor's eyes shifted left then right. He didn't like this. They were surrounded. 'But we can't, we are on an urgent mission.'

'To see the Font, we know, but you have to come with us.'

'How did you know that?' demanded Salor, standing defiant.

'That doesn't matter,' said the chief gnome, stepping aside. His hand tightened around the thing in his hand. His companions did likewise. 'But first you must put these on.' He handed blindfolds to all but Sid; which was strange.

'Looks as if we have little choice,' said Twinkle, who had weighed up their chances and come up with not a snowball's chance. Although they stood less than two feet in their little boots, there were just too many of them. Besides they were armed with dibbers.

'Can't we rush them?' whispered Danrite, having had the same idea as Twinkle.

'Not with that many dibbers,' Twinkle whispered back.

'Oh,' he said, 'that's what they are.' A puzzled Danrite looked at the gnomes, then back at Twinkle. 'Aren't they something to do with allotments?' He hadn't the faintest idea where he had gleaned that bit of information from. Probably Percy, he decided.

'Usually,' said Twinkle, 'but these are a little bit more dangerous.' And just like that, as if he had been waiting for a cue, the chief gnome flicked the dibber in his hand and a blade suddenly protruded from the end of it. 'Those are sword dibbers.'

'Oh,' said Danrite, the hand that had gone back to resting on the hilt of his sword, now gently eased away from it. Any appetite he may have had regarding any swashbuckling swiftly disappearing from his mind. He put his blindfold on.

'Quickly now,' said the chief gnome, as twenty more dibbers were flicked. 'The king doesn't like to be kept waiting.' Jose, for the moment, was forgotten.

CHAPTER 57

Though the village and its alleyway were well behind her now, Frida didn't let her pace drop. As she ran she pondered on who it might be she was supposed to be meeting, perhaps one of the owners of the voices she had spoken to on the telephone, perhaps another agent, but whoever, she was determined they were going to tell her where she was and what the heck was going on before they said anything else.

Twenty minutes later Frida had still not seen a soul, and her running had turned into a jog. She was beginning to wonder just how far she was supposed to go before she met this person, whoever it was, that she had to meet up with. Over hill, over vale she had travelled, and looming large was another hill; the highest so far, but it looked easy enough to jog up. It could be high enough for her to see the lay of the land ahead of her; see what was waiting for her, perhaps who. And if the hill wasn't as high as she hoped it would be then she could climb the tree that was standing alone on the top of it.

The hill was steeper than Frida thought it was, but she was there now, at its summit. The tree was an old oak, and standing beside it was a table; not the picnic type, but one you might find in a kitchen or small dining room. Frida shook her head. Could things get any weirder? It could. The tree spoke to her.

'Frida?' said Leif, tentatively. The girl fitted the description he had been given, but…

Frida stopped dead. Someone had spoken her name, but there was no one in sight. Unless… Frida cautiously took a look behind the tree. But there was no one there. 'Hello?' she said, wondering if the person who had spoken was the one she was supposed to meet. There was a noise like wood tapping on wood. Had the table's flaps just moved?

'I know,' said Leif, answering Rosie.

Frida span on her heels looking for the owner of the voice. 'Who's there?'

'Me, Leif,' said Leif.

'Show yourself.' Frida had been trained in self-defence and took a defensive position.

'I am,' said Leif, who then rustled his leaves to prove it.

Frida looked up. Aha! she thought, he's hiding in the tree. 'I won't tell you again.' But the only answer was the sound of wood tapping on wood again. A weapon? She backed off a little.

Leif rustled his leaves again in agreement with Rosie's suggestion that the girl appeared to be short-sighted. Perhaps she had lost her glasses. He decided to bend forward a little so that she might see him better. Trouble was, as he did this, he accidently did something else. Frida dropped as if she had been shot. She hadn't, she'd been clubbed by a branch.

Rosie rattled her flaps frantically.

Leif rustled his leaves apologetically.

What did they do now?

Frida came round, slowly. Her head was hurting. Perhaps something to do with the lump the size of a goose egg that she had on her head. She now opened her eyes, slowly. The world was spinning. She held on. It gradually slowed to a stop. But her head still hurt. She then realised she was lying on the ground. What had happened? But she couldn't quite remember, the part of her mind holding her memory was pretty fuzzy. She went to sit up.

'I'd rest before doing that,' said Leif helpfully, hoping she wouldn't be too angry with him. And Leif was helpful, only not in the way he had intended.

On hearing Leif's voice, Frida's memory flooded back. She quickly rolled onto her front and assumed a crouching position, all in one painful, fluid movement. But the assailant she had been expecting to find standing over her wasn't there. She was alone. Her head buzzed. She must have been hearing things; her mind playing tricks as she tried to remember. All was the same as it had been before the attack; the tree, the table, except…

The hill, what had happened to the hill? Frida's mind filled with confusion. She felt dizzy. There had been a hill, hadn't there? Yes, she remembered, the climb up it had been steeper than she had been expecting it to be, but now it was gone; in its place a field filled with wild flowers.

Struggling to make any sense of things she decided to, and somehow managed, to get to her feet without falling. She was now in a field. Okay, she got that. But how did she get there? She didn't get that. Had someone carried her here? Perhaps whoever it was she was supposed to meet had found her and carried her? But if so where were they now? Nothing made sense, not even the lump on her head. How did that get there? Had someone crept up behind her? Jumped from the tree and lumped her one? And where was he? *The tree*. Frida's focus was suddenly on the tree. How could the tree be here? No one could have carried that. Whoa, slow down, she told herself, there are plenty of oak trees about, just a different one that's all. She took a deep breath. She was getting somewhere. She was managing to find explanations; sort of. At least she had one for the tree being there, the tree… but oh dear, then there was *the table*. How did she explain that? She doubted there were plenty of them about. Frida stared at it. She suddenly felt very dizzy. Her legs were giving way. She felt herself start to fall. And then suddenly she wasn't. Something had stopped her. The tree had stopped her. She blacked out.

This time, Frida's eyes opened with a start and the first thing they saw was the table leaning over her. It had been the table's shadow falling across her that had roused her. Frida jumped. The table jumped. It then ran away and hid behind the tree. At the same time Frida had scrambled backwards on her elbows as fast as she could go. 'What the…'

'You frightened her,' said Leif, turning to look at Rosie.

Frida stopped scrambling. It was that voice again, the one that belonged to her attacker. Although shaken by what had just happened with the table, she was feeling better than she had the first time she had woken up, and managed to get to her feet a lot quicker this time around. She looked this way and that. 'Where are you?' Frida demanded. The table could wait, she wanted answers.

She really did need to see an optician, thought Leif. 'Here,' he said, waving a branch in front of Frida, but then quickly pulling it back when he realised what he was doing. One goose egg lump was enough for anyone.

Frida had taken a step back when the branch had waved towards her, and had then taken another one when the table had reappeared, flapping its flaps like a huge wooden bird, and then another one when whoever owned the voice started talking to it.

'My bad,' said Leif, in reply to Rosie telling him off for getting his branch so close again, 'but see, she's okay.' Leif took a step towards Frida.

Frida took another slightly bigger step back. Was the tree moving? The tree was moving. The blow she had taken to her head must be worse than she thought.

'Don't be afraid,' said Leif, his knotty face full of concern, 'we're here to help you find Danrite.'

Frida stopped. She was confused, dazed, and a little bit rattled, but more than that she wanted answers. And as it appeared she wasn't going to be attacked again she decided to take a chance and throw caution to the wind. 'Who?' she said, not entirely sure who or now, what, she was talking to.

'Danrite,' said Leif, relieved the girl could hear a lot better than she could see. 'The one Mister Power is looking for.'

Frida had no idea who this Danrite was, but the mention of Power had her attention. 'What do you know of Mister Power?' she asked.

Leif told her. He also told her that he had been asked to meet her; to tell her about a change of plan. He also told her the reason behind her unfortunate accident.

'Okaaay,' said Frida, when Leif had finished his tale. She wasn't sure how much she did believe, especially the bit about the branch, but he had said a lot that had made sense to her, this Leif character. 'But if what you say is true, why won't you show yourself?' To this point she had managed to ignore the table that now and then had peeped at her from behind the tree. She was putting it down to blurred vision or something.

'But I am,' said Leif, who then noticed that Rosie was still hiding, 'unless you mean Rosie here. Rosie.' He ushered Rosie from behind him with a branch. 'Say hello, Rosie.'

Rosie flapped her flaps at Frida.

Okay, not blurred vision then. Had to be a trick of sorts? Perhaps this Leif was some kind of stage magician or puppeteer. She couldn't see any strings. Still, if that's the way he wanted to play it. 'Nice trick,' said Frida. 'Now how about if Leif shows himself?'

A puzzled Leif looked at Rosie and then back at Frida. What was wrong with the girl? '*Here*,' he said, suddenly leaning forward. He moved his branches well away from his face as he did so that she could get a better look at his knotty face. It ended up within a couple of feet of Frida's; a lot closer than he had meant.

Some people might have screamed, but not Frida; her mouth had dropped open much too far to be able to do that. She did some more backing up. 'Wha-what are you?' she said, when she finally found her voice.

'I'm a wood elf,' said Leif proudly. He straightened up. 'And Rosie here is a wood nymph.' Rosie did some flapping.

Course you are, thought Frida. She must be dreaming. That was it, the knock on the head; it explained it all. She was still unconscious; had to be. But everything seemed so real. She could feel a slight breeze on her skin. She could definitely feel the lump on her head. Frida gave it a tentative touch. 'Ouch.' Her shoulders suddenly slumped. She thought about the people back at the village; the giant. Oh good grief, she thought, what was going on?

'But I'm a tree at the moment,' said Leif, oblivious to the girl's sudden paleness. Rosie flapped. 'Oh, and Rosie is, well, I suspect you can see what she is yourself.'

Frida could, but that didn't mean she believed it. She suddenly squeezed her eyes tightly shut and then opened them again. Nope, they were still there. A walking table and a smiling, talking tree, called Leif. And why not? Most of everything she had seen so far on her mission had been weird. A walking table and a talking tree fitted right in. Frida felt dizzier than before so she squeezed her eyes shut again; it hadn't got rid of the weirdness, but it might help ease the sickly feeling she was having. It did, in a way, but this time her eyes were closed for a little bit longer than she had been expecting.

When Frida came round for the third time she found a concerned tree looking down at her, its knotty brow knitted. It asked her if she was all right, and you know what, when she thought about it, as she looked up into those knotty eyes, apart from the lump on her head, she decided she was. She felt strangely serene considering everything. Should she be worried about that? Not if it got her through the day. She had always been one for “seeing is believing”, so why go against her own advice now. It wasn’t as though she had a choice. It was what it was, time to go with the flow, and she had a mission to complete. And gosh darn it she was going to do just that. Frida had awakened with a new determination. And the first thing she was going to do was ask those questions she had promised herself she would ask.

Rosie flapped her flaps. Leif frowned. ‘You don’t know where you are?’ he said.

‘No,’ said Frida. She had decided when she left the village that she was no longer in any county she had heard of. She had briefly flirted with the idea that she had somehow got to Ireland (how, she didn’t have the faintest), and the village was nothing but a film set. She had heard that they do a lot of films there recently. But the giant had looked too real, and now, as she talked to a tree, that idea was blown well out of the water. Frida told Leif all this and, after a moment or two of wavering on whether she should do or not, she told him everything that had happened to her thus far, including her mission.

‘Wow,’ said Leif. Rosie flapped her flaps. ‘She says, double wow.’

‘Wow indeed,’ said Frida.

‘And you really don’t know where you are?’

‘All hush-hush,’ said Frida.

‘The Otherside,’ said Leif.

‘The other side?’

Leif explained. He then told her what was happening on the Otherside, why it was happening, where it was, the land she was in, and why she had to change her mission from following Power to finding Danrite before Power did. He also told why he thought the Font was the voice on her phone, and why she had sent her sidekick Basil with the news of the change of mission instead of just phoning her.

‘Drama?’ said Frida.

‘She loves it so I’ve heard,’ said Leif.

So now Frida knew everything or as much as she needed to. It was time to move; find this Danrite character and save him from the clutches of Mister Power.

'So,' said Frida, carefully touching the lump on her head. It had gone down quite a bit, but was still pretty sore. 'Where is this Danrite?'

'There,' said Leif, pointing a branch at the distant forest Frida had noticed. 'In there.'

CHAPTER 58

The trees were closing in on him, slowly, but with purpose.

A trapped Jose had so far held them at bay with the odd cock of the leg, but all it had really done was to cause some hesitation amongst the trees and the occasional step back. Still they came, relentless, and in a few moments they would be on him.

'Ay caramba!' wailed Jose, as his hopeless situation pressed about him. 'It is as if my fondest dream turns into my worst of nightmares.'

And then they stopped. Dead, just like that. Suddenly, for no reason, as if the whole thing had just been a nightmare. Not waiting for an answer, Jose saw his chance to escape and took it. He bounded between the two nearest trees, into an open space, landed on all fours, spun round to make sure they were still not moving, sniffed the air, whined, and bounded back to where he had just come from.

There, in the undergrowth, between the two trees that just earlier were threatening to do something tree to him, Jose took refuge, and peeped. Something large had entered the Enchanted Forest. It looked bad. It looked ugly. It was sniffing the air where Jose had just stood.

Mister Power had finally caught up with Hewie, a dirt and grass spattered Ergo, and Rogi. He had done it in his own time. There had been no need to rush; all he had to do was follow the furrow Hewie had made with Ergo and Rogi. And when he had caught up, he demanded to know why they were where they now were, standing in front of the largest forest he had ever seen, instead of following the boy Danrite into the next land. The simple answer was the boy hadn't gone into the next land; he had come to this forest; gone into the forest. Hewie's nose had said so. And now they were in the forest as well. Even though Rogi had explained that the forest was the Enchanted Forest, and how dangerous it was. But the boy had gone in, and therefore so would they.

'What is it?' said Mister Power, wondering why they had suddenly stopped as soon as they had stepped inside the Enchanted Forest.

'It's Hewie, sir, he smells something,' said Rogi.

'The boy?'

'Hard to say, sir, but his hackles are up.'

'What does that mean?' said Mister Power, not familiar with the word.

'I'd say he doesn't like something he smells, sir,' said Rogi.

Mister Power took a tentative sniff and instantly wrinkled his nose. He could sympathise with the beast. What was that smell? But idle sniffing was getting them nowhere. 'Find out what it is he doesn't like.'

Rogi went to investigate. After a moment or two he returned.

'Well?' said Mister Power.

'It's puddles, sir.'

'Puddles?' said Mister Power, frowning.

'There are lots of them on the ground, sir, and he won't go near them, or past them,' said Rogi, shrugging. 'He goes cross-eyed every time he tries.'

Mister Power pushed past Rogi to see for himself what the fuss was all about. Rogi was right; there was a puddle for nearly every tree in sight. Mister Power reluctantly sniffed at them, and then wished he hadn't. 'What is that?' he spluttered, between coughs.

Rogi immediately went to one of the puddles, knelt down beside it, and stuck a finger in it. He then sniffed the finger, and then licked it. Mister Power looked as if he were about to share his breakfast. 'Chihuahua urine, sir,' said Rogi, standing up, 'and pretty powerful too in such concentrations.'

'Dog wee?' said Mister Power, managing to contain his porridge.

'Magical dog wee, sir,' said Rogi.

'Magical?' said Mister Power, not liking the sound of that. 'Is it dangerous?' He started to rub his nose.

'Not as such, sir,' said Rogi, 'but Hewie there has a pretty sensitive snout. If it was from an ordinary chihuahua I doubt there would be a problem. This is stronger; it's affecting his senses you see.'

Mister Power could understand that, it had made his eyes water, but smell or no smell, the longer they idled the further the boy got from his clutches. He then had an idea. 'What about the whistle?' he said, thinking if it got the creature out of a cave, perhaps it could get him over some puddles.

'Good idea, sir,' said Rogi. He shook his head. 'Why didn't I think of that?' He took the whistle from his pocket and blew on it.

Because you're extinction fodder and I'm not, thought Mister Power rather cruelly. He watched Hewie starting to react to the whistle.

'I believe it's working, sir,' said Rogi, as Hewie rose onto his back legs.

'Keep at it then,' said Mister Power, eager to get on.

Rogi put the whistle back to his lips and, carefully stepping across the puddles (he was wearing Gucci shoes), started to lead the entranced Hewie deeper into the Enchanted Forest and away from the smell.

Ergo, still holding the lead, but now free of most of the dirt and grass, followed. Mister Power held his nose and did likewise.

Phew, thought Jose as Mister Power and his cannon fodder disappeared from sight, that was a close one. And talking of close ones, Jose quickly bounded back between the gap and away from the trees that had been closing in on him. This time they would not trap Jose so easily.

But now in the open, Jose was in a quandary as to what to do next. He had recognised the two humungous beings that had entered the forest with the large ugly creature, from the skirmish at Danrite's house. They were Mister Power's henchmen. And from what he had overheard in his hidey hole, the man in the sharp suit was the main man himself, Mister Power. Ay caramba! What was he doing here? Jose started to walk, in a circle. He had to warn the others. But how, he didn't have the faintest idea where they were? He had to think. Keep a wary eye on the trees, and think. He continued with his walk in a circle, but now with his other eye watching his tail. He picked up pace. He started to chase his tail. It helped him think. Mostly about catching his tail, but it was something.

CHAPTER 59

The journey to the king of the small fellows akin to the garden variety wasn't a particularly long one, but it had proved to be fairly precarious for the blindfolded captives. Danrite had managed to trip over twice, and Salor three times, but they finally arrived.

The blindfolds were removed. Salor, Danrite and Twinkle blinked, while Vlad rubbed at thin air. Sid, the only one who hadn't had to wear one, looked puzzled. A voice demanded their attention. It was the king of the small fellows akin to the garden variety.

The king was sat on a throne in the shape of a toadstool; he was a traditionalist. He shifted as he sat, as if uneasy. He was uneasy. What he was going to demand was outrageous. It was a thing to be frowned upon most vigorously. It was a bad thing he wanted to do, but he had his people to think of. He pointed at Sid. 'I want the unicorn,' he said.

It was an outrageous demand. Salor frowned at the king most vigorously. This was bad. 'Never!' said Salor.

'You have no choice,' said the king, looking most uncomfortable, as he waved his guard forward.

'You will have to come through me,' said Salor, wielding his staff.

'Magic,' said the king, 'I think not.' The king's guards' hands went to their dibbers.

'I still possess enough to stop you,' said Salor, hoping it was true.

'Again I think not,' said the king. 'Belief wanes in you wizard?' Salor looked puzzled by the king's words. 'It's going, magic, and with it myth and make-believe.' The king got to his feet. 'Imagination is dying, Salor, and with it belief in your kind; all your kinds.'

'Our kind?' said a bemused Salor. 'Aren't you our kind as well?'

The king smiled. 'Yes, but think about it, we are everywhere in the human world, gardens, rockeries, beside ponds. The humans will not be able to forget about us, so we will survive.'

'So why have you stopped us?' said Twinkle.

The king's smile dropped. 'Because we need insurance,' he said grimly.

'Insurance?' said Salor. 'For what?'

'Against the memories of humans,' said the king, raising his hand.

'I don't…' But then Salor did, understand. 'You think there's a chance that your survival will be set in stone.' Set in stone as of that of the garden gnome.

'Precisely,' said the king.

'But what has Sid got to do with it?'

The king's hand hovered, but like all baddies he liked to talk, so it stayed where it was for the moment. 'The alicorn,' said the king. The alicorn is the name for the unicorn's horn; the purest of magic and the most powerful of all things magical.

'But he hasn't-'

'So I see,' said the king, 'but no matter.'

'Then I don't understand,' said Salor. What use was Sid to the gnomes if he no longer had his alicorn? Unless…

'Then better we discuss it no further.'

'His blood!' roared Salor. 'You want his blood?!' It was said that unicorn's blood was but second only to the alicorn in magical force. Sid whinnied in dismay. 'You fool, if we don't save magic none will exist, not even Sid's.'

But the king's mind was set, and he would not be swayed. He let his arm fall and the small fellows akin to the garden variety stepped forward.

CHAPTER 60

The Font flicked from one image to another. What *was* going on? Perhaps Rosemary would throw some light on the situation when he got back from the errand she had sent him on? Until then the Font could only second guess; something she wasn't used to, or happy about.

Basil eventually made an appearance, if it was somewhat dishevelled.

'About time,' muttered the Font. 'Well?'

Basil had a little mumble to himself.

'What was that?' said the Font, not quite catching what he had said; luckily for him. 'Speak up.'

'I said, that if you'd seen fit to give me a long range talky-walkie, I could have told you what I'd found out ages ago.'

'I've told you before, they're too expensive. Now, what news have you got for me?'

Basil sighed deeply. No, "how are you?". She must have seen his landing on Leif. No, "well done.". He might have had the "luxury" of a flight out there, (which reminded him, the catapult needed new elastic) but he had had to scurry back under his own steam, and she knew how he suffered with his bunions. But oh no, no "how are your feet?". No nothing, but he told the Font all he had found out anyway.

'The nightmares?' said an astounded Font. She didn't know what to make of that.

'Yes, your Fontness,' said Basil, knowing full well she hated to be called that.

But the Font didn't appear to notice, she was much too busy thinking. She came to a conclusion; no harm had been done. The nightmares had poked their noses in, but at least for the good. Danrite had been given a helping hand and she wasn't going to complain about that. And the girl Frida wasn't far behind. But was that enough? They still needed to find the centre and Mister Power was lurking somewhere between them in the forest. Perhaps more help was needed. She decided it was and she knew just the person; Sage, or was that Thyme? Anyhoo. 'Rosemary, I have another little job for you.'

CHAPTER 61

Jose had no idea how long he had been thinking. All he knew was that he was growing tired, and that annoying tail of his just wouldn't stop wagging. Just one more snap at it. Just one more thought. But he couldn't. He was much too tired to think. Much too tired to catch his tail. It had won again. But one of these days, he was sure, one of these…

On entering the forest Frida found it wasn't as dark as she had been expecting it to be, but it was a whole lot smellier. She then found something else she hadn't been expecting.

In the middle of a small clearing was a small dog. Frida thought it looked like a chihuahua. She stepped closer. It was a chihuahua and it was frantically running in circles, chasing its tail. It looked tired, as if at any moment it would suddenly stop and keel over sideways. A moment later it did just that.

Frida ran to the dog-tired dog. As she did she wondered where it had come from. Maybe it was lost. She looked at the chihuahua's collar, thinking she might find a name and address tag, but then thought better of it; the collar was studded with nasty looking spikes. No way was she going anywhere near them. If it was lost it would have to stay lost. But she couldn't just leave it there, lying on the ground as it was; even if it was a few currents short of a bun; which it had to be, running around as it had. She decided a drop of water from her flask might help.

'Aaagh!' spluttered Jose, water spraying everywhere. 'Who is it that is drowning me?'

Frida sat back in surprise, but not amazement. How could she ever be amazed again after what she had been through just lately? But surprise, well, that was still hanging on. 'You spoke,' she said, after a second's pause.

Jose snorted water from his nostrils. 'So did you,' he said. He then coughed, spluttered and blinked a couple of times to get a clear look at his assailant. What he saw startled him. He blinked a few more times. He was still startled. He shook his head and blinked again. This time he saw a young lady with short blonde cropped hair. Ay caramba, he thought. I am more tired than I am thinking.

'Are you okay?' said Frida, her initial surprise at finding a talking dog, giving way to concern for the small canine. 'You look as if you've just seen a ghost.' Yeah, she thought, I really am conversing with a dog.

Jose meanwhile had pulled himself together. He stared up at Frida with a look that wasn't quite a glare. 'What it was I was seeing, was my poor little life flashing at my eyes.' He should have been angry with her, trying to drown him like that, but for some reason he couldn't. It was as if he knew her.

'Yeah, sorry, my bad,' said Frida, finding she was slipping into a surprisingly comfortable groove where chatting with dogs was concerned, 'I missed your mouth.'

'It is the thing here that is with tiny white things.' Jose bared his teeth, and the ice was completely broken.

Frida laughed. She couldn't help it. He looked so funny. The little dog looked as if he was giving her a manic grin. 'Sorry, again, I shouldn't have.' She held out a hand. 'My name is Frida.'

Jose stopped his grinning and frowned, he gave Frida a long hard look. Not because she laughed at him, but because he was sure he had seen that laugh before. As he was sure he had seen her before. The frown quickly disappeared though as he struggled to remember where. Thinking was not on the top of his list of favourite things to do right then. He held out a paw. 'My name is Jose.'

'No wa-'

'No, please, do not say it. It is getting old with me,' Jose sighed.

Smiling, Frida got to her feet. 'I can imagine.' She wished she could stay longer and chat with the little chap, not a thing one often gets the chance to do; have a conversation with a dog, but she had a job to do. She brushed a twig from her shorts. 'Well, I better be on my way,' she said. 'Again sorry for nearly drowning you.' She put a hand up and went to step deeper into the forest.

‘Sí, it is okay, I-whoa, where you go?’ said Jose, when he saw where Frida was heading. ‘There, it is dangerous.’ He gave the trees a wary sideways glance.

‘That as well might be the case,’ said Frida, thinking the dog might not be wrong, ‘but I’m looking for someone.’ Ah, she thought, perhaps she shouldn’t have said that. ‘Is it?’ she said quickly, hoping to deflect attention from her slip.

‘Who?’ said Jose, ears pricking, suddenly alert and suspicious. ‘Very,’ he added.

Frida could have bitten her tongue off. ‘No one important,’ she said, not liking the look that had appeared in the chihuahua’s eyes. His teeth were showing. She took a step sideways. Weren’t his teeth smaller than that just now?

Jose wasn’t sure he liked the way the girl was moving, as if trying to get behind him. ‘I too am looking,’ he said, moving so that they remained facing each other, ‘for someone.’

It was Frida’s turn to be suspicious. ‘Who?’ She took another step sideways. Was the chihuahua trying to get behind her?

Should he say? He decided there would be no harm doing so. ‘My friends,’ he said, keeping his cards close to his chest.

Frida stopped her side-stepping. Friends? The tree had mentioned there were others with the Danrite boy, but had not elaborated on who, or what. Could this little dog be one of them? ‘Friends you say?’ she said, cautiously.

‘Sí,’ said Jose, equally cautiously.

We could go on like this forever, thought Frida, cagily going to and fro. But she didn’t have forever; she really had to get moving. If this chihuahua was one of Danrite’s friends, as she now erred on the suspicion that he might be, then that could be handy, even if only for his sharp little teeth. She suspected Jose might be a good one to have beside you in a tight corner; if he wasn’t too busy chasing his tail that is. It was time to make a decision. Had that tree just moved? ‘Do you know someone called Leif?’ she said, gambling. Her hand slowly went to her whip; just in case.

Jose looked shocked. ‘What is it he is saying?’ he said. ‘It is all lying.’ Jose was suddenly an indignant little chihuahua. ‘I am innocent!’

Frida's hand relaxed and slipped past her whip, she smiled. 'Nothing about you,' she said. She thought she saw another tree moving. Trick of the shadows she decided.

'Ay caramba!' groaned Jose, on realising the mistake he had just made. 'I am undone. Vlad, he say Jose would never be a spy. He say they smell me coming, but now I estúpido as well.'

'It's okay,' said Frida, finding herself feeling sorry for the little dog, 'I'm not much of one either. I was the one to slip up first remember, when I mentioned I was looking for someone.'

Jose brightened up. 'Sí, it is so, we are both being no good spies.'

'So, you're one of Danrite's friends?'

'Leif did not mention so?'

'He said Danrite was with friends, but didn't elaborate; nor did I ask I'm afraid,' said Frida, who in her defence, had had rather a lot on her mind at that moment. She gingerly touched her bump, which thankfully had gone down quite a lot, taking most of the pain with it.

'Sí, I am a friend, but I am losing him.' Jose looked sad. He then looked up at Frida. Had he just made another mistake?

'Then we'll find him together,' said Frida, putting Jose's mind at rest. 'I've been sent to protect him by someone called the Font.'

Jose's eyes widened. 'You see her?'

'No, it's what Leif told me.'

'Ah,' said Jose, a little disappointed. As he spoke he saw a tree move, from out the corner of his eye.

Frida noticed as well. 'Did you just see what I think I just saw?' she said, realising that perhaps it hadn't been her imagination before.

'Sí,' said Jose, turning towards the tree. 'It is what they are doing.'

'Perhaps we should get going then,' said Frida, nervously watching as another tree made a slow, but definite movement in their direction, 'I don't think the Enchanted Forest likes uninvited guests.'

'Sí, that is being true,' said Jose, moving beside Frida, 'but I am thinking it is more a Disenchanted Forest that moves towards us.'

'Which way?' she said, looking at the gap Jose had jumped through earlier, when Mister Power had arrived.

'There,' said Jose, his nose pointing towards a wider gap; the one Hewie had taken earlier. The trees had not liked the look of Hewie so perhaps the going would be easier that way; more dangerous, but easier. 'It is the way the man himself went.'

'The man himself?'

'Sí, Mister Power.'

Grief, thought Frida, but there was no point worrying about that now, there were more immediate dangers. 'Shall we?'

'Sí,' said Jose.

Together they ran for the gap.

CHAPTER 62

Mister Power was now certain the trees around him were moving. At first he had thought it was his imagination getting the better of him, but then he remembered he didn't possess one, so therefore the trees had to be moving; especially when Hewie drew close to them. This in mind, and as he didn't like the idea of trees that moved, especially his way, he had decided to stick as close to Hewie as was safe to do so. It was nearly his undoing.

A moment later Hewie suddenly stopped dead. Ergo, taken by surprise by the sudden stop, overbalanced and landed on his bottom. Mister Power, in his eagerness to keep close, but with one eye on the trees, failed to notice in time and, sprawling headlong over the top of Ergo, tried to grab onto something hoping to stop his fall. This he managed to do, but sadly it failed to check his momentum. Worse, the something he had grabbed was Hewie's tail.

There was a howl, a growl, and snarling of the most vicious kind as Hewie turned on Mister Power. Massive jaws, strong enough to snap a tree in two (could be a reason the trees were getting out of his way) snapped shut.

'Aaargh!' screamed Mister Power.

Luckily for Mister Power they didn't snap shut on his arm; instead they clamped onto and smashed to smithereens a thick branch the size of a small tree trunk that Rogi had managed to wedge into Hewie's mouth. If the knotty eyes of the watching trees had been able to, they would have watered. Maybe they had.

'Whoopsie there, sir,' said Rogi. He held Mister Power in one extremely strong hand, as a small child might hold a rag doll, and swung him away to safety. 'If he's anything like his brother El Yograg was, he'll be apt to be a bit playful when he gets his tail tugged.'

'Playful?' said Mister Power, as he landed safely in a patch of moss. 'Are you mad? He nearly took my arm off!'

But Rogi just shook his head in a "boys will be boys" way, and blew on the whistle he had taken from his pocket. The effect was immediate. Hewie stopped his snarling, went glassy eyed, and spat the last of the sawdust from his mouth over a rising Ergo.

'There,' said Rogi, putting the whistle back in his pocket, 'all's well again.'

With his heart rate just about returning to normal, but with his anger rising, Mister Power brushed moss from his backside and demanded to know what had happened to make Hewie stop so suddenly.

The question went from Mister Power, to Rogi, to Ergo, to Hewie, and back again via the same route. It appeared Hewie's senses had been suddenly overwhelmed by a flood of scents all hitting his snout at once, and so many and so strong were they that they had confused him to a sudden dead stop.

Mister Power needed further explanation.

Rogi pointed to the ground a little way ahead from where Hewie was swaying. 'Look there, sir,' he said.

Careful to give Hewie as wide a berth as possible whilst also giving the trees the same respect, Mister Power went to look at whatever it was Rogi was pointing at. He looked. 'What am I looking at?' he said, wondering how he was supposed to see scents.

'Small footprints, sir,' said Rogi.

In his mind Mister Power wanted someone to give him strength. 'I can see that,' he said, 'but what has it got to do with the creature's snout?' He was about to point at Hewie, but then changed his mind. Better safe than sorry.

'They belong to the small fellows akin to the garden variety,' said Rogi, in way of explanation. 'They've got a rather pungent musky smell to them, sir. It causes havoc with noses as sensitive as Hewie's and it's much stronger than chihuahua urine. Through living in damp conditions so the theory goes. They smell a little bit like mushrooms.'

Mister Power took to rubbing his eyes and then pushing his hands through his hair in frustration. 'Who?' he asked.

'Ah,' said Rogi, 'gnomes, sir.'

'Really?' said Mister Power, looking again at the small footprints. 'They really exist?' he said. 'Like those you see in gardens, looking jolly and holding fishing rods?' Mister Power nearly shuddered, he hated jolly-looking things.

Rogi nodded. 'Yes, sir, but these cause more of a nuisance of themselves.'

A mind-boggled Mister Power sniffed. There was a faint smell of mushrooms, but not so you would notice if you weren't sniffing for it. He then noticed something else; several something elses. A few paces from the trampled area of small footprints were larger ones. He went over to them. There were several. He assumed belonging to several of the larger fellows akin to people. He afforded himself a small smile at his little pun, but it was only small and soon faded as he drew Rogi's attention to his find.

Rogi investigated. 'Some could belong to the boy, sir,' he said, 'but there doesn't appear to have been a struggle.'

A meeting perhaps, thought Mister Power. Or perhaps just groups passing like ships in the night? He then frowned. Perhaps a joining of forces? Mister Power didn't like the thought of that. He ordered Rogi to have a scout around to see if the larger footprints had gone off in a different direction.

When Rogi returned he announced he could find no trace of the larger footprints moving away, but had found hoof prints to one side of the larger footprints.

It appeared the two groups had joined forces then, but…'They're on horseback?' said Mister Power, a little alarmed by the idea. How would he catch them if they were on horseback?

'No, sir,' said Rogi, with just the faintest hint of alarm in his eyes, 'not a horse, a unicorn.'

Mister Power's eyes had widened, not so much by the mention of a unicorn, but more by the first hint of fear he had ever seen shown by his muscled minion.

'Should we be worried?' said Mister Power, trying not to be.

'Depends, sir,' said Rogi. 'Depends on how he's being affected, having said that, unicorns are the epitome of goodliness, so we being not so good could be a problem, however he's affected.'

Mister Power stared at Rogi, the creature's mind had changed. He was getting as intelligent as he was handsome; not good, especially as he had been expecting Rogi to start to deteriorate now he was back in his own world. Next thing he'll be questioning why he isn't good; definitely not good. It was time to quickly move on; but where to? The footprints lead away together, but it didn't follow that any belonged to the boy; he still needed the creature's snout.

Thankfully the musk, so strong a few moments ago, had already started to fade; enough for Hewie to once again pick up Danrite's scent. It was faint, but as long as the musk of the gnomes stayed as weak as it was now, it was enough for him to be able to continue tracking the boy, along the track all the hoof and footprints had taken.

CHAPTER 63

Basil was sat in a clearing, which was the centre of the Enchanted Forest, which was the gateway to everywhere, and most importantly to the Font, picking at his bunions. He was also talking to himself.

'Never easy, oh no, not for poor old Basil,' moaned Basil. 'And what's with the Rosemary? Only been in her service for I don't know how many years, and still she can't be bothered to remember my name.' He shook his head, and continued with his picking.

After a little while he looked up at nothing in particular and shook his head again. 'And that's another thing,' he said to himself, 'why hadn't she gone and got the boy Danrite when the time had come? Why all the dilly-dallying?' He continued picking.

A couple of minutes later he decided perhaps it might be a good idea to start doing what the Font had sent him there to do; keep a look out for the Danrite boy and act as his guide. He put his socks and sandals back on and then paused. He got up. He felt under his robe; it was there, his copy of the television programme guide. Dare he? Why not? The Font wouldn't know what the Font couldn't see. It was well-known to him that the Font's seeing machine couldn't see into the Enchanted Forest; there was much too much interference. He sat back down again. What was another ten minutes between disgruntled employee and mean boss? He started to read.

CHAPTER 64

This doesn't look good, thought Danrite, as the small fellows akin to the garden variety advanced menacingly towards him; not good at all. He and the others were slowly backing away, but there was nowhere to go, they were surrounded.

Ground now had to be stood. Salor, with his staff held out before him, faced front. Twinkle, with some nasty-looking, sharp-edged, snowflake-shaped objects which she had produced from somewhere, turned to the right. On the left, Sid pawed the ground and snorted. Behind them, which was where he liked to be when danger came to call, but in this case was also in front, depending from which side one was looking from, was Vlad. He was hissing and baring his fangs (though no one could actually see them), and saying "ah-ha" repeatedly in his Transylvanian accent. Danrite was in the middle. It was where Twinkle had pushed him. He fiddled with the hilt of his sword. He wasn't sure whether to take it out or not. Should he or shouldn't he. If he did, there would be no going back; he would have to use it. But could he? Some hero he was, he thought.

'Wait!' demanded Salor, 'We can talk about this.'

'We can't,' said the king.

'You can't do this.'

'We can,' said the king, stepping forward, 'and we will.'

'Take another step and… and woe betide you,' warned Salor, but the lack of conviction in his voice matched what he was feeling inside; the fear that he no longer possessed enough magic with which to stop the gnomes.

'Enough of this,' snarled the king. 'Get the unicorn, alive or dead!'

Shock reverberated through everyone at the king's words. Even his mens' step faltered a little. But he was their king. He was the law. He was to be obeyed.

Without realising what he was doing, Danrite had taken his sword from its scabbard after the king's words. He stood with it raised. The time for dithering was over. It was time to be that hero. He looked at his friends. Vlad had stopped his hissing and "ah-ha's" and was now crouched as if ready to pounce. Twinkle, her face a picture of determination, held her snowflakes at the ready. Sid was showing his teeth. The sword weighed heavy in Danrite's hand. He looked at Salor. Salor had his staff raised above his head. Danrite wondered what Salor was going to do with it.

'Your last chance,' warned Salor. But the fellows akin to the garden variety kept moving. 'Then you give me no choice.' Salor thumped the end of his staff into the forest floor with all his might.

What followed next could only be likened to standing in the eye of a storm. All was suddenly deathly quiet where Danrite and his friends stood. It was as if the world had suddenly ceased to exist around them. As if time had been suspended. But if magic had been used, there had been no flash. No explosion from unleashed energy. Just silence. Ear-popping silence. Yet magic had been unleashed, and now noise was rushing back into the void it had left. The noises of the forest suddenly filled Danrite's ears again. Noises he hadn't really taken any notice of before; leaves rustling on their branch, the creak of those branches, the breathing of most of his friends. All those sounds were suddenly loud in his ears, as if he were hearing for the first time. And then he saw.

'Blimey,' said Danrite, as he stood and stared.

A low whistle came from Vlad's hood.

'Grief,' said Twinkle, her snowflakes still poised for throwing.

Sid neighed nervously.

None could believe what they were seeing.

On the ground, split asunder, was Salor's staff. He lay beside it, face up and motionless. Surrounding him and everyone else for that matter, were dozens of small grey statues akin to the small fellows of the garden variety, but even more akin now. But though none were holding fishing rods, or smiling, a bit of paint here and there and Bob's your uncle, a whole army of garden novelties just waiting for delivery to the nearest garden centre.

'What the fang just happened?' said Vlad, finding his voice after a second or two of gaping disbelief.

‘He… he used it,’ said Twinkle.

‘Oh, gosh,’ said Vlad.

Sid meanwhile had wandered over to where Salor lay and gently nuzzled him, Salor didn’t move.

Sheathing his sword, Danrite stumbled forward amongst the small statues and stood beside Sid. He stared at Salor. He didn’t look good. Danrite spoke. ‘What did he do?’ he asked, his voice nothing more than a whisper.

‘He used up the last of his magic,’ said Twinkle, her death snowflakes now safely tucked away.

‘Is… is he…’ Danrite couldn’t bring himself to say out loud the terrible thing he was thinking.

‘No,’ said Twinkle.

‘But?’

She turned to Danrite and smiled. ‘It was his magic. Your own can’t hurt you. Well, not much; a singe here and there perhaps, maybe a bruise. A broken leg has been heard of, but no, not what you were thinking.’ She looked at Salor and gave his leg a kick. He groaned.

‘Twinkle!’ said Danrite, appalled by her kicking a defenceless wizard.

‘He’ll be all right, just magic-less, that’s all,’ said Twinkle, giving Salor another prod of her toe. ‘Dramatic effect, that’s all. Wizards love it.’ She prodded again.

‘Okay-okay,’ said Salor, eyes flicking open. ‘Less of the boot, I get the message.’ He had rather enjoyed all the attention. He raised his head. ‘Did it work?’ he said, surveying what he could see of the immediate area around him.

‘Depends on what it was you were trying to do,’ said Twinkle, giving Salor a hand up.

‘Stop them in their tiny little tracks,’ said Salor, his knees creaking.

‘Well you certainly did that.’

‘Oh,’ said Salor, as he caught his first glimpse of what he had done. ‘Not quite what I’d had in mind, but hey-ho.’ He had been thinking more along the lines of rooting the gnomes’ feet to the ground. He then saw what was left of his staff. ‘Oh dear,’ he said, ‘that was my best one.’ He bent down and inspected the crystal that had been on the end of it. It was dark; spent. No good to anyone. The magic was gone. Salor's face clouded over, but he was determined he wasn't going to cry. Even though the advert said the mascara he was wearing wouldn't run, he wasn't about to test it; not after the day he was having. Sad of face he picked the crystal up and placed it in one of his numerous pockets.

'What now?' said Vlad, stepping among the stone gnomes.

'We go on,' said Twinkle, looking at a dejected Salor. 'Salor?'

'Er… yes?' said a distracted Salor.

'I said we should get going?'

Salor blinked as if nudged from a daydream. 'Yes, yes, of course.'

'But which way?' said Danrite. They had been brought before the king blindfolded, but it wasn't hard to see, by the tracks that they had left, which way they had come. But did they need to go back that way?

Salor turned to Sid and patted his nose. 'Which way old friend?'

Sid raised his head and then pawed the ground to his left, away from where they had come.

'That way it is then,' said Salor.

After a quick check to make sure no harm had come to anybody, they continued their quest to find the Font; Sid leading the way again. Sadly, as he passed the king of the small fellows akin to the garden variety, one of Sid's hooves accidently caught the king, knocking him some twenty feet through the air into a tree, smashing the gnome to pieces. Clumsy Sid, thought Sid.

CHAPTER 65

The Font was sat, thumb-twiddling. There was nothing more she could do but wait. She changed channel on the seeing machine to see if Basil was in place. The Font knew that Basil couldn't understand why she hadn't just gone and got Danrite when he was born, but she had her reasons; reasons that held little secrets. All of which would be revealed when she was ready to reveal them. The screen changed and the scene that appeared made the Font shake her head in despair.

Basil was sat down reading that magazine of his. And this was why, thought the Font, I keep little secrets; you just couldn't trust anyone these days. The Font had fed and purposely fanned the flames under the rumour she had put about that the seeing machine couldn't see into the Enchanted Forest because its magic caused interference to the machine, but it was not true. On the contrary, the magic within the forest actually strengthened the signal to the seeing machine. So much so that she saw everything in the forest in high definition. The speaking machine on the other hand really didn't work, if it had, she would have been using it that very second to give Basil a right royal ear-bashing.

'You, Rosemary my boy, are in big trouble when you get back here,' said the Font to Basil's image. But Basil in truth wasn't the highest thing on the Font's list at that moment, she flicked the remote and the picture on the screen changed again.

What she saw caused her to frown. She couldn't remember there being ornamental gnomes in the forest. Real ones, yes; those that were akin to the garden variety, but not stone ones. The Font suddenly had a bad feeling in her stomach. What was going on?

CHAPTER 66

Back in her castle the Font had just changed channels again, so just missed out on seeing what happened next in the little clearing inhabited by little stone statues.

The yell from Mister Power was a mixture of surprise and pain. The surprise was from suddenly stumbling upon a multitude of little stone statues, and the pain because of stumbling into one of them with his shin.

'You all right there, sir?' said Rogi, reaching a supporting hand.

'What? Yes-yes,' said Mister Power, hopping on the spot, a grimace on his face. He rather fancied he may have broken something. He swotted Rogi's hand away. Then hopped into another statue, overbalanced and fell over.

'Magic I'd say, sir,' said Rogi, stabbing the toe of his shoe at pieces of stone that had once been the king of the little things akin to the garden variety. He helped Mister Power to his feet.

'Magic?' said Mister Power, not liking the sound of that. He shrugged himself free of Rogi's helping hand, but only when he was safely upright.

'Yes, sir,' said Rogi, kneeling to inspect the pieces of the king. He picked up what had once been the king's nose, 'and powerful stuff too; powerful enough to turn a whole tribe of gnomes into stone, sir.'

Mister Power stopped rubbing his shin as he realised what Rogi was saying. He stared at the stone gnomes. 'These are the same ones whose smell caused the creature's snout to overheat?'

'I'd say so, sir,' said Rogi.

Magic strong enough to turn creatures to stone; something else Mister Power didn't like the sound of. Sounded as if magic wasn't as dead as he hoped it was. But as he wondered what it all meant, his train of thought was interrupted by Rogi drawing his attention to something else on the ground.

'Look, sir,' said Rogi, sounding rather excited.

Mister Power looked. Rogi was now kneeling beside what appeared to be a length of burnt wood; two pieces of burnt wood. 'Something I should be excited about?' said Mister Power, doubtfully.

'The remains of a wizard's staff, sir,' said Rogi, standing. 'I believe it to be Salor's, sir. He may have used it to cause this.' He pointed at the gnomes.

At the mention of Salor's name, Mister Power's interest in the pieces of wood suddenly increased. So he *is* with the boy, thought Mister Power, who hadn't been totally certain up until now, that he had been. This meant the other footprints must belong to some of Salor's little helpers. How many that might be, he didn't know; but not many and he wasn't really bothered by their presence anyway, they didn't matter, from what he had heard they were more a liability than a help. Apart from the unicorn that was; he was an unknown quantity, but what did matter though was Salor's staff, or more to the point, its destruction. A wizard without his staff meant a wizard without power; or at least one with a lot less than he had before. The thought pleased him. He went to pick a piece up.

'I wouldn't do that, sir,' warned Rogi, 'there could still be magic lingering.'

Mister Power, a sudden vision of fingers turning to stone, quickly backed off.

'Boy close,' said Ergo, out of the blue, causing Mister Power and Rogi's heads to turn. But if they had been half expecting to see Danrite standing amongst them, they were disappointed. What they saw was Hewie pulling on his leash for all his worth, his snout hard to the ground. 'He go this way.'

Stone gnomes and broken wizard's staffs were suddenly forgotten. The boy was close. 'Then what are you waiting for?' said Mister Power, eagerly. 'Seek him.'

CHAPTER 67

'You thinking what I'm thinking?' said Frida, as she and Jose inspected the multitude of footprints they had just come across.

'Maybe,' said Jose, looking up at her, 'if it is needing the cocking of the leg against a tree that you are thinking.'

'Uuuugh,' said Frida, disgusted at the thought. 'No.'

'Then I am not.'

Frida let the thought drift from her mind then told Jose what it was she was thinking. 'I think someone may have been ambushed by pygmies.' She pointed at the small footprints.

'Pygmies?' said Jose. 'What is this pygmies?'

'Small people,' Frida explained, 'they live in forests, well, jungles really.'

'Sí, small fellows,' agreed Jose, 'but not made by these pygmies you speak of. The footprints they are made by the small fellows akin to the garden variety. I smell them.' Jose took a sniff at them which caused his eyes to cross.

'Who?' said Frida.

'Gnomes,' said Jose, eyes returning to normal. Thankfully the smell was now barely noticeable, just a faint smell of mushrooms lingered, but still strong enough to have some effect on the owners of sensitive noses.

'Gnomes!' said Frida. 'Like the ones back home in the garden?'

'Sí,' said Jose, 'but these are not having the fishing rods.' Jose had met with the small fellows of the garden variety before, both kinds; the flesh and blood ones and the stone ones. 'And are not being as friendly.'

Frida took in what Jose was saying and it then occurred to her that pygmies might not leave prints made by small hobnail boots. Gnomes, she thought, who knew. But it was as good an explanation as any in this mixed up world she had walked into. She now noticed the hoof prints. Jose had filled her in on who was keeping Danrite company, which meant he had surely been here, but at the same time as when the gnomes had appeared? And that went for Mister Power as well. Had they all converged at the same time? Perhaps the gnomes were working for him? And then again, perhaps the meeting of the footprints was merely coincidence; paths crossing paths. There was only one way to tell. Frida had a quick scout about.

'Nope,' said Frida, when she had finished scouting, 'no more tracks. They all lead off together.' But were they together?

'Then we follow,' said Jose.

'Looks like,' said Frida. She just hoped she wasn't too late to offer Danrite her protection.

They followed the trail, along the way managing to work out who some of the prints belonged to. The hoof prints, Sid. The big, wide, weird ones which left claw marks they suspected belonged to the creature Mister Power had with him. Then there was the size fifteen and sixteens that had to be those of Rogi and Ergo. The ones that were slightly bigger than the gnomes' prints, Jose said, belonged to the fairy Twinkle. Some fairy, Frida had thought, as she noticed how deep the prints were stamped into the ground; almost as deep as Rogi's. They couldn't distinguish the footprints of Salor and Mister Power however. And when Frida had asked Jose about Vlad, he had explained that Vlad didn't walk so much as glide, which meant he didn't leave any footprints. They had been unable to tell if anyone else was with the group. But now they had come to an abrupt stop.

'Ay caramba!' exclaimed Jose, suddenly.

'Flipping 'eck!' said Frida, a microsecond later.

They had ambled into the clearing that was filled with small statues.

'Gnomes,' said Frida, amazed to see so many in one place. But her amazement disappeared as she soon realised these weren't like the ornamental ones back home. For one, they all had such angry faces; nothing jolly-looking about these at all. And for two, they were all holding nasty-looking stone knives with funny handles. She had never seen a dibber before. She looked to Jose; perhaps he had an explanation. But his attention was on something else. Carefully sidestepping the gnomes, Frida went over to see what it was that was interesting him so.

‘It is Salor’s,’ said Jose, as Frida approached. ‘It is broken.’ He looked as worried as a chihuahua could.

‘The singed sticks?’

‘Sí,’ said Jose, ‘it is his magic.’

Frida didn’t understand a lot regarding the world she now inhabited, but from the look on Jose’s face, the burnt sticks meant something and it wasn’t something good. ‘I don’t understand,’ she said, wondering how a couple of sticks could be magical. Unless they were wands; but they looked too big and ragged for that. Or some kind of divining sticks; but weren’t they used for finding water; nothing magical there.

‘It is the remainings of Salor’s staff,’ said Jose.

Frida knelt down to get a better look. Now closer, she could see that the two pieces had indeed once been one. A wizard’s staff, just like the ones she recalled seeing in films and books from her childhood; how cool was that? She remembered they always seemed to have lightening sprouting from an orb on top of it. That would explain the charred remains, she supposed, which wasn’t so cool. She looked to see if she could see the orb, but she couldn’t. If that was really the remains of Salor’s staff, and it had an orb, then she doubted it would be in one piece either; probably disintegrated or the like. ‘Any idea what could have happened to it?’ she asked.

‘Magic,’ said Jose, turning away. ‘Perhaps it is used on them.’

Frida looked to see what Jose had turned to look at. ‘The gnomes?’

‘Sí,’ said Jose, ‘and I am also thinking that we will be finding no more of the small footprints.’

The frown on Frida’s face lasted only a second as she realised what Jose meant. Her eyes grew wide. ‘The footprints we were following belonged to these?’

‘Sí,’ said Jose.

‘We should go,’ said Frida.

‘Sí,’ said Jose.

CHAPTER 68

'Ooh,' said Basil, as he read a juicy bit about one of the daily soaps, 'I didn't know that.'

CHAPTER 69

The Font flicked to another channel. ‘Bah!’ she said, when she saw that Basil was still reading his television guide. ‘I don’t know why I pay you?’ And a fair question it would have been too, if she actually paid him.

CHAPTER 70

Sid was angry. Who could blame him? Being wanted dead or alive for your blood would make anyone in that situation at the very least a little perturbed. But Sid was angry, very angry, and determined. He was going to get everyone safely to the Font, and woe betide anyone who got in his way. This though was not the normal way for Sid to behave. Generally he was a placid chap, a happy go lucky sort of character, one who liked a little horsing about now and again. But angry does that to you sometimes.

'Is he all right?' said Twinkle, as Sid lashed out at a tree root that had ventured too close for his liking.

'I think so,' said Salor, 'but I have to admit I have never seen him like this before.'

'The thing with the gnomes?'

'I'd think so.'

Behind them, Danrite and Vlad were also discussing Sid's behaviour, and the "battle" they had just been involved in.

'Had my sword out,' said Danrite.

'Yes, I saw,' said Vlad. 'Could have taken them.'

'Good hissing by the way.'

'Makes them think.'

'Is he okay?'

Vlad gave this thought and then shrugged. 'Suppose so, but I've never seen him like this.'

'Glad he's on our side.'

'Too true.'

Up ahead Sid came to a sudden halt, lifted his head high, and let loose the loudest whinny any human, beast, or magical being had ever heard. It was the battle cry of the unicorn.

CHAPTER 71

The blood went cold in Mister Power's veins; proving to the contrary those that thought him to be a constantly cold-blooded creature. 'What in all that's wrong with the world was that?' he said in a hushed voice. Even the relentless Hewie had stopped in his tracks at the terrible sound that was now echoing its way to the farthest reaches of the forest.

'That I believe, sir,' said Rogi, warily glancing at their surroundings, 'was the battle cry of the unicorn.'

'Battle cry?' said Mister Power. 'Good grief. Do you think it's the one with the boy?' He wondered if the cry was aimed their way, and if it was, would Hewie be able to stop a battle-ready unicorn. Mister Power grudgingly moved a tad closer to Rogi.

'I couldn't say for sure, sir,' said Rogi, 'it is the Enchanted Forest after all; there could be any number of unicorns in here.' But before Mister Power could take heart from Rogi's words, his next ones chilled his already cold blood further. 'But as the noise came from directly in front of us, sir, and down the track we are currently following, I'd say there's a good chance it may well be that very one, sir.'

CHAPTER 72

So engrossed was he by the latest goings on in the world of television soaps, Basil, at the sound of Sid's battle cry, very nearly managed a somersault from a seated position.

He gingerly got to his feet, dusted twigs and dirt from his white robe, and rubbing the back of his neck, as that is what he had landed on, that and his television guide, Basil went to the edge of the clearing and faced the direction the cry had come from.

'About time,' he muttered.

Basil wandered back to where he had been sitting to retrieve his television guide. It looked the worse for wear as it *had* managed a somersault, two in fact, before finishing under a bouncing Basil. He picked it up and uttered a mild curse as he tried to flatten the pages. It was to no avail. Shaking his head, Basil turned back the way he had come and waved a hand.

CHAPTER 73

Frida's blood had also run cold at the sound of Sid's battle cry, but not as cold as Mister Power's had; no one's blood could get as cold as his. The main reason was she felt fear for what might be happening ahead, unlike Mister Power who only had felt fear for his own safety.

'What the heck was that?' said Frida, abruptly coming to a halt.

'Sid,' said Jose, from between her feet.

'The unicorn?'

'It is the cry of his battle,' said Jose, the fur on his back rising.

'Oh no.' Frida suddenly had a bad feeling run through her. In her mind's eye a battle was raging up ahead. 'Quickly,' she urged, 'we have to get to Danrite.' But was she already too late?

CHAPTER 74

Glued to the seeing machine, the Font watched events unfold. All was roughly going to plan; a few hiccups, the timing was slightly out, the route not the one she had planned, but they were still in one piece.

The time was nigh. The Font pressed a button on her remote control. She rose from her chair and left the room; the characters in the scene on the seeing machine paused live; literally. The characters not on the screen, but playing their part also paused live. It was better to leave them like that while she set the final scene. The Font wanted nothing to go wrong while she was away.

The Font entered a large hall, large enough for the final scene. All was set. No, something was missing. The Font entered a small room adjoining the hall and returned carrying a bucket, a cardboard bucket, like the ones cinemas fill with popcorn. This one was filled with popcorn. The Font placed it on a small table beside a chair, large enough to be called a throne. The Font paused. She couldn't resist. The Font took a handful of popcorn and put some in her mouth.

Munching happily the Font returned to the seeing machine room, sat, and resumed the action on the screen.

CHAPTER 75

Shocked, stunned, and a little bit in the way of frightened witless because of the unexpectedness of it, the ones in the group that weren't Sid or Salor had instantly huddled together in a defensive triangle. Salor was lying on the ground yet again but, to be fair, he had been standing beside Sid when he had let rip his near earth-shattering call.

The triangle now broke apart as no imminent danger had presented itself and hurried to Salor's aid. Salor was now sitting, shocked, stunned, a little bit frightened witless, and for the moment totally deaf in his right ear and slightly deaf in his left.

'You okay?' said Twinkle, the first to reach him.

'WHAT?' said Salor, cupping his right ear with his hand.

'I asked you if you are okay,' said Twinkle, trying again. 'Are you?'

'ER?' said Salor.

'Never mind,' said Twinkle. She left him with Danrite and Vlad and went to speak with Sid. She knew a unicorn's battle cry when she heard it, and had explained it to Danrite, but she now wanted to know why Sid had made the noise when there wasn't any obvious danger in sight.

Sid turned his head towards her as she approached. 'What is it Sid?' Twinkle asked. 'What did you see?'

He had seen nothing. But he had felt the centre of the Enchanted Forest was now very close. Close enough for his primal instincts to take over and give a warning. The call was not only a battle cry, but also to tell those who might be close by that he was near.

Twinkle frowned and looked, she could see nothing. There was nothing but trees surrounding them. Nothing but the forest and…

CHAPTER 76

'There,' said Rogi.

'Where?' said Mister Power.

'Straight ahead,' said Rogi.

'Ah-ha!' said Mister Power.

'Where?' said Frida.

'There,' said Jose.'

'Straight ahead?' said Frida.

'Sí,' said Jose.

'Ah-ha!' said the Font. And, 'Yes!'

Relief was what Mister Power felt when nothing had come charging at him from the trees. Then apprehension as he had cautiously continued his pursuit of the boy, Danrite. And when Rogi pointed out that their quarry was at last in sight, the feeling was sheer delight; sheer evil delight.

There had been no sign of battle; that was good. The noise may not have come from the unicorn with the boy. Mister Power looked and saw no danger. The boy was slightly away and behind the others; he was just waiting to be captured. And if there was danger, his cannon fodder minions and Hewie could take care of that. This was the moment he had been waiting for.

Frida hadn't seen Mister Power at first, and if Jose had not warned her, she may well have run smack bang into the back of him. She quickly crouched down and hid from sight.

'There,' said Jose, in an excited whisper, 'beyond the bad man, it is Danrite.'

Frida craned her neck to look past Mister Power and his gang, but she couldn't see. She moved a little to one side, being careful not to give herself away as she did, and looked again. She saw a horse, a huge white horse, and people, three of them, dressed in what appeared to be fancy dress. Her minded returned to the village and its occupants for a second. She shook her head to clear it. There was also a cloak that looked as if it was hovering in mid-air. She took that to be Vlad; Jose had explained who and what his friends were along the way.

'Wearing the Roman stuff?' said Frida, wondering why. Jose had failed to mention that little piece of information. Not, she supposed, that it mattered; not here.

'Sí,' said Jose.

'Who the flipping heck is that?' said Twinkle, as she noticed a small man in a white robe waving at them from a clearing she had not noticed before.

'Beats me,' said Vlad.

'Perhaps we should see what he wants,' said Danrite.

Salor said nothing as he hadn't noticed the little man, or heard the others talking about him. He was busy staring straight upwards while clamping his hands over his ears, again and again, as he tried to get his hearing back.

'Could be a trap,' said Twinkle.

But Sid had other ideas and set off in the direction of the small man at the trot.

'Ay up,' said Vlad, which was difficult to say with his Transylvanian accent, 'I think Sid's made our mind up for us.'

'Grief,' said Twinkle, setting off after him. 'Come on.' She grabbed the shell-shocked Salor as she went. Vlad and Danrite followed in her wake.

'Where are they going?' said Mister Power, as the moment he had been waiting for suddenly took a turn for the worse.

'Someone waved at them,' said Rogi, his eyesight as keen as his looks were handsome.

'Who?' said Mister Power, peering into the distance. He now saw the little man in white. Who was he? What did it mean? 'Do something,' ordered Mister Power, as he saw his opportunity disappearing.

‘What goes on?’ said Jose, his view now obscured by the urgent movement of Mister Power and his minions ahead of him.

Frida gripped her whip. ‘I think Mister Power’s making his move.’ She got to her feet. ‘Come on.’

Jose, his teeth surely larger than they were a moment ago, fell in by her side.

Basil’s wave of his hand had released the barrier of invisibility that surrounded the centre of the Enchanted Forest, hiding it from prying eyes. Not all that sort the short cut found it; the Font saw to that. Basil had then used that same hand to wave at Danrite and his friends to beckon them forward.

As he watched the unicorn trot his way, he wondered if the Font would see fit to reward him for getting the boy safely to her. A portable television for his bedroom would be nice. Never had someone been so deluded.

Sid boldly trotted to where Basil waited. Danrite, Vlad, Twinkle and a towed along Salor were not far behind. But just as they were within reach of the clearing that was the centre of the forest they were forced to stop dead in their tracks. Something terrible, with slavering jowls and frightening teeth, had appeared to stand between them and the waiting Basil. Holding onto its straining leash, a monster of a man with a slight resemblance to a monster.

‘Wo!’ said Twinkle.

‘Ye gads!’ said Salor, the fright of seeing the creature working on his hearing as it might for someone with hiccups. ‘What the dickens is that?’

Danrite went for his sword.

Vlad went for his fangs.

Sid pawed the ground.

Salor went for his staff. ‘Drat!’ he said, when he remembered it wasn’t there.

Twinkle put her hands together and cracked knuckles. Death snowflakes would be no good here.

‘Now, now,’ said a voice, from behind them, ‘no need for violence. Just give me the boy and we’ll be on our way.’

Salor spun on his heels. He knew that voice; it was his; or rather it sounded eerily similar to his! It belonged to Mister Power. 'Never!' he said, thrusting his hand forward menacingly. It would have been even more menacing if he had had the staff in it. 'Drat it.' He wondered if another fright might do something for his memory.

'Well, hello Salor,' said Mister Power, 'we meet at last.' They knew of each other's existence, but had never met.

'Grrr,' growled Salor, as he rolled up his sleeves. He might be without his trusty staff, but he still had his fists. His sleeves unrolled. He rolled them up again. They unrolled again. They were rather baggy sleeves. 'Bah,' said Salor, deciding to leave them as they were. He raised his fists.

'Ah,' said Mister Power, 'such barbarity, but if that's the way you want to play it, Rogi!' He smiled as Rogi pushed his way from the forest. 'I elect Rogi here as my champion. He'll fight you one on one. I suggest the winner gets all.' The smile now broadened as Salor backed away. 'No? Oh well.' His smile dropped. 'Now give me the boy,' he demanded.

'You can't have him,' said Twinkle, pushing in front of Danrite.

'No,' said Danrite, peering round her, 'you can't have me.'

'Show them the whistle please, Rogi.'

Rogi frowned, but took the whistle that controlled Hewie from his pocket and held it so everyone could see it.

Mister Power pointed to it. 'One blow on that,' said Mister Power, 'and Hewie there,' he pointed to the slavering beast straining at the leash, 'will tear you to-'

Rogi had interrupted him, speaking in a whisper.

Mister Power angrily whispered back. 'I know what it does,' he snarled, after Rogi had pointed out that one blow on the whistle would in effect stop Hewie, and not send him into a slavering rage. 'But they don't know that.' Grief, thought Mister Power, surrounded by cretins, how he wished it would all end.

'But I do.' The crack of a whip followed and the whistle was torn from Rogi's grip. Frida knew what the whistle was used for; Jose had told her.

'No!' yelled Mister Power, as he turned to see who the voice and whip belonged to. 'You fool, you…' His eyes suddenly became like saucers. His jaw dropped. He surely recognised that face. But surely it could not be? Where was the long auburn hair? The horn-rimmed glasses? 'Miss Manager?' he said.

On Danrite's side, everyone gave one another confused looks to match the one on Mister Power's face.

'Yes,' said Frida, picking the whistle from the end of her whip, 'the very same.' She blew on it, after first wiping the mouthpiece on her shorts, and Hewie lulled by the sudden blast of silence, rolled on his side and lay there, as harmless as a sleeping crocodile. Hewie's reaction to the whistle depended on which note that was blown. Without knowing it, Frida had blown the note for roll over and sleep like a crocodile.

'But…' Mister Power was lost for words. His mind was a whirr. What did this mean? The whirr stopped. He focused. He knew what this meant. Someone else was trying to stop him from getting the boy. And no one, no matter how attractive they had looked in horn-rimmed glasses, was going to stop him. Hewie was down, but he still had his cannon fodder. He clapped his hands. 'Rogi, Ergo, get the boy.'

Twinkle, Vlad, and Sid stepped to meet them. A second later, so did Salor. Danrite was once more shielded from harm between them. But Danrite no longer wanted to be piggy in the middle; he was a hero for goodness' sake. And it was about time he acted like one. So, with sword raised, Danrite pushed past his friends, and went forth to prove himself.

The scene was set, but would it be the final one?

Watching the events unfold on her seeing machine, the Font decided that she had seen enough and that it would be; at least where the seeing machine was concerned. You see the Font had other plans for where the final scene would be played out. She pressed a button on the remote control and paused the live action on the screen. She then made her way to the large hall.

The Font took a seat on her throne-like chair, took another handful of popcorn from the bucket, popped some of it into her mouth and, happy with the way of things, waved her other hand in a most magical way.

Now it was time for the final scene.

CHAPTER 77

The flash, which was a flash, but not in the sense most people would think of one, startled everyone by its presence. It did not blind with its brilliance, leave spots before eyes, or precede any sort of explosion. It was felt more than seen. It just was.

'Wah,' yelled Basil, who was the most startled of everyone. The most startled because, even though he had expected something to happen when things beyond the clearing started to go wrong, he had still held out hope that it wouldn't. He also knew the dream he had had of owning a portable television was in tatters. None of it had been his fault, but he knew who would get the blame; who it was that always got the blame. Full of woe, Basil felt rather than watched the flash spread out from where it had started; from between his feet.

'Wah!' yelled Danrite, as he felt the flash engulf him.

'Wah!' yelled Mister Power.

'Ay caramba!' said Jose.

And then, before another yell of surprise could be heard, everyone was somewhere else.

CHAPTER 78

There was disorientation. There was dizziness. There was puzzlement. There were questions to be answered.

'Wah…t just happened?' gasped Twinkle, as she took in the new and sudden surroundings. The forest had gone. In its place was one of the largest rooms she had ever laid eyes on.

Salor promptly added his wisdom. 'I think we may have left the forest,' he said, looking very puzzled.

'You don't say,' said Vlad, the spinning in his head thankfully slowing.

Danrite, feeling a little bit sick, but with his sword still held high, noticed another change. 'The creature's gone,' he said, with considerable relief. It had.

'Look, there's Jose,' said Twinkle, spotting their little canine friend across the hall from them. But the smile, on seeing Jose again, disappeared as she noticed he wasn't alone. The girl with the whip was standing beside him. 'Who's that with him?' she said, her eyes narrowing. The girl looked familiar. Had she seen her before somewhere?

But the other's attention had turned to other things.

'Grief,' said Vlad, as he noticed Mister Power was also in the room, 'Mister Power's here as well.'

Salor's attention had been grabbed by the person sitting on the chair that looked like a throne. 'Oh my,' he said, 'is that who I think it is?'

'Who what is?' said Twinkle, now watchfully glaring at Mister Power after Vlad's warning.

'There, on the chair, right there,' said Salor, looking on in awe.

As Mister Power looked as disorientated as the rest of them, everyone chanced a look. Sid instantly whickered and bent a knee.

'It is,' said Salor, getting all the verification he needed from Sid's reaction. He suddenly felt very excited.

'Who is it you think it is?' said Danrite.

'The Font of course,' said Salor, 'the Font. The quest is over.' Salor was finding it hard to contain his excitement. At last they would find out how Danrite would save Myth, Magic, and Make-believe. And then all would be right again.

Mister Power, standing between Rogi and Ergo, and as befuddled as the rest of them in the hall, didn't bother demanding to know what had happened when the dizziness he had been feeling wore off, because he doubted he would get an answer that would please him. Instead he stared at the huge hall, glared at the worried-looking little man dressed in white that no one else had noticed, and glowered at Salor and his gang. But no one was glowering back at him; they seemed far more interested in staring at the far wall of the large hall. At someone sitting in a chair that looked mightily like a throne, and who was eating popcorn from a rather large cardboard bucket. He didn't particularly like the look of whoever it was. He didn't know why. Perhaps because the hood hid their face.

The hall fell silent. You could cut the tension with a knife. Something was about to happen; everyone could feel it.

Well, not everyone.

'Ay caramba,' said Jose, only now recovering his wits, 'the trees, they are being missing.'

CHAPTER 79

'Welcome to you all,' said the Font after a silence that seemed to go on forever. Beneath the shadows of a hood that hid her face from sight, the Font smiled at everyone and put her bucket of popcorn to one side. The smile though had disappeared when she looked up again. 'I am the Font,' Salor was right, 'but before I say more to you I have something I have to do. Basil, come here.' Heads turned until they came upon the small man in white standing at the back of the hall.

Shocked, stunned, shaken, and any amount of other words starting with "S" that might describe how Basil was feeling at that moment, best described Basil's feelings as, for the first time in since he couldn't remember when, the Font had called him by his proper name.

It took a moment for the Font's words to sink in, but when they did, Basil was overcome with joy. Sadly the feeling didn't last long. When he looked up and saw that the Font wasn't looking very pleased, the joy was quickly replaced by a new feeling; dread. The fears he had held in the clearing came flooding back. He gulped. The Font could even be said to be looking a little bit angry. The dread deepened. No television then. He started forward. It was a stumbling walk.

As Basil took his slow stumbling walk to face whatever fate the Font had in store for him, the scene around him started to change. Jose, seeing his friends, darted across the hall to greet them. Frida, wary of what Mister Power might do now he knew Miss Manager wasn't all she was supposed to be, gave the man a wide berth and edged after Jose. But Frida need not have worried for the moment, she was not high on the list of Mister Power's priorities right then, he would deal with her, but not now. Nor had he given Jose so much as a second glance as he had passed by. His focus was on someone else, the person he felt was responsible for the loss of his prize, just as he had had him in his grasp. He called Rogi and Ergo to him. It was time he had words with this interloper. He faced the Font.

'Do you know who I am?!' bellowed Mister Power, drawing everyone in the hall's attention.

The Font kept her stare on the dawdling Basil, but gave Mister Power an answer. 'Yes,' she said. 'And if you would be so polite as to wait until you are spoken to, I will speak to you soon.' She now looked away from Basil and cast a glance around the hall. 'I ask just a little patience. Once I have dealt with business I will speak to you all.'

Halfway down the hall a worried Basil became even more worried. She called me business, he thought, oh woe is me.

Mister Power was furious. No one spoke to him like that. She, if it was a she, he couldn't quite make out if it was a woman on the big chair because of the hood she was wearing, would pay, but first he had business of his own to finish. The boy was there, in reach, and important. He needed rid of him, but circumstances had changed, he was somewhere he didn't want to be and put there by someone with a power, magical or otherwise, that needed to be handled with caution. What he needed now was leverage. He needed a hostage and the Danrite boy would do just fine. He ordered Rogi and Ergo to grab Danrite.

' !' ordered Mister Power. Only nothing came out. He had tried to shout "Get him!" but for some reason he couldn't. He tried again. But as hard as he tried, Mister Power couldn't utter a word. A horrified look spread across his face. A face that now looked at the Font.

'Don't worry, you'll get your voice back,' said the Font, 'but as I told you, before we talk I have a little problem to deal with first.'

Basil had almost, despite serious feet-dragging, reached where the Font sat waiting. Little problem, he thought, she said little. Perhaps he had been worrying over nothing. A small sunbeam now peeped through the clouds in his mind. It needn't have bothered. The sun wasn't going to shine for a while where Basil was concerned. He finally arrived, false hope shining, at the foot of the Font's large chair.

'Right,' said the Font, looking down on the little man, 'why did you do it?'

Basil gave her a mystified look. Not that he didn't know what the Font was talking about, he knew everything he had done that she wouldn't be pleased with, it was more he wasn't sure which particular *did* it was she was referring to. How worried should he be? He thought. There was the not so bad *did*, the *go to your room and think about it* sort of one, to the… oh good grief! Basil suddenly went quite weak at the knees. Surely she didn't know about that.

'Well?'

'I… er,' said Basil. He was playing for time. Could he bluff his way out? But what if it wasn't the one he was thinking she meant. What if he owned up to the wrong *did* and dropped himself in it? But who was he kidding; she knew. She always knew. She had called him Basil, things had to be bad. But Basil was a trier if nothing else. 'Do what, your Fontness?' he said, putting the ball back in her court. Calling her your Fontness might not have been the wisest move considering the situation, but he had thought what the heck, he might as well go out in a blaze of sarkiness.

The Font's glare hardened. 'Leif, Basil, why did you do it. Did *he* put you up to it?' The Font pointed at Mister Power. 'Are you in his employ?'

She did know. Basil went as white as his robe. He had guessed she was talking about Leif, but to actually hear it was a different thing entirely. But he took a little solace from learning she didn't know everything. It would not help him though. 'No,' he said, without turning round. He knew who she meant.

'Then why? Why did you have Leif lead everyone on a wild goose chase?' The Font was at a loss; she couldn't understand what could have gotten into Basil to make him act in such a way.

Basil's top lip began to quiver. His eyes began to fill with tears. He went to speak, but found he couldn't. Not because of a magical spell, but because he felt embarrassed. It had been a silly thing to do, but at the time… He looked at the floor, wishing it would open up and swallow him.

'Basil,' encouraged the Font, 'why?'

Basil managed to mutter something, but the Font didn't catch it.

'Pardon?' said the Font, 'I didn't quite catch that.'

Basil looked up. His face had taken on a defiant look. 'The television,' he blurted. 'I did it because you wouldn't let me have a television.'

The Font was taken aback. 'Because of a television set?' she said, hardly believing what she was hearing.

But it wasn't the only reason and so Basil, now certain something terrible was going to happen to him and nothing he said or did would make any difference, opened the floodgates on his woes and let them flow.

The Font stood up. 'Enough!' she said, putting a dam in Basil's river of complaint as he got to the bit about her never remembering his name. 'We all have our problems,' she said, 'but your whining and complaints, whilst obviously valid to you, does not excuse you from the way you acted. You kidnapped Leif's family, and that is wrong.'

Basil gulped. He had forgotten all about the kidnapping. And he had done that because he hadn't really kidnapped them. What he had done was tell Leif's family that the Font was sending them on holiday as Leif was so important, but they would have to go without him as he was on a secret mission. He told them he would tell Leif where they had gone as he was on his way to see him that very moment with a message from The Font. They had believed him, packed and went on their merry way and then, when the coast was clear, he had left the note telling Leif his family had been kidnapped and what he had to do if he ever wanted to see them again. 'But I-,' said Basil, looking desperate.

But enough was enough as far as the Font was concerned. With a click of her fingers Basil disappeared. She had sent him somewhere where he could ponder long and hard on what he had done. Kidnapping was a serious thing. He should be punished severely. But, as the Font already knew he hadn't really kidnapped Leif's family, it wouldn't be that severe. She had discovered the truth when the so-called kidnapping had come to light. But a good hard pondering on one's lot never did anyone any harm. But punished he would be. Leif had suffered because of Basil's stupidity. The Font sat down.

While the Font was having her discussion with Basil, the hall had been filled with a multitude of stares, glares, and muted discussions.

Mister Power, his power to have a conversation none existent, muted or otherwise, chose to stare and glare instead. He glared at Salor, he glared at the Font, and he stared and then glared wholeheartedly at the new version of Miss Manager. So she *had* been up to no good in his office. He was fuming. You couldn't trust anyone these days. But there was nothing he could do about it for the moment, not while the hooded creature was calling the shots. But he could wait. He would bide his time and then both of them would pay for the way they had treated him.

Across the way, Jose had taken no time to tell everyone about his adventures with his new friend, who had tried to drown him when they had first met, but that was okay. They listened, and told their story; all the while glancing from Mister Power to the Font to Jose's new friend who, standing a little away from them, had thus far kept herself very much to herself. She seemed to be weighing things up. Salor, hearing nothing, saying nothing, and glancing at nothing, just stood and stared at the Font, a silly puppydog look etched on his face.

As for Frida, she was weighing things up. Who was her friend? Who was her enemy? What should she do now? She saw Jose's friends looking at her and guessed Jose was telling them all about her; not that there was much to tell. She had also noticed Mister Power glaring at her. She guessed she wasn't his favourite secretary any more. And then there was the Font, or at least that was who she guessed she was, going on about what Leif had told her. She sighed; there was a lot of guessing going on. But of one thing she was certain; the voice on the phone most definitely belonged to the person sitting on the chair. And if that was true, then the Font was her boss.

That voice now spoke again.

CHAPTER 80

With Basil dealt with for now, the Font focused on the real business of the day.

‘I’m sorry about that,’ said the Font, cutting through the hall’s mutterings and stopping them dead, ‘just a small matter that needed my urgent attention. Now, where was I?’ She surveyed the hall, scanning faces as she did. ‘Oh, yes. Welcome to my humble abode. I am the Font.’

An eager Salor, the silly look still plastered on his face, took a step forward. At last he was in the presence of the all-knowing Font. He could hardly believe it. The journey was at an end. Soon they would know how Danrite was to save them. But before he had a chance to say anything, Mister Power took two steps forward.

Mister Power glared at Salor daring him to take another step, and then glared at the Font. The Font returned his glare with an unseen smile.

‘I take it you want me to give you your voice back?’ said the Font. Mister Power nodded. ‘Okay, but before I do, I want you to promise me that you will behave yourself. Will you?’

Surging with fury, but powerless to do anything, Mister Power, with narrow vengeful eyes, could do nothing but agree. He nodded.

Good,’ said the Font, who then snapped her fingers, lifting the spell from Mister Power’s lips.

With his speech restored, Mister Power took no time at all to go back on his word. ‘Rogi, Ergo, get the boy.’ It was time to get his plan back on track.

‘Oh,’ exclaimed the Font, who had been expecting Mister Power to go back on his word, but was disappointed all the same when he did, ‘STOP!’

Rogi and Ergo stopped, but not because they had been ordered to. Frozen in a moment of time by the Font’s command, they stood rooted to the spot. The Font gave Mister Power a disappointed look before snapping her fingers once more. Ergo and Rogi were no more, or rather, no longer what they had been. She watched Mister Power look on in horror, but she knew the look wasn't one of concern for the poor creatures he had been using; only one of concern for his own safety. 'I know you don't care, but they are back as they belong.' This included Hewie, who was at that very moment happily doing what grotesques do best; sitting on a parapet of the Font's castle, watching the world go by. She sighed and shook her head. 'Nothing changes; you were just as naughty as a child.'

The Font was right; Mister Power was furious, not for his cannon fodder, he couldn't give a flying fig about them, but because he was seeing his whole life's work unravelling before him. His only concern now was his own safety and finding a way out of the nightmare he now found himself in. He made a break for it. But a second later, he too was frozen.

The Font now spoke to Rogi and Ergo, calling them by the names Mister Power had given them. 'And do you like these names?' she asked. They both shrugged. She spoke to the frozen Mister Power. 'I can see why you hate imagination so much; you haven't got an ounce of it in you, have you?' Mister Power didn't answer; he couldn't really, his face frozen like it was. The Font spoke again to Rogi and Ergo. 'Well, I shall call you by your proper names. Igor…' She stopped. She realised that for once there was something she didn't know; a small thing, but important all the same. The Font knew what Ergo was; an ogre, and so why Mister Power had called him that, but not his real name. She asked.

'Fred,' said Ergo the ogre, though it had sounded more like "Freeeed" when he had said it.

'Well Fred, and Igor, you are free to go.' Two doors, not unlike the ones used to travel from one land to the other, shimmered into being beside them. 'The only thing you are guilty of is falling in with a bad crowd, and I can't punish you for that.' The Font gestured to the doors. 'The one beside you Fred will take you home.' Fred stepped towards it, into it, and he and the door disappeared. Igor went to do likewise with his door, but the Font stopped him. 'Just one thing Igor before you go, please try to stay away from mad scientists, there's a good fellow.'

Igor gave the Font a sheepish look, said he would try, and stepped into the waiting door. Then he too left the building.

As before, the others in the hall had looked on as the Font provided justice, and as before there were muted discussions and stares, but no glares. Glares had gone for a break as most of them had been either from Mister Power or at Mister Power which meant, as he was frozen and didn't appear to know what was going on around him, there didn't seem much point in carrying on with them.

And many stares there had been. Everyone had stared in differing degrees of amazement and horror as Ergo and Rogi had changed back to their original forms. Rogi from the most handsome man ever seen to… to one of the many Igor's of legend. And Ergo to Fred the ogre; though not so much of a change there; more colour than anything but…

Danrite's stare was that of amazement. He watched as Ergo shrank and changed. His square shoulders becoming rounded, so rounded they were often mistaken for a hump. He watched as Rogi's face changed form; a badly sewn scar here and a badly sewn scar there, one of his eyes becoming slightly higher than the other, his hair thinning to a few strands. Until finally Rogi was no more; in his place an Igor of myth and make-believe. Danrite continued watching as Ergo changed; colour and become a little bit lumpier. And so amazing were the changes, when they were done, he started staring at everyone else in the hall, wondering in turn what some of them must really look like. Twinkle, Vlad, Salor, Jose, Sid, Frida… He stopped at Frida and stared harder. There was something about her, something that was trying to ring a little bell in his mind. Did he know her from somewhere? She did look familiar. And then it hit him, where he had seen her before. Because he *had* seen her before, many times, in his dreams, in his nightmares. She was the nightmare the nightmares hadn't shown him; the nightmare without the cheese in it. She was his worst nightmare. The nightmare the nightmares said would be waiting for him. Danrite's mind whirred. What did it mean? How did they know? He felt dizzy. He felt faint.

As Frida watched the transformations come to their conclusions she suddenly felt as if someone was watching her. She turned. Someone was, it was the boy Danrite and he was staring at her as if he had seen a ghost. He didn't look too good. Whoops, she thought, as his legs give way beneath him.

'Is he okay?' asked a concerned Font.

'I think everything proved a little bit much for him, your…er,' said Twinkle.

'Please call me Font, Twinkle.'

'Oh, yes,' said Twinkle, 'thank you your er… Font. He's fainted.' Twinkle wasn't quite sure calling the Font, Font, sounded right, but if that was what she wanted.

'Oh dear,' said the Font. 'Put him on that.' A small bed had appeared from thin air. 'And when he comes round, give him some water. I believe Frida still has some.' The Font nodded at Frida. 'And now, if you wouldn't mind, I wish you all to gather round, I have some rather important things to tell you all.' She then remembered Mister Power and clicked her fingers. He also had to hear what she was about to say.

To the frozen Mister Power no time had passed at all and when the Font freed him he at first continued with his attempt to escape as if nothing had happened but then, as the others watched him and wondered why the Font wasn't trying to stop him, his stride began to falter and slow, until gradually he came to a full stop. What did she just say? He turned. He looked at the Font. His eyes narrowed. He spoke. 'What did you just say?' he said.

The Font looked at him. 'I said I have something important to tell you all.'

'No,' said Mister Power, who hadn't heard her say those words as he had still been frozen, 'you said something else, something about a child.'

'A child?' said the Font.

'Just now,' he said. Mister Power was slowly walking back towards the Font. He had a strange look on his face. A somewhat puzzled look, as if he had just found something out he didn't quite understand. 'You said something about me, about me as a child.' He was sure that was what he had heard; what she had said. But that didn't make any sense. How could that be? What could this popcorn-muncher possibly know about his childhood?

‘Ah,’ said the Font, ‘before you were frozen you mean. I said you were just as naughty as a child as you are now.’

If someone could turn someone to ice just by looking at them, then Mister Power’s stare at that moment would surely have turned the Font into a tray of ice cubes. ‘You lie,’ he said, his look of puzzlement had been replaced by one of anger. No one knew of his childhood. He hardly knew of his childhood. He had had enough; it was just some ploy to trap him there. And it had almost worked. But he saw through her tricks. He had wasted enough time. Mister Power again looked for a way out, and when he saw none, he ran anyway.

Mister Power was halfway across the hall when the Font’s voice echoed from its walls. She asked him a question; one that caused him to stop dead in his tracks, his heart to skip a beat, and the blood to drain from his face. He turned; his face ashen. She had asked him about his book; did he have it with him? What did she know about his book? How could she know about his book? It was a secret; known only to him. Then a thought occurred to him. She was talking about some other book. That was it; some other book. She must be talking about some other book that he knew nothing about. All the same, his hand had automatically pressed against his chest; against the secret pocket in his jacket where his secret lay hidden; against his book. He couldn’t help himself; it was the guilty reaction of someone with a secret to hide. ‘What book?’ he heard himself say defensively. The words had just slipped out. He wanted to bite his tongue. He should run.

‘You know which book,’ said the Font, noticing Mister Power’s reaction. She smiled again. ‘It’s in your pocket, isn’t it?’

Mister Power’s eyes grew wide and wild; alarm caused by the Font’s words. Panic, something he had never known before, started to build. No one could know of the book’s existence, no one. It was his; his secret. A secret he had always guarded. He clasped his arms across his chest. But she seemed to know. She really seemed to know. How?

The Font raised a placating hand. ‘Don’t worry Mister Power,’ she said, ‘yours is not the only secret book in the hall.’ She turned to Salor and smiled at him from the depths of her hood. The smile was warm; knowing. ‘I take it you have yours here as well, Salor? Perhaps also hidden in some deep dark recess of your robe?’

It was Salor's turn for his face to grow pale and grey as he, like Mister Power before him, automatically pressed a defensive hand against his chest, against the secret pocket in his robe that held his most guarded secret.

'Ah-ha,' said the Font, 'I see you do.' She held out a hand towards Salor. 'Please be so kind and pass it to me.'

Salor didn't want to, it was his. He hesitated. His book was a secret no one knew about, and he wasn't sure he wanted anyone to know about it now. But they did. The Font had seen to that. He still hesitated. But it was the Font, and she knew everything. So was it really a secret? He felt the book-shaped lump beneath his robe. He looked up at the Font. She was the Font. He reached inside his robe and removed his beloved book. A further, short reluctance followed. But she was the Font, the all-seeing, he couldn't not hand it over. So, handling it like the precious thing it was to him, he very carefully, passed it into the Font's waiting hand.

The Font took it, looked at it, smiled, thanked Salor and then spoke to Mister Power. 'And now yours,' she said. She held out her other hand and waited expectantly. But she knew it would be harder for Mister Power to hand over his book than it was for Salor. Whereas Salor's book was his *little* secret; Mister Power's book was his *dark* secret. Dark secrets were harder to share by their owners than little secrets were. Mister Power ignored her and clamped his arms tighter around his chest.

'Okay,' said the Font abruptly, 'not to worry. I only need the one book for now.' The Font opened Salor's book at the first page and studied it. There was an inscription written on it, or rather a jumble of mixed up letters. Salor had tried for years to make some sense of them, but however hard he had tried, he had always failed to find a meaning to them.

The studying went on for some time. Until it seemed the Font would never look up from Salor's book ever again. Salor became nervous and agitated. Not because his book was no longer in his safe keeping, though its loss wasn't helping, it was because as yet he hadn't had an answer. He needed, they all needed, to know how Danrite was going to save them. It was why they were there. It was important; time was running out. The world of Myth, Magic, and Make-believe was crumbling; not so much in the Font's hall obviously, but how long before even that was affected? So Salor needed an answer, but before that, to get to that answer, he had to ask the question. He politely coughed.

'Yes?' said the Font, looking up from the pages she had been turning.

'I… that is we,' said Salor humbly, while waving a hand towards his friends, 'are, here to ask a question.' He wondered if perhaps he should have removed his hat. A bit late for that he supposed. 'It's a very important question.'

'And?' said the Font.

And? puzzled Salor, what did that mean? He didn't have the foggiest, so he carried on regardless. 'As I expect you know, our world is on the edge of disaster. And we, as I also expect you know, have found the hero that, as it is written, will save it.' If Salor had taken his hat off, he would have now been nervously fiddling with it. 'It's just that, now we have him, we were wondering if you could perhaps tell us-'

'How he is going to do it,' said the Font, finishing Salor's sentence for him.

'Why, yes,' said a relieved Salor. He knew he had been right in seeking out the Font. He could hardly contain his excitement; they were going to be able to save the world. He almost did a jig, but didn't. 'But time is short you see, so if it pleases you, could you be so kind as to tell us how, and then we can be on our way.' He thought about asking for his book back, but decided against it, one thing at a time.

The Font looked thoughtful. She closed one eye. She opened it again. 'He isn't,' she said, frowning at Salor. She returned to the book.

CHAPTER 81

'Sorry?' said Salor, fearing his hearing was playing up again. Behind Salor mutterings could be heard.

These mutterings were varied in content. Sid, Vlad and Jose, were as shocked as Salor would be when he eventually got his head round what it was the Font had said. Twinkle was not so stunned by the news, as she had made her doubts about Danrite known from the beginning. But still… shame. As for Danrite, if he had been conscious at that moment, he would have roughly been in the same boat as Twinkle and, if truth be told, more than a tad relieved. Frida was nonplussed; it was just a job. Mister Power on the other hand was delighted. The so-called hero was a mere nobody which meant there was nothing to stop his plans now. Except that he was trapped. That and he had wasted his time, energy and cannon fodder for nothing. He was no longer as delighted as he was a moment ago.

The Font looked up and for a moment was puzzled by everyone's reaction. A stammering noise now caught her attention. It was Salor.

'But… but,' said Salor, who was still having trouble with his head, as in getting it round things. 'That… that cannot be, he is the one. He was prophesised.'

She then realised why all the discontented mutterings, she had quite forgotten to tell everyone what she had been meaning to tell them; the whole story. No wonder they were in a tizzy. It was the book's fault; she hadn't seen it in such a long time, her mind had wandered. Right, she thought, I had better explain why I said what I have just said.

'Oh dear,' said the Font, 'I've confused you, sorry about that, it's the book you see; I haven't seen it in such a long time. It brought back memories.' She held the book up and then placed it on her lap. 'Now, as I said I have something to tell you all, so it's about time I told you. Things will then become clearer, I promise.' She caught movement out of the corner of her eye. 'And that means you too,

Mister Power.' Mister Power had started to sidle away, hoping to find a means of escape while the Font's mind was elsewhere. 'Come closer.'

As if, thought Mister Power, but then found he was now closer to the Font than he had been when he had started to sidle away. How had she done that? He hugged himself tighter.

'There,' said the Font, pleased that Mister Power had decided to join everyone else; even if it hadn't been his idea. 'Now, I will get on with that explaining.' She stood up, placed Salor's book on the table beside her, and started to remove the hood, that up until then had hidden her face from sight.

The room filled with gasps of shock and looks of surprise from all but Danrite as the hood was removed to reveal the face beneath it. The surprise belonged to Frida and Mister Power as they had been expecting to see a woman. The shocked gasps belonged to those who had been expecting to see someone that wasn't dead.

'Percy?' exclaimed Salor, as he fought against the reeling feeling going on in his brain.

'But you died,' said Twinkle, stunned by what she was seeing.

'Fluttering bats,' said Vlad.

'What the?' whinnied Sid in horse.

'Ay caramba!' said Jose, just managing to not do a mischief for once. 'I am thinking someone should be waking Danrite.'

'No!' said a voice from behind them. Everyone span on their heels to see that another hooded figure had entered the hall. Jose looked worried, but the hooded figure wasn't talking to him. 'It's not Percy. Percy never existed, not as a person at least.' The hooded figure removed its hood to reveal the face of a woman in her late fifties, a kindly face, framed by straight white hair that reached to her shoulders. 'He was just an extension of myself; an avatar if you like.' The woman, the real Font, appeared to glide over the floor, rather than walk, as she approached. When she reached where everyone was standing, she raised a hand. Avatar Percy did the same. 'For now,' said the Font, talking to Percy. She clicked her fingers and Percy the avatar, robe and hood, folded in on itself and disappeared.

Seeing Percy again had been a shock, but the reeling feeling had lessened a little inside Salor's head as Percy's appearance was explained, but it didn't go entirely; there were too many questions filling his head for that. But he started with a statement. 'I don't understand,' he said, saying what most of them in the hall were thinking.

'Stop! I wouldn't do that if I were you.'

Mister Power stopped. As soon as Percy had disappeared, he had seen an opportunity to get closer to Salor's book. As to whether he was going to steal it or just look at it, he hadn't yet made up his mind. 'And if I don't?' he said, still reaching towards it.

'It would be too soon,' said the Font.

But Mister Power wasn't listening; he had to see if Salor's book was the same as his. His fingers touched it, clawed at it, disappeared.

They reappeared with the rest of Mister Power on a gurney. He was strapped to it. He wriggled and struggled to get free, but it was useless, the straps were magical, as was the gag the Font had placed on his mouth. She hadn't wanted to do it, but her patience with him had grown thin. She needed to explain and it was sadly obvious he wasn't interested in what she had to say. He wasn't just a naughty boy anymore; he was a very dangerous man with thoughts only for what he wanted. The Font leaned over him and opened his jacket. Mister Power threatened to tip the gurney over, such were his struggles, but struggle as he might it was for nothing; the Font reached in and removed his secret.

'You won't need this anymore,' said the Font. Mister Power had never been without his book, and as the Font lifted it from him, his eyes grew large with pleading. So much so, that the Font thought for a moment that her heart was going to break. But it was for the better good in the end. With tears in her eyes she gently touched his forehead. 'Sleep,' she whispered. 'Soon all will be revealed.' But Mister Power never heard those last words.

As the gurney wheeled itself to a far corner of the hall, the Font took her place in the large chair that looked like a throne. She placed Mister Power's book with Salor's and prepared to tell all. As the Font gazed down on everyone she wondered if perhaps they should all be sitting down as well. For what she had revealed to them so far was nothing to the shocks that still awaited them.

CHAPTER 82

The hall was full of stunned silence, and all the chairs that had appeared from nowhere were still empty. No one had moved. All were gobsmacked. Especially Danrite who had come round from his feinting fit just in time to find he wasn't the hero they had all been waiting for after all; Frida was.

'Ay caramba!' exclaimed Jose, the first to break it. 'It is you.'

But Frida, who was more puzzled really than gobsmacked, had no idea what the Font was talking about. 'What do you mean?' she said. Up until that moment she had been quite happy to take a backseat to everything that was going on, as she figured her job was done there and she would soon be going home, or given another assignment. She had been waiting to ask.

'Yes, what do you mean?' demanded Salor, who was starting to regret coming to the Font, especially as she was turning everything he knew on its head. The puppy-dog look had started to slip when the Font had taken his book. It had totally vanished now.

'Told you he wasn't the hero,' whispered Twinkle in Vlad's ear.

Sid nuzzled Danrite's shoulder. 'It's okay,' said Danrite, being brave. 'I'm kind of relieved in a way.' Though really, he wasn't sure what he felt, but if you were to mix relief and disappointment together and add a sprinkle of bewilderment, it wouldn't be far from what he was feeling at that moment.

'Sorry, I'm not explaining this very well am I?' said the Font, not far from the mark. 'He is, a little bit, but not as much as his sister is.' There, thought the Font, that should make it a little clearer; as mud.

'I've a sister?' said Danrite, looking as though someone had just fed him a spoonful of cod liver oil.

'Yes,' said the Font, thinking they were at last getting somewhere.

'Where is she?' said Danrite.

And there was the Font thinking things were finally swimming along nicely. 'There,' she said, pointing at Frida, 'Frida.'

'Her?' said Danrite. And now he could see it, why he thought he had seen the blonde girl before. She looked like him; which in turn sort of explained his worst nightmare. In it he always appeared dressed as a girl; perhaps in his subconscious he had always known he had a sister somewhere. At least he hoped it explained it.

'Yes,' said the Font. 'Haven't I made that clear?'

'No,' said nearly everyone at once; Danrite was still staring.

'My brother?' said Frida, now looking as if she had shared that spoon of cod liver oil with Danrite.

'Yes,' said the Font. 'You're twins.'

'But the book said there was only one hero,' said Salor, frantically treading the water of confusion he was floating in.

'And you've seen the book have you?' said the Font.

'Well, no,' Salor had to admit.

'No,' said the Font, 'but there is one, and it does foretell the coming of a hero. It also foretold when that day would come and you Salor were put in charge of being there when it did; which you were.' The Font drew breath. 'But there were complications. Instead of one baby, two were born; twins. A decision had to be made, so the more magical of the two, the oldest by seconds, was whisked away before the forces that seek to destroy the hero noticed.'

Salor turned on Vlad. 'Vlad,' he said, scowling at him. 'You were there all day and night, why didn't you notice?'

Vlad's mind turned to that fateful night. Whoops, he thought.

'Don't blame Vlad, Salor; it was all done with sleight of hand. And done so quickly that when he saw first a girl baby, and we know he did, and then a boy all on his own, he honestly thought he had made a mistake. He never knew there were twins.'

'So I was never a magical hero,' said Danrite, fiddling with his sword.

'A little bit magical,' said the Font, 'and I believe more than a little bit of a hero.'

'That's why he collapsed amongst the flowers,' said Vlad.

'And why he recovered so quickly,' said Twinkle.

'Yes,' said the Font.

But Danrite wasn't listening. He was suddenly feeling very angry and very used. 'I was a decoy, wasn't I?' he said, glaring at the Font.

The Font gave him a sad smile. 'Not at first Danrite,' she said. 'At first all I wanted was to get you somewhere safe. But as the years passed, and the rumour grew that you were the hero, I decided to let it grow; and sometimes, I'll admit, I added fuel to that fire.' The Font rested her hands in her lap. 'But you were looked after at all times. First by the people you called your parents, and then by Percy. You were never in any danger.'

The words took a minute to soak in, but soak in they did. 'They weren't my parents?' said Danrite, as the last segment of the little world he called his life was pulled from under him.

'Avatars,' said the Font. 'Both you and Frida had avatar copies of your parents before you were old enough to be moved on.'

Did that mean they were still alive; hidden? Danrite and Frida looked at the Font, a mixture of hope and anger on their faces, and spoke as one. 'Are they here?'

'No,' said the Font, 'they disappeared shortly after you were born. We have no idea where they went or where they are.'

Danrite fell quiet; there was a lot for him to take in. But for Frida there were still questions to be asked. When her parent avatars had disappeared she had been adopted by a strange maiden aunt she had never heard of before; until that is, that maiden aunt happened to die in a freak accident. It was soon after, the same day of the funeral in fact, that she was suddenly approached and enrolled into an organisation who had been watching her and felt she was just the person they were looking for; a spy. She never gave the timing of it a second thought, she was just happy to be wanted. She looked the Font in the eyes. 'You were Auntie Paula, weren't you?' said Frida.

'Yes,' said the Font, 'at least an avatar was.'

This Frida took in her stride, but what she wasn't happy with, and she couldn't understand was why, if she was this hero everyone kept on about, had she been dumped in the lap of the enemy; Mister Power? She demanded to know.

'Because he isn't the enemy,' said the Font, bringing even more puzzled looks, raised eyebrows and the like, into the hall. At least from those that were still following. Jose had lost the plot a long time ago and was now scratching behind an ear. 'Well not the one we need the hero to save us from anyway.' The Font suddenly looked very tired. 'He's my son.'

CHAPTER 83

'What?' said nearly everyone at once. Jose was now concentrating on doing a little licking.

It was a shock to everyone; it would be too for Jose later, but for one, an even bigger shock was in store. The Font now hit him with it.

'As are you, Salor,' said the Font.

Imagine for a moment the look of someone who had just been hit in the face with a wet fish. Now imagine the look as a second later they were hit by another one. That was how Salor looked as the Font's words echoed around his head.

'Me?' managed a flabbergasted Salor. Like Mister Power, Salor did not remember much about his childhood.

'Yes,' said the Font, 'and we have been waiting for this day a long time.'

'We?' said Salor, who was holding himself together remarkably well considering the slapping he had taken.

'The Otherside and myself,' said the Font. 'You see, Salor, there are other things written in the book besides the description of the hero.' More surprises gathered on the horizon.

Not quite what anyone had expected when they set out to find the Font. A clue as to how the hero was going to save everyone was all they had wanted. To do their job; spying. To get rid of the hero so he could destroy myth, magic and make-believe. Their quests had been turned on their heads. Everything had changed, and no one so far could yet decide if that was good or bad. Least of all Jose, who at that moment was puzzling over a place he found he couldn't reach to lick. Danrite wasn't the hero. He had a sister who was. Percy had never existed, or Frida's Paula; the same for their parents. Mister Power wasn't the evil that everyone thought was threatening the Otherside. The Font was Salor's mother, and also Mister Power's. Mister Power was Salor's brother. Or was he?

As the hall was filled with wonderings of what the Font could possibly mean about there being other things written in the book, Salor's mind had stalled on just the one thought; a rather alarming one.

'Grief,' exclaimed Salor, suddenly, 'that means Mister Power is my brother?!' He looked as if he had eaten something that only people on television in survival programmes might eat. He looked at the Font with despair in his eyes and disgust on his face. 'That's why he sounds like me.'

The Font gave Salor a haunted look. 'No,' she said, 'he isn't.'

Salor puzzled over the Font's reply. He brightened a little. Perhaps, he thought, things aren't as bad as he thought. 'My stepbrother?' At least that might explain the difference between them.

The Font's look didn't change. 'No.' she said.

No? thought Salor. What did that leave? 'Sister?' he ventured. That didn't make sense; did it? Salor in truth was not sure *what* made sense anymore.

'No,' said the Font, a slight smile flickering at the corners of her mouth. 'None of those, he is you, Salor.'

'Me?'

'And you are him.'

'He?' Salor's eyelids did some flickering. His knees did some wobbling. His body did some collapsing. His mind had done some closing down.

'BASIL!' yelled the Font, bringing her sidekick back from where she had sent him. It was time.

CHAPTER 84

A door, no one had noticed before, opened and Basil, his white robe ash-smeared, scorched about the hem, and slightly smoking, entered the hall wheeling a chair that appeared to be a cross between one of those chairs that the patient sat in on a visit to the dentist and one of those chairs with a dryer attached that ladies sat in in hair salons. Neither of those though came equipped with the extras this chair possessed; restraining straps on the arms and footrest.

Basil, his recent banishment to the top of an active volcano, where he had been sent to think about his recent actions, pushed the chair to where Salor lay on the floor. He nodded at the Font, and without saying a word left and reappeared a few moments later with a second chair which he placed opposite the first. A third chair was then wheeled in and placed between the two, facing them. This one lacked the restraints of the other two. The Font clicked her fingers.

Salor woke with a start to find Mister Power glaring at him from a chair opposite him. A chair similar to the one he found he was sitting in, but with one main difference; the restraining straps on his chair hung loose, whereas the ones on Mister Power's chair were doing what they were supposed to do; restrain their occupant. He was confused. What was going on? Then he noticed a third chair to his left, placed facing his and Mister Power's chairs. The Font was leaning against it. 'What happened?' he said, as his mind tried to make sense of things. The last thing he remembered was… oh good grief. 'I'm… he's…'

'Stay calm, Salor,' said the Font, as she left the chair she was leaning against and faced him. 'You just suffered information overload, that's all.'

'But…' said Salor. He started to get out of the chair.

'Relax,' said the Font, 'all will be explained.' She gently pushed him back. 'Mister Power there didn't want to stay seated either.'

Salor looked across at Mister Power, who was obviously gagged again as he was mouthing all sorts of things at him, and taking the hint, he sat back again. 'But what did you mean?' he asked. 'How can I be him and him me?'

'As I said,' said the Font, as she returned to her throne-like chair, 'all will be explained.' She sat down. 'Now,' she said, 'let me tell you what is actually written.'

The book told of a darkness that was coming which would threaten the very existence of myth, magic and make-believe. This, to a certain extent, everyone knew. But the dark power wasn't Mister Power, it was far worse than ever he could be; beyond anyone's imagining. And that was why the book told the coming of not one hero, but seven heroes. Yes, there was mentioned a hero, a hero that would be born on a certain day, who the Otherside would need to look after and protect in readiness to face the dark power. Everyone knew this, but only a few knew the real identity of that magical hero, fewer less that that hero had a much less magical brother. This was because it was not written in the book. This hero, when ready, would go forth and meet the approaching darkness, but not on their own; they would be aided by six other heroes. Heroes that would only be made known as the day of facing the darkness approached. To find them a test was needed. But, as there was nothing that existed in the Otherside or the human side that was anywhere near as evil as the approaching darkness they needed to create something. So the Font created Mister Power; a creature that would help them find what they were looking for. Those six had now been found. The quest to find the real dark power and defeat it could now begin.

'You made him?' exclaimed an astonished Twinkle, as the Font finished.

'I did,' said the Font. In the chairs, both Salor and Mister Power stared at her, and the most puzzled and disturbed by the news was Mister Power. 'You see, as I said, there was nothing in the Otherside or the human world dark enough for the test. So I divided my son, a powerful wizard, and took all the best that existed in him to form Salor, and all the worst in him to create Mister Power. It wasn't an easy decision, but it had to be done.' The Font looked at Mister Power and Salor with a sad glint in her eye.

'So can you put them back again?'

'Oh yes,' said the Font, 'now I have the books.' The Font took the books from the table. 'The books had been left with each new born as a fail-safe; a secret to be guarded by them so there could be a return to one when the time was needed.'

'No!' screamed Mister Power, surprising himself as he hadn't realised the magical gag had been removed. But now he knew, he took advantage of it. 'It's all lies. Lies I tell you. Let me out of this.' He started to wriggle and fight against the restraints, but when he found struggling was useless and he was going nowhere fast, he slumped back in the chair and started to whimper. 'It's not true.'

'But it is,' said the Font. She raised the books so Salor and Mister Power could see them. 'Did you ever wonder what the inscription that is written inside meant?' Mister Power didn't answer, but Salor admitted he had. The Font smiled and then read the letters out.

Mister Power's inscription read: I I L L A S E I H O L V M T E.

Salor's inscription read: W L A W Y B W T Y U O E O H R.

'What do they mean?' asked Salor. 'Are they spells?'

'I will show you.' The Font brought the two books together, both opened at the page with the inscriptions, and as they touched they began to slowly merge into one. 'There,' said the Font, when the merging had completed.

Everyone looked at the inscription written in the one book the Font now held in her hands. It read: I WILL ALWAYS BE THERE FOR YOU LOVE MOTHER.

A gasp came from one of the chairs. It was Mister Power. 'You are my mother,' he said. And for the first, and the last time, a tear rolled down his cheek. He then ceased to exist; as did Salor. Like the books, the two had just become one.

CHAPTER 85

What was written had come true. Salor, the Font had told him that Salor had always been his name, had woken up in the middle chair after becoming one again. And the seven heroes had been named. Frida, the hero that was written, and six others; Danrite her less-magical brother, Salor the wizard, Twinkle the fairy, Vlad the vampire, Jose the werechihuahua, and…

'Me?!' wailed Basil as the Font told him the good news.

Sid, his alicorn, the spiral horn that gave him his magical power, having been returned to him, was a unicorn again, but he would not be going, as he needed to stay behind and act as a last defence should all else fail against the darkness that threatened. Rosie, who was a wood nymph again, would also stay, but not as a last defence; for some reason, she would now get into a terrible flap at the tiniest of things. The Font said she would keep an eye on her.

Sadly, the others were not able to change back. The Font had the magic to change the magical and mythical into the form they had once been, a few anyway, but she could not change Twinkle, Vlad or Jose as they had to stay in the forms in which they had become heroes, at least until the darkness was defeated.

Those heroes now waited on the castle roof, waiting for their journey to begin; waiting for the Font to see them off. The Font arrived and her heart lifted. There might be hope for the Otherside yet. She then looked at Basil and sighed. Why him she did not know, but he had been there from the start, and there had to be seven. Never mind, she thought, he will be useful as her eyes and ears. She inspected the troops.

'Looking good, Twinkle,' said the Font, complimenting her on her camouflage tutu, all khaki and leaves. 'Lifelike.'

‘Thank you, Fonty,’ said Twinkle, beaming.

‘Font will do,’ said the Font, smiling and walking on to Vlad.

‘Nice camouflage,’ said the Font, recognising a theme appeared to be going on. Vlad’s was more “dusty dungeon” than foliage though. His robe was a slate grey and covered in dusty looking cobwebs.

‘He copied me,’ said Twinkle, glaring at him.

‘Did not,’ pouted Vlad.

‘Imitation is the sincerest form of flattery,’ the Font whispered to Twinkle. She walked away from a happier, smiling, Twinkle.

Next were the twins, who appeared to be getting on a little bit better after the shock of discovering they each had one. Danrite had decided not to follow the others down the camouflage route, preferring to keep the armour the nightmares had given him. He had gotten kind of used to it. Frida on the other hand was wearing khaki shirt and shorts with just the faint touch of leaf.

‘Nice outfit, Twang,’ said the Font, using Frida’s surname for the first time. It would out sometime, better now than later.

‘Twang?’ said Danrite loudly, causing the others to look over. He proceeded to titter.

‘Twang?’ said Vlad.

A slightly blushing Frida looked embarrassed. ‘Just a name,’ she said. ‘Anyway, it’s better than Willocky.’

‘Got a point,’ said Twinkle.

A point at which the Font felt she should step in. ‘It’s an anagram,’ she said. Mister Power wasn’t the only one playing that game.’ She smiled at Frida and explained. ‘Frida Twang - giant dwarf. There.’

‘Is mine an anagram?’ said Danrite, trying to make something with the letters in his name, but failing.

‘Afraid not,’ said the Font, ‘Basil gave you yours, said it was a statement? I never understood.’ It was Frida’s turn to titter. Danrite now reddened. The Font walked on.

‘And how are you?’ said the Font, catching Jose with one leg half-raised against the parapet.

‘Ah,’ said Jose, quickly lowering it. ‘Sí, I am being good.’ He, like Danrite was sticking with what he knew best attire wise; fur and a spiky collar. 'But I am not feeling too much like the hero.' He looked worried.

'Oh, but you are Jose,' said the Font, bigging him up. 'And one day soon the others will look to you.'

'They will?'

'They will.'

The Font left Jose with his tail wagging happily. Something he immediately noticed and started to chase.

'Yes?' said the Font, as Basil sidled up to her.

Basil was not happy with the situation one little bit. In a few moments he was to be flung into who knows where, and did he have a choice about it, no, no he didn't. 'Why me?' he demanded, and not for the first time.

'You know why,' said the Font.

'I said I'm sorry,' said Basil.

'You know that's not the reason.'

'But I'm not a hero.'

'Everyone has a hero in them waiting to get out,' said the Font.

'Mine must be hiding.'

The Font gave Basil one of her famous smiles. 'Cheer up, think of it as a holiday.'

Basil stared hard at the Font.

'Okay,' said the Font, breaking under Basil's gaze, 'not a holiday. But go you must. Now put the haversack on, it's nearly time to go.'

Basil became gloomier. The haversack was almost twice the size of him. Thankfully, he had had the foresight to attach wheels to it so it didn't drag. It was still heavy though.

'Mother,' said Salor, as the Font left Basil to it.

'Salor, you ready?'

'For anything,' said Salor, holding out his new staff for inspection. If only he felt as confident as he sounded. So far there had been no side-effects since his merging with Mister Power. The Font had said it was because he had the stronger personality. He hoped it was true.

'A tie?' said the Font, raising an eyebrow. It was a rather snazzy one, all stars and moons.

‘Yes,’ said Salor. ‘I don’t know why, but I just fancied a change. Salor reached up and tightened the knot. He hadn’t needed to. Just felt the need.

Oh dear, thought the Font, but too late to worry now. She walked to the centre of the roof and stood beside the aerial. There she spoke some words that no one, not even Salor understood and then stepped back.

Nothing happened for a moment or two then gradually the air began to shimmer a few feet in front of her. The shimmering began to grow. Until a doorway, like the ones they had used to travel from land to land took shape. But this one was not the same. It looked darker, uninviting.

‘Ready?’ said the Font.

Six heads nodded. One shook.

Ignoring Basil, the Font wished them all good luck. She stepped aside as Frida stepped forward. With just the slightest of frowns, Frida stepped up to the doorway and into it. Danrite followed. As did the others until only Salor and Basil were left.

‘Good luck son,’ said the Font as Salor stepped up and in.

Only Basil now remained. ‘Do I…. AHHHHH!!’

‘Yes,’ said the Font, who was stronger than she looked. She closed the portal. All she could do now was wait and hope; and other things.

CHAPTER 86

'Blimey,' said Vlad.

'With you there,' said Twinkle.

'Ditto,' said Danrite and Frida as one. They stared at each other.

'Ay caramba, with knobs on,' said Jose.

'Ooof,' said Salor, falling forward.

Basil said nothing. He was just happy he'd had such a soft landing.